WALKING IN THE DARK

OLLIE WIT, BOOK TWO

DONNA AUGUSTINE

Chapter 1

PEOPLE ALWAYS THINK THEY KNOW WHAT'S IMPORTANT. THAT it's not something you need to spend hours debating. You just *know*. Or you should. I'd always thought I'd known.

When I lost my family, I didn't need to think about how it was going to feel. It was instant devastation and it nearly broke me. According to some, it had broken me.

But I was realizing that sometimes you don't know what's important at all, not until you've really gone and botched things up so badly you aren't sure if you can ever make things right.

As I stood in the alleyway, the Underground loomed ahead, casting me in its massive shadow. It was a large converted warehouse where the paranormal came to play, but it wasn't only home to creatures better off not named. This was Kane's lair.

The last time I'd set foot in this place, there'd been snow on the ground. Now the trees had buds and the smell of spring was fresh in the air.

As I struggled to catch a deep breath, I knew it wasn't allergies clogging up my lungs but fear. Three months ago, almost to the day, I'd walked out of here without so much as a note, and today I'd find out how badly I'd botched things up.

I hadn't lived at the Underground for long, and yet as I walked toward the steel door, I felt like I was coming home. This wasn't my home, but I hadn't been able to shake the longing to come here, no matter how many times I reminded myself that it hadn't been all good. Still, every step forward I took felt better than the last.

The door swung open before I was close enough to knock, and an attractive man in his early twenties stood there, looking at me as he filled the opening with his large frame. Jerry didn't look like he belonged manning the door of a club in Boston, let alone this place. With his sun-kissed skin and blond glints in his brown hair, he looked like he should've been dropped behind a bar on some tropical island, wining and dining attractive patrons as they sipped piña coladas, instead of sleeping his way through the female vampire population while they sipped on his blood. Although I'd never confirmed whether the vampires feasted on him during sex. My overactive imagination had made that addition.

Jerry stood there silently as he soaked in the shock of seeing me here. Considering how I'd left, he was probably checking to see if I'd grown horns in my absence. It took him a moment to get his voice back, but when he did, he finally began to speak.

"Whoa." His one word sized up my appearance better than anything else.

Yeah, that was exactly how I was feeling about my visit too, except hopefully I wasn't being as obvious about it. "Nice to see you, too," I said as I closed the distance.

"And I thought today was going to be boring." He

stepped back, offering me entrance, and I walked into the Underground.

The place was as electric as I'd remembered it, the energy seeping into my pores. The music was pounding while people milled about the industrial-looking space, drinking, playing cards, lounging at tables and in the few booths.

I caught a couple of nasty stares from the witches; the shifters mostly ignored me, disregarding me as unimportant to their lives. The vampires weren't awake and up yet. Yep, everything was exactly as I remembered.

Our booth in the corner—Butch and Leon's booth in the corner—was empty. I'd caught glimpses of Butch and Leon a handful of times over the last few months. I'd wanted to approach them but they never came close enough, and I feared having to chase them down the street if I was headed in their direction. After I left the way I had, only a fool would think things would be the same. That if they'd been here, I'd be able to slip into the booth like old times and joke with them and laugh like we used to. Nothing was like it used to be.

My eyes shot to the office up above. I feared just how different things would be now. Kane had never struck me as the forgiving type.

I'd stalled long enough. I'd come here for a purpose and I wasn't chickening out now.

I leaned slightly toward Jerry, who was standing beside me, while keeping my eyes on the office. "Kane upstairs?"

"Oh yeah." Even that simple answer and the way he dragged out the O was telling.

I'd only taken a step before Jerry asked, "You want me to go see if he's free?"

What he really meant was take the temperature of the

room for me and make sure it was safe for entry. Jerry had always been the softy of the group.

Some things had definitely changed. I hadn't expected a warm welcome, not after the way I left. But Kane needing a warning of my arrival? That didn't bode well. I turned back toward Jerry. "Is that necessary?"

"Probably not? It's not like he'd kill you anyway. Otherwise he would've already done it." He shrugged, looking as unsure as I felt.

I wasn't sure if that was supposed to make me feel better. If it was, Jerry was going to have to spend some serious time working on his people skills. Worst part was, he'd always had the best skills out of the whole gang.

"Thanks, but I'm good." I headed toward the stairs with a confidence that was all bluster with no meat. Whether I was actually good didn't matter. I had to do this, and now. If I talked to Jerry for another couple of seconds, I might not make it to the office at all.

Isabella, Kane's stalker—or assistant, as they liked to call her around here—was leaving Kane's office as I hit the first step of the metal staircase. The gloating smile on her face prepared me for my reception and was better than a warning flare out of the door.

So, he already knew I was in the building, which wasn't surprising, and guessing from her level of happiness, it was going to be really bad. Isabella didn't say a word as she walked past me on the stairs, and her smile seemed cemented in place. It made me even edgier.

As I climbed though, excitement mingled with the fear. I hadn't seen Kane in a long time. I'd missed him so much more than I ever imagined I would. I almost wanted to run up these stairs, like I used to. Back then, I'd always been running from something. Now it was as if I wanted to run to something: Kane. Wanting to be around Kane was a very bad idea, considering my current situation. I was only here because I had to be, even if part of me was happy about it.

I knocked on the door before I could think about it any longer. I'd avoided thinking about Kane, and the shit that bubbled up inside of me when he came to mind, for three months. I could do another day standing on my head with one hand tied behind my back, or at least pretend to.

There wasn't a response from inside, so I tested the doorknob. It was unlocked, so I let the door swing forward.

Kane was standing by the wall of windows that overlooked the main floor of the Underground, looking out.

He looked better than I'd remembered, and the memory was already pretty damn good. The dim lights reflected against his black hair. His profile seemed a little more hawkish, predatory. The woodsy, masculine scent of him was subtle in the air as I took a deep breath, remembering how much I liked his scent. His posture was relaxed, his white shirt sleeves rolled back, his arms crossed over his chest. I had to remind myself that even though he wasn't looking directly at me, he was probably aware of my every move.

I could feel the tension in the room as I took a few hesitant steps forward.

He finally turned toward me, and his deep-set hazel eyes seemed much colder than they used to be. That wasn't exactly unexpected, not after the way I'd left. No note, no goodbyes, just a bag packed in the wee hours of the morning.

When I first came here, I'd never thought of it as a permanent situation. It had been a means to an end, that *end* being a normal life at some point, one without crawlers breathing down my back at every turn. But along the way, the *means* had morphed into something else, something maybe just as important as the end goal. Even before I formed relationships with these people, not once had I imagined slinking out without a word. If I imagined a hundred different goodbyes, none of them would've been like that, if I'd wanted a goodbye at all.

Still, I'd had to do it, and I knew from the second I made the choice it was going to be hard. I just hadn't expected it to be downright agonizing.

Kane lifted a single eyebrow. It was the subtlest *what the fuck do you want* I'd ever gotten. Kane was good like that, making you feel like dirt without saying a word. In the time I'd known him, I'd seen him do it to countless people. Being on the receiving end sucked much worse than I'd imagined it would, and I gripped the back of the chair I'd stepped beside.

I was here now. I couldn't exactly go running from the room. Well, I could, but how stupid would I look then? Maybe if I warmed him up with some chitchat? I had to do something, because I feared I was about to get booted out of here on my ass.

"So, how are you?"

Both eyebrows rose now, as if to ask, *Did you really come here for small talk?*

He tilted his head slightly, getting the angle of his stare just right. I knew there was no way I'd get a warm welcome, and I was prepared for it. I hadn't been ready for the look in his eyes that called me an ingrate at best, a traitor at worst. I felt like my legs had been chopped out from underneath me and I'd shrunk a couple of feet.

He cleared his throat, in a *spit it out type* kind of way.

This was turning out to be much harder than I'd thought. I figured leaving the way I had might have hit the reset button between us—perhaps it would be similar to the tension when we first met, or maybe a couple of steps back. As I stood here in front of him, his stare harder than I'd thought it could be, I felt like I'd fallen to the bottom of a deep ditch and had nothing but my bare hands to claw my way out.

But I wasn't a quitter, and I'd come here because I was running out of options, so I'd claw until my fingers bled. "Everything looks like it's going well." Dead silence, and he turned back to his previous view of the Underground. I kept talking. "I've been meaning to stop by one of these days."

I groaned inwardly as I heard my small talk. It wasn't my forte under good circumstances, let alone a hostile environment. I might have been better off spitting out why I'd come and let the chips fall where they may, or come shooting back at me, if that were the case.

I forced myself not to look back at the door as I calculated how much of a mistake this had been.

He glanced back over at me before turning away again and saying, "I saw your commercial. All those Sesame Street-looking characters running around painted black? Stroke of genius to be sure. How did that work out? Get any bites from Shadow Walkers?"

My spine stiffened even as I felt my skin heat, in spite of the fact that I thought I'd forgotten how to blush a long time ago. Even if I hadn't heard the sarcasm that laced his voice, I would've known he was poking at me. After all, I'd seen my own commercial and I wasn't delusional.

Maybe that hadn't turned out the way I hoped, but I'd been trying to save Shadow Walkers. My intent had been good. What had I known about commercials? The director had a hundred good reviews online—all probably sock puppets, now that I thought back.

Even if Kane was mocking me, at least he was speaking to me. One hurdle crossed.

He straightened, still not looking at me as he said, "I've got a busy day. What do you want?"

There it was. The dismissal. He was finished with me. Yes, I'd left in a bad way, but I hadn't committed mass murder on the way out.

His eyebrows rose slightly with the silent question: *Why are you still here?*

Small talk was over. I wasn't ready to run out the door, but trying to get the words out felt a little like trying to cough up dirt.

It shouldn't be this hard to say. He needed me too. Our relationship hadn't been a one-way street, and I was sure after how long it took to find me, he hadn't replaced me. This was mutually beneficial. Nothing to sweat over. "I'd like to get back to work."

"Get back to work?" he repeated, as if he couldn't believe what I'd just said.

My fingers tightened a little more on the chair beside me. "Yes. I know from firsthand experience how hard it is to keep Shadow Walkers, so you can't say the position has been filled. We both need things, I'm sure." He was looking at me like he needed nothing except me out of his office.

He took a step toward me, and it didn't feel in the least friendly. It felt like I was about to be helped to the door.

"I already have what I need. Your services aren't required here. If you need money or resources, maybe you should ask that new boyfriend of yours."

I'd known Kane had eyes on me. That's who Kane was. He had eyes on everyone and everything. There was a reason he had this club, rented to all walks of life. He knew everything. Or thought he did.

But he definitely didn't know who he was calling my new boyfriend. So at least from afar, Asher passed for a regular guy. I'd been worried about that, and some of the tension I carried in here with me seeped out. Not all of it, though. I was still in the same mile-deep hole, and I desperately needed the man in front of me.

"I'm fine financially," I said, knowing that broadcasting my desperation would only hurt any slim possibility of negotiations. "I would like to shadow walk again, is all."

He walked over to his desk and perched on the corner of it as he gave me a grin that chilled. "Really? No problems financially? I heard you paid nearly double what you should've for that building. From what I heard, it was nearly eight million."

It had been him. He'd screwed up my deal. Every time I put a bid in, more bidders seemed to jump into the deal. I'd considered whether Kane had been behind my bad luck but told myself I was being paranoid. "It *was* you."

"I like real estate. What can I say if we have the same taste in buildings?" He picked up a pen and drummed it on the desk. "Then there was your commercial. Primetime is pretty expensive air."

"Are you willing to work with me or not?" I blurted out, not needing the accounting of my last three months. I knew it well. And he didn't know the full extent of it, like how the last million had disappeared out of my account.

"No." It was succinct and firm.

"No?" I thought he'd make it hell to work with him for a while, but I hadn't expected not to work with him at all.

"Yes. That is what I said. *No.*"

"But you had said—"

"My offer has expired."

"You didn't tell me there was an expiration on your job

offer." I was entering into a precarious place, and I knew that desperation was starting to cling to me like the stink of day-old gym clothes.

"There was. It expired the day you walked out without a word."

I could beg. I didn't know if it would make a difference, but it was either that or walk out. I'd never begged, no matter how hard my life had gotten, but I was damn close right now. I knew what would happen if I walked out. I didn't have family or friends to lean on. I'd eventually lose the building, and Asher and I would be homeless.

His eyes shifted to the door and back to me.

No. I still didn't have it in me. These knees didn't hit the floor for anyone. I'd rather sleep in my car than kneel for him.

I walked out, fairly certain I was entering worst-case-scenario territory.

Chapter 2

"YOU WENT OVER *THERE*, AND SPOKE TO *HIM*."

Asher was pacing the small living room of the apartment we shared in one of his full-blown fits, his brown hair now a shaggy length blowing back from his pale skin as he walked.

At first, I'd thought him coming out of his room and speaking to me was an improvement. Now I found myself preferring his initial reaction of refusing to speak to me for two hours.

If I wasn't positive he'd follow me, I would've gone downstairs and tried to hide out in the office. When I bought this building, I'd thought that space would be crawling with Shadow Walkers looking for help. I should change the lock on the door so Asher couldn't get in, and at least it would save one person.

"You know how I worry for you," he said, pacing in front of where I sat with my laptop.

"I know you do." I meant it, too. My gaze dropped to my keyboard as a wash of guilt fell over me. I repeatedly thought of ways of running away from him, and all he'd ever done was help me. Even now, as I sat here, the closest crawler was barely visible all the way across the room where it huddled. Asher had done that for me. He'd made my life livable.

When Asher had shown up in my room that night back at the Underground, with no idea how he'd gotten there, asking me—no, begging me—to help, I knew I'd do whatever I had to. I owed him my life. I owed him everything I had. If it weren't for what he'd done for me, I would've had to give up my own magic or else live a life that would've driven me mad.

And I might have to give him everything. I'd thought protecting and getting him on his feet after he'd landed out of the Shadowlands was going to be a few weeks, not a few months, and looking closer to a few years, if ever. Leaving him would be like abandoning a puppy at the side of the road.

I heard him grumbling again, and even though I couldn't make out the words, he'd been stuck on repeat for a while, so I already had a good idea.

"Asher, I had to do it. I had to try something." I'd lost count of how many times I'd said that today. It was like we both had a bad case of a stomach flu where we regurgitated the same argument over and over again.

If he knew what I had planned for later on today, he'd still probably be locked up in his room. I was wishing I told him I'd gone for a pedicure earlier.

He stopped right in front of me, and I kept my eyes on my screen, not wanting to deal with this anymore.

"You didn't *have* to. You *wanted* to. And look what happened. You looked near to tears when you walked in."

"I stubbed my toe on the way in." I hadn't, but I wasn't telling him that. And if I had been upset, it certainly wasn't because Kane had rejected me. It was because of our current circumstances, no matter what ideas Asher might get in his head.

"You wanted to see him."

I grabbed a pile of the bills that were spread out on the coffee table and held them up. "These things, they're bills. People want money for the things they give us, and I have no money left." He wasn't human, but I still thought he'd understand what the pile of bills on the table meant. It wasn't that hard of a learning curve, and I'd been explaining it repeatedly.

Three months ago I'd had a suitcase full of cash. Now it was all gone.

His shoulders rose and his head was shaking back and forth. "Can't you just talk to these people, the ones that give us things, and tell them we'll give them stuff later?"

I put my computer off to the side so I could run both hands through my hair, reminding myself that I didn't want to go buy a wig when I was ready to start pulling it out. No, I had to remain calm. Losing myself would get me nowhere. "Asher, remember how I told you about that? It works differently here. People don't just give you things on an IOU." I watched, hoping this was the time it was going to sink in.

It looked like he was on the verge of believing me when all of a sudden the *aha* light shone in his eyes. That light never boded well.

He was off and moving again. "We get free things all the time. What about the pretty pictures they give us as we walk?" He walked over to where he kept his flyers in a stack.

"Those are advertisements meant to tell us what we should buy. They're trying to sell us stuff so that we give them more money." Money I no longer had. I hadn't been completely irresponsible. I'd kept that separate account with the emergency money, enough to pay the taxes on this building and pay the bills for a long while. And when I needed it, it was all gone. That hadn't been the worst moment, though. That had come when the bank officer informed me that because it hadn't been reported within sixty days, they wouldn't reimburse me a dime of it.

If there were a bright side, Asher had fallen quiet, as if reality was finally seeping in.

He took a few paces to the left and then back, and I wondered if he'd picked up the pacing thing from me.

I'd gotten all my pacing out of the way earlier today before I'd gone over to see Kane.

"I'll work. I'll get one of those human jobs that pay lots of doppers." His pacing picked up until I was feeling dizzy.

"It's not doppers, it's dollars, and it's not that easy, Asher." Times like this, I wondered if I'd made the right choice. Maybe I should've taken my chances when Asher showed up and talked to Kane. Except they weren't my chances, they had been Asher's.

His pace seemed to slow as he walked the length of the living room a couple more times until stopping completely in front of the love seat. "Are you going to go back?"

"No. I told you. He wouldn't work with me." I was going to do something worse than that.

"I can't believe he'd refuse to work with you." His voice was soft, as if the insult of today was finally sinking in to his mind.

It had hit me like a hammer.

Asher came and sat down beside me, head bent as mine now was. "I'm sorry, Olivia, but it's for the best. I don't trust him. He's dangerous. You don't know what you're getting involved with."

There was no strength left for another conversation replay. I'd just made it to the other side of one argument when he wanted to rehash another. I didn't have it in me today. Definitely not today.

"As I said, he won't work with me, so it doesn't matter." *He's dangerous*, Asher would say. I'd heard it over and over again from Asher, but he never said why. He'd never even been face to face with Kane. He wasn't giving me anything to go on, and he hadn't shown great judgment to inspire confidence, and it was a moot point anyway.

"Are you hungry? I've got a fantastic meal planned for tonight." He jumped off the couch and walked toward the kitchen. This was what Asher did when he was trying to make peace or cheer me up. Feed me. As if that were key to the world's woes.

Asher had taken to the Food Network like a cat to tuna. As to how well he actually cooked, that was closer to a cat in the ocean. As far as shopping for the stuff, he was somewhere in between, but had been gaining speed.

"Lobster Fra Diavolo tonight, with a caviar appetizer. Got all the ingredients this afternoon."

"You bought that with the silver card?" It was a stupid question. There was only one card he had, and it was already overdrawn. The fees would add up to what he'd just spent on groceries, maybe more. The idea of food right now, or this week, wasn't even a little appealing. "Asher, I told you, emergency only."

"Eating food is critical for life."

"We're going to have to do cheap food. No more lobster."

His eyes dropped to the ground. Shit.

"It's all right. Just don't do it again, okay?"

His head shifted up, but not all the way. "You're sure it was okay?"

"Yeah. I'm sure." I patted him on the back as I stepped

toward the door. "It sounds so good I'm going to go get bread, okay? I'll be back by dinner, okay?"

He perked up and nodded.

I paused, looked at the charred wall over the range, and pointed to the corner where the fire extinguisher hung. "Don't forget, that gets rid of fire."

"I know."

Chapter 3

If Kane wasn't going to help me, I only had one choice left...that I knew of, anyway, and that was all that mattered at the moment. I climbed into my red Mini Cooper that still had the new-car smell clinging to it, amazed that I could drive all by myself, and plugged in the address.

I hadn't meant to commit this place to memory, but from the moment I'd overheard its location at the Underground, it had sort of burned itself in, as if I'd always known I might end up there.

The place wasn't that far away, but the price of the real estate here would've made you think it was a state away, but I guess that was to be expected when you were right on the Boston Harbor.

There was a valet as I pulled up to the curb, and I handed my keys over reluctantly as I toyed with the idea of finding a spot. I'd probably have to park so far away it wouldn't help me if I did have to make a quick getaway.

A man in a uniform pulled open a grand wood and glass door for me and I stepped inside a marble foyer. I walked over to the receptionist seated at yet more marble. This couldn't really be the place, could it?

I stopped in front of the desk where the young man was sitting and took another glance around.

He raised his eyebrows. "May I help you?"

"I'd like to speak to Collin?" I didn't know the alpha werewolf's last name. That might've been a good thing to have remembered along with the address. I reasoned that if I was in the right place, it wouldn't matter—he should know who I meant.

He nodded, and I nodded in return. Okay, I *was* in the right place.

"Your name?" He said it as if he'd been waiting for me to offer it already.

"Tell him Olivia Wit is here to speak with him. He'll know who I am." And that was all I was willing to tell him.

The phone on his desk started to buzz before he'd picked it up.

"Yes," he said, looking at me. "Yes, sir." He placed the phone back on the cradle. "Proceed up to the twentieth floor. Mr. Bard is waiting for you."

"Thank you," I said, in my politest tone, as if nothing untoward had happened.

I walked past him to the interior hallway lined with elevators while I tried to figure out what the hell I was going to say. This meeting needed to work out better than my last negotiations.

The elevator doors opened. And what a surprise. More marble. What was it with him and marble?

A brunette with a waterfall of thick, dark brown hair and a doll face rose from a desk situated to the right of double doors. "Ms. Wit?" she asked, smiling.

"Yes." I walked toward the double doors where she stood, motioning me to follow her.

She left the door open and waited beside it, asking, "Can I get you anything?" when I passed her.

"No, thank you."

She closed the door behind me as I stepped into the massive office, windows overlooking the best view of the harbor you could buy. I didn't want to be impressed, but sometimes it's not optional.

Collin wasn't too bad himself. There was a bit of an unrefined look to him, even dressed in a suit as he was. I wasn't sure if it was his protruding brow or jaw that seemed a bit too large for his face.

Thinking about suits, the one he was wearing could probably feed me for a month, and Asher for a weekend. The only issue with the suit was he didn't appear like he belonged in it. When Kane wore an expensive suit, he was still the main attraction.

Why was I even comparing him to Kane? Kane and I were over. I needed to evict him from my thoughts.

"Nice place you've got." Had to prime the pump here, as Collin was my last chance. I walked closer to where he was standing beside two couches facing each other.

He smiled like a man who liked getting complimented a little too much. "Thank you."

If all I had to do was fluff his ego, this was a done deal. Just with that small interaction, it had already surpassed my meeting with Kane.

Damn it, I was comparing again.

He waved a hand at one of the sofas. "Please, sit."

"Thank you." I situated myself square in the middle, hoping he'd take the hint and sit on the opposite couch.

There was only so much fluffing I'd do, and I wasn't crazy about the way his eyes were flickering over my neckline.

He settled across from me. "So, what can I do for you?"

"You've shown interest in working with me in the past." I left out the other things I'd thought he might want from me at the time. I knew that interest might still be there, but that offer wasn't on the table. "Are you still interested?"

His eyes narrowed, but I saw the uptick of his lips as he leaned back into the sofa. "You really did break ties. I knew you'd left, but Kane doesn't normally let go of his favorite toys."

Too many things about that last sentence burned to want to think on it more. I wasn't dwelling on Kane. I wasn't even going to think about him anymore.

"I've got no other obligations." There. Hadn't even said his name.

He nodded, way too happy with himself right now. I didn't think Collin was a really bad guy deep down, but he had some pretty annoying superficial qualities for sure. I didn't plan on sitting here all day while he smiled over stepping in shit.

"Unless you're scared to work with me?" That should speed up his massive ego a little.

He leaned forward, resting his elbows on his knees and losing the smirk. "What terms are you offering?"

Terms? I hadn't thought of terms. I hadn't thought past desperation. I went with the first thing that came to mind. "We alternate. I get the first spell, you get the second, and so on." That sounded pretty reasonable, and he must've agreed, because he nodded. Maybe too agreeable?

"But no wild goose chases. If I can't get a spell you want on the first try, it's done and over unless you want to keep using your turns." I wasn't wasting weeks for a spell like I had for...that person. I didn't have time for that. I had bills that had to get paid, and a quasi-human who had very expensive tastes to feed.

"I can live with that." He was rubbing the thick stubble on his chin as he sat there nodding again.

This was almost too easy. Maybe he was the desperate one? "Not to insult you, but are you sure you can do this?" Note for future self: if I had to warn someone that what I was about to say wasn't meant to be insulting, then odds were the person I was saying it to would get insulted. Prime example sitting in front of me, with red spreading over his cheeks. "I only say that because this is life or death for me."

Collin stood. "Kane likes to think he's the only one capable of anchoring, but he's not."

I wanted to laugh as I heard him lay blame for the insult at Kane's doorstep. "It's not that *I* don't trust you." Well, actually, I didn't, but if he wanted to heap blame on Kane, I wasn't fighting him.

His body was facing the door but he turned his head my way. "When did you want to start?"

"I'll call you tomorrow." I had one piece left to this puzzle.

———

I was stopped beside the oldest building I'd been able to find a few blocks away from the Underground. It was as close as I was willing to get to the place.

I got out and walked into the alley beside it so I could avoid looking crazier than necessary to anyone who might happen upon me. Plus, I didn't need anyone from the Underground spotting me here.

"Is there a gargoyle here?" I called as loud as I dared as I walked a circle in the alley. "Gargoyle?"

I spent another ten minutes calling for a gargoyle before one showed up. It was an especially ugly one with a cement pot belly.

"What? Who are you?" It leaned toward me in a way that a person might feel was slightly menacing.

I stood my ground. "I need to speak to Zee."

"So? Why are you here?"

"Don't you have a way of communicating?"

It was stone still for a moment before it said, "I'll call Zee, but don't come back here."

"Sure."

I crossed my arms as I moved a little further into the shadows and heard a few people passing by close to the alley. There wasn't anyone that walked these streets that I'd want to bump into.

And then Zee was standing in front of me, with her side pony, red stretchy pants, and white halter top.

"What? I'm busy and you aren't on the rolls anymore. You've been removed from service. You shouldn't be calling for me." Her words were much harsher than her expression.

I smiled in spite of them, and she rolled her eyes, even though I thought she might've been happy to see me.

"I've got a business offer for you."

She tilted her head, definitely interested. "What?"

She was in. That was all I needed. I just needed to negotiate a deal where she didn't take ninety percent of what we'd make. "I'm going shadow walking again, but I need someone who's good at sales to broker deals for me. I know you could move the spells."

And then we hit a brick wall, or a cement one in this case.

"Who are you shadow walking with?"

Did everyone feel like they should be running my life? "It doesn't matter. I'm going to be getting spells soon. Lots of them." I swept my hands wide. "Lots and lots. Can you move them or not?"

She looked down at her red claw nails and buffed them on her shirt before she finally said, "I probably can. I'll need a fifty-fifty split."

"No way. You're not getting fifty. I'll give you ten percent."

"Thirty."

"Fifteen."

"Twenty."

I took a moment to respond, as if I had other people in the wings willing to move all these spells I didn't have yet. "Deal."

She held out her hand and then pulled it back. "But I get spells for personal use on the house." She held her hand back out.

I pulled mine back in. "Within reason."

"Five a month."

"No, two." I held my hand out again.

"Fine." Zee took it. "I'll get you a list."

Chapter 4

THE WEBSITE WAS DOWN. THE COMMERCIAL HAD BEEN A HUGE miss and now the site was down. This was the worst host ever. How was I going to save other Shadow Walkers if they couldn't find me?

I flopped my head forward into my hand when it hit me.

Maybe it wasn't the host? That bill had been connected to the last account I'd had open, the one that Asher had ordered his lobsters with and was now as frozen as the tundra in the middle of a Russian winter. I reached forward to the basket that sat on the edge of my desk, the place where debt notices went to die a slow, unpaid death. I pulled it over and shuffled through it for the hosting company bill while I did a mental inventory of what pennies I could scrape together.

The door jingled.

"Hi, Sam." Sam, my mailman, was the only person besides me and Asher that ever stepped into this building. I waited for the new notices to hit the desk, and the friendly hello that accompanied the pile of dread. Once upon a time, I'd liked getting mail. It was hard to believe at the moment.

Wait, I'd already gotten the new stack of bills. That was when I caught his scent.

I raised my head to see Kane walking around my office. I quickly tucked the basket underneath my desk, where I nearly tipped it over.

I went from not seeing him at all for months to seeing him daily. I wasn't sure if it was a good thing. Had he changed his mind? Did he want to go back to work? Why else would he be here? I thought we'd said everything that was needed yesterday. Had he really changed his mind?

He didn't say hello as he took the place in.

I didn't say hello, either. It wasn't like we'd left each other feeling all warm and fuzzy. Plus, I'd already looked desperate enough, and it was understandable if I still had a bit of frost clinging to me after the way he'd acted. He'd shown up here. Let him state his case. If he wanted to work with me now, he was going to have to do some major groveling. Or a little groveling.

Who was I kidding? He'd have to ask, and that was about all the effort he would need to extend. But he hadn't said a word yet.

He stopped beside a poster painting, then tilted his head as if trying to understand the point of it. I understood. I'd hung it quickly in an attempt to give the place a warmer atmosphere with little effort.

His attention shifted down to the braided area rug that did very little to enhance the white ceramic tile. If he didn't get on with it, I was going to have to point out that his office at the Underground looked like the inside of a disorganized filing cabinet. But I'd let him ask me back to work first.

A really unpleasant thought popped into my head. Had he heard about my meeting with Collin? Collin wouldn't have said anything—to Kane, anyway. But I didn't put it past him to blab to all his people, many of which hung out in the Underground. It had only been yesterday, though. We hadn't even set a time frame yet. How many people could possibly know?

I watched him finish his lap around my office. The chill of his expression had me mentally scrambling.

Zee knew about it too. Could it have been her? Why would she give me up? She was standing to benefit from it, and she didn't even know who I'd be shadow walking with. Except that there was only one other person around that made any offer of being able to anchor someone. Still, why would she go run and tell Kane?

The bigger issue was it didn't matter. Even if he knew, it didn't matter. None of this was Kane's business. And before I picked this fight, it might be a good idea to make sure that was why he was even here.

Finally, he came back around. He moved until he was on the same side of my desk as I was seated and perched a hip on it as he stared down at me. I glared right back.

Oh yes, there was definitely going to be a fight. I wouldn't strike first, but I was preparing for a brawl.

"Collin isn't going to be able to help you out."

Stay calm. He could be bluffing. I didn't think he *was*, but it wasn't out of the realm of possibility. I mean, I'd just talked to Collin yesterday. He'd said yes. Would he roll over that quickly? He had more fight in him than that...I hoped. Even if he had rolled over, it was surely lip service to Kane.

I crossed my arms and narrowed my eyes. "According to you?" I leaned back, as if I had nothing to worry about. "My situation with Collin has nothing to do with you. You can't dictate to me. I came to you first, even though I didn't have to. If you don't want to work with me then I don't see how this is any of your business."

He nodded and shrugged, listening in the most arrogant and placating way until I was finished.

"I spoke with him and he agreed with me that it was a bad idea." He was so calm and condescending as he delivered what he knew was a huge blow.

Shit. So Collin had said he wouldn't. But then again, this was Collin. I wasn't sure how reliable his word was.

Don't lash out. Stay as calm as Kane was, the arrogant ass, as he leaned and looked at me as if he had all the answers. *Don't let him see how you want to tackle him to the ground right now.*

I slid my chair back and lifted my feet to rest on top of my desk as I leaned back. "Really? That's what he said, is it?" I didn't need to add *because we all know how much Collin's word is worth*. Unless he'd suddenly become deaf, Kane heard it in my tone. He knew the score.

If he was skeptical about Collin, the confidence in his expression didn't portray it. "I think you'll find he's fairly dug into his position now that we've discussed it. And if he does have a change of heart? It won't last long."

I was screwed. He'd officially boxed me into a corner. No, a bottomless pit. I might've been able to work my way out of a corner.

"Why are you making things difficult for me? Because I left without telling you? It wasn't that bad!"

His expression didn't change as he stood. He turned his back on me and walked toward the door, leaving without bothering to answer my question.

I waited all of two minutes, or however long it was for him to get in his car and pull away before I called Collin.

He didn't answer the first call. I got dumped into voicemail and my mouth grew dry. It was the second time I got dumped into voicemail that my palms grew slick. It took two more tries before he answered the phone.

When he answered the phone with a generic "Hello," as if he didn't know who was calling, my hope was slipping down into the gutter.

"It's Ollie. I want to start tonight." I pressed my phone hard to my ear, afraid I'd miss his answer somehow and hoping it would prove Kane wrong—praying that Kane hadn't really gotten to him yet. I paced to the back of the office, out of sight if you were looking through the front windows. I wasn't sure if I was being careful or paranoid.

He wasn't speaking. I looked down at the phone and checked to make sure I hadn't lost my signal before putting it back to my ear. "Did you hear me? We should meet tonight."

There was a long pause before he said, "Uhm, yeah...I'm not sure tonight is good for me."

"How about tomorrow night?" I asked, swallowing down the acid that was gurgling up and threatening to choke me.

"Let me check my calendar and get back to you. I think I have a couple of bad weeks coming up." His voice held none of his normal swagger, and was bordering on brittle.

I stopped pacing and thudded my hips into the wall, rattling my cheap poster prints. "Check your calendar or check with Kane?"

"Olivia...he says he'll kill me. When Kane says he'll kill you, it's not a saying. It means. He'll. Kill. You." He sounded as desperate as I was feeling.

Neither of us spoke, and the silence was thick.

I was screwed, completely. I took a couple of deep breaths before saying, "I get it. Let me know if anything changes."

There was a quick "sure" and then an even quicker

hang-up. I pocketed the phone and then scrubbed my face with my palms. What was I going to do now? I had no money. No options. Going back to work was useless, as I had more debt than a cashier could even hope to keep afloat. I didn't have a spell to my name, and Asher's magic dried up the moment he'd crossed out. He was in worse shape than me in that department. I'd at least been able to set some butterflies to flight. He couldn't even say the words.

I'd had such big plans. I was going to save all Shadow Walkers, help them have normal lives. Instead, I couldn't even save myself. I was about to lose the roof over my head because I didn't have a dime to pay the tax bill and the utilities were going to be shut off.

And then there was seeing Kane again. I'd thought—hoped—he was going to say he'd changed his mind. That he wanted to work with me. When he didn't, I realized, things weren't going to be the same between us, not now and probably not ever.

"Ollie?" I straightened as I looked over to where Asher was standing beside the stairwell that led to the apartment above. "What's wrong?" He made his way over toward me.

The hurt was still too tender to speak of at all, let alone hash over for hours, as was Asher's way. I forced a smile. "Nothing at all. Just a long day and I'm tired." I straightened and made my way back to my desk, where I sat down and started flipping through some of the papers there, as if he'd merely caught me in a momentary break.

I could see him wavering between stepping forward and turning around. "Okay. Well, dinner is done."

I nodded, afraid to ask what we were having tonight and where he'd gotten the money. "Great. I'll be up in a few minutes, after I lock up."

I turned back to the stack of bills, praying he'd leave. I

didn't breathe until I heard the door shut and his footsteps on the stairs.

I got up and walked out of the room and then out the back door, my breathing even and my spine straight. Squinting into the dark, I didn't see another soul, and I didn't hear any sounds.

That was when I sagged against the brick of the building. I wasn't going to cry. It was stupid to cry. I'd been in worse situations, way worse.

So why was I acting like such a ninny over some bills?

Then I pinpointed the problem. For a while there, I'd had hope. Mountains of hope. I was going to become the magical phenomenon who would save all the Shadow Walkers. I'd had the resources to do it.

Now here I was. I hadn't saved one. Kane wouldn't work with me. I had no magic left and I had no money for bills. I'd had windows of opportunity months ago and I'd failed epically.

And Kane hated me.

I let the sobs shake my body, not caring about holding back anymore.

Chapter 5

I WALKED OUT OF THE CAR LOT WITH SLOW STEPS, LEAVING MY pretty little Mini Cooper behind, along with another chunk of my pride. It had been one of my first purchases after I left the Underground. I remembered it hitting me, that not only could I drive in peace without crawlers rubbing shoulders with me, I had the money to buy a car. I'd had lots of money, courtesy of Kane.

I'd taken a hit on the car, but because I'd paid cash, at least I had enough money to feed me and Asher...for a bit. I was on foot but we'd be eating dinner tonight. Plus, cars weren't much fun if you didn't have gas for the engine. Without gas, they were more like awkward street sofas that blocked the wind, and this would buy me some time to come up with another solution.

The one thing I'd been good at doing, the thing that would've paid the bills, was over unless I could find another anchor. There *had* to be more anchors out there. Except I didn't know exactly what made an anchor. Might've been a good thing to ask before I left the Underground months ago while Kane was still speaking to me.

Until Kane scared them off too. Bottom line was he wanted to screw me, and if Kane wanted to screw with you, you might as well hand him the screwdriver yourself, because it was over.

I could always sell the building. I'd overpaid, but it had been another cash deal. These were all things that would be pondered after some chicken chow mein.

I popped into Mr. Lee's, grabbed the Chinese food I'd ordered before I left the car lot, and was back out walking in under five minutes. That was when it became obvious that I was being followed.

The guy all the way at the end of the street, in the dark blue sweatshirt and white cap, had been walking behind me before I'd went in for Chinese. After going in and getting my dinner, he was again walking behind me at the exact same distance. A couple of right turns confirmed the guy was following me, unless he'd also meant to do a U-turn at the exact time as me.

Damn, Kane. As if screwing me with the Collin situation wasn't enough? I had no choice but to slowly sell off everything I could, but that wasn't bad enough. Now he was having me followed.

He was really pulling from the bottom of the barrel now, though. The guy was sloppy, *really* sloppy. Butch and Leon might have their faults, but I'd never seen them until they wanted to be seen. They'd managed to leave a note in my apartment, an apartment I'd barely left, without me knowing.

Or maybe it wasn't Kane? He had better people than this. But if it wasn't him, who was it?

Damn if my fingers didn't want to reach into my purse, grab my cell phone, and call up Kane to ask. If someone would know why I was being followed, it would probably be him. But that wasn't our relationship now, and I doubted if he'd answer my call. This was my problem, and I was fully capable of working it out myself.

I started checking off the list of who could be following me and realized there were quite a few potentials. I not only had monetary debts, I had magical debts. I still owed the dwarves for the clothes, I owed the fae for the location of the retired shadow walker, and I owed the gargoyles. Some of them were probably getting tired of waiting to be paid. If I had access to magic, I would've settled them all, but as it was, unfortunately for everyone, I had nothing.

I didn't have to owe the vampires. Alexandria, queen vampire, hated me either way, and it was dark out, so they were contenders. Couldn't forget that the shifters hadn't been particularly fond of me, and the witches downright hated me. It would be great if I knew who was tailing me, but it might have been any number of supernatural breeds.

When I really thought about it, it was surprising I hadn't been followed before now. Bunch of slackers.

I picked up my pace as much as I could without it being too obvious. There was a row of stores coming up on the right, almost all of which I'd been in, and at least some of them had a back exit. Luckily, I knew this area. Hopefully the guy following me didn't know it nearly as well.

I held my jacket closed with one hand as a cool spring breeze off the harbor nailed me, and resisted the urge to check if he was still there. It was better if they thought I was oblivious. If he knew I was watching my back, it might make it that much harder to figure out who was watching me.

There it was, the candle shop I liked, and it definitely had a back exit they let the public use. Unless you were a regular customer, you wouldn't know about it.

I ducked in and got a smile and a wave from one of the

workers as she was helping another customer. I walked around and sniffed for a couple of minutes so they didn't think I was using them for their back door, while working my way farther into the shop.

I sniffed my way through the store for another ten minutes as the smell of the Chinese food clashed with Sugar Cane Candy.

Maybe my luck was changing—the alley was clear except for a cat by the dumpster. I didn't make it two steps before there was a blow to the back of my head and I went crashing to my knees.

———

There was a rough bag over my head when I came to. I was lying on my side with my hands tied behind my back. I could feel the rope digging into my ankles. Whoever had done the tying must've thought I was Houdini.

I could feel the cold of the floor seeping through my clothes, and from the musty smell, I was definitely in a basement. There weren't any voices, but I heard the shuffling of feet a short distance away.

I had no spells, no magic. I was as vulnerable as I'd ever been in my life. At a complete loss of what else to do, I did nothing. I pretended I was still out cold.

More feet shuffling, and this time they were closer.

"She still out or is she faking?"

There was a strange accent to the man's voice. Similar to an Irish brogue, but different somehow. Was it distinct to the individual or his race?

"Hasn't moved, but I think she's awake." A second male voice, same accent. So, seemed it was connected to the race. I'd never heard it before, but I'd guess it was the leprechauns. Yes, I owed them a debt for getting Flip the address of the Shadow Walker, but wasn't this overkill on collection? Flip had warned me they were hardcore.

I heard someone's phone ring and then muffled words, like the person who called was talking really loudly.

"Leave her for now. She's not going anywhere, and it might be a long night."

Both sets of feet moved, and then I heard the sound of a door, one that sounded horribly heavy.

I wiggled the loose bag off my head and tried to get my bearings. Definitely in a basement. There were two windows down here, and they both had bars over them. Inching backward, I used the wall to help edge up into a seated position.

There was nothing down here, not even a heating system. The place had dust and dirt piled up in the corners, but nothing that was going to cut through these ropes.

There was also a crawler in the corner, a smaller one in the furthest corner from me, its attention completely focused on me, as if it knew my thoughts.

Could I talk to it without someone anchoring me and not blow this place up, taking me with it? It was a risk, a huge one, but it might come down to that. If I could, and I managed to shadow walk, alone and unanchored, would it matter if I got a spell if I couldn't make it out?

Was I that desperate yet? No. Not yet, anyway.

The door swung open and I met my captors face to face. Not *too* scary looking, though one had a scar running diagonally across his face, as if he'd come out on the bottom of a knife fight. The other guy's nose looked like it had tried to take a left turn halfway toward his lips. They wore the appearance of violence the way Zee wore lipstick.

Scar came and kneeled a foot away from my side. His reached a hand out toward me, and I jerked my face to the side. His hand followed me, gripping my chin with his fingers. "How the mighty have fallen."

My eyes shot to him and then shifted away.

"Oh, we know all about you. Us leprechauns are always keeping our ears to the ground. You're the Shadow Walker no one was allowed to touch. Kane's precious." He let go of my chin to run a finger down my cheek.

Weren't leprechauns supposed to be short? Probably not the time to ask. "Is this about the debt? I was going to pay you next week," I said, hoping they weren't looking for a different type of payment.

Crooked squatted next to Scar, nudging him with his elbow in a *cut it out* manner. "Where did you put it?"

Huh? "Put what? Money? I told you I'll pay."

Crooked shook his head slowly, his eyes never leaving mine. "We don't want money. We aren't playing around. We want what you took. Where is it? Where's our map?"

Even if I wanted to tell them, I had no idea what they were talking about. "I have no idea—"

"No one ever believes us." Crooked shook his head. "Chuck here, he likes hurting little girls." He nodded toward Chuck. "Give her a little taste."

Chuck pulled a knife from his ankle, and then Crooked was yanking my shoulders forward. The rope around my wrists was cut, along with a bit of my skin, and before both arms fell forward, Chuck had one arm in his hand and was twisting it upward at an angle it wasn't supposed to move.

The air whooshed out of my lungs with a small squeak, and then I was panting as I was held leaning partially forward, trying to brace myself with my free arm.

Crooked shifted lower so he could look me in the eyes. "It only gets worse. Are you sure you don't want to tell me where the map is?"

"I'd tell you if I had it. I don't." They were violent, but I hoped they weren't insane. "Why would I take your map?"

"Because you are the most likely culprit. Are you sure you have nothing else to say?"

"It's hard to say anything else when I don't have it."

"Chuck?"

Chuck placed both hands on my arm and then yanked it. A searing pain ripped through me. When he let go, I was gasping for air and my arm was dangling at a weird angle. I fell forward, my cheek pressed to the cement.

"Can I do the other one?"

"Not yet. Let that one marinate for a while. We'll come back in an hour or so, after she's had some time."

"I think I should do it now," Chuck said.

Crooked stared down at me as he said, "Patience. You'll have plenty of time with her."

Chapter 6

I pushed with my feet, moving farther into the corner, every move shooting pain into my arms. They'd held true to their word, and now both arms were useless, and I felt a stabbing pain with every breath.

I heard footsteps above me and muffled voices I couldn't make out, all while I prayed they wouldn't come back downstairs.

They were going to question me again, ask me about the missing map. I didn't know how many more beatings I could take. If I had any idea, I would've told them. If I had any magic, I would have made them a map just to get rid of them.

There was light streaming in the window, and even though I knew I hadn't been here for a full day, it was already feeling like a lifetime. Or the rest of my lifetime, as I wasn't sure if I'd set foot out of this place again.

I looked over at the farthest corner. The same crawler was there, watching me. It was waiting for its opportunity, and it might get it. I'd rather go out in a blast, or get lost in the Shadowlands, than sit here and wait for them to kill me. At least I'd go out trying.

Whatever this building was, it was old. Was it possible that maybe it was gargoyle-worthy old? Was I somehow still wired in, maybe? I'd been able to call a gargoyle before.

Even if I couldn't get Zee, maybe I could get a gargoyle like I had before. On my list of options, it was definitely higher up than burning to death or fading away in the Shadowlands.

"Zee? Can you hear me? I need a gargoyle," I whispered.

Zee popped in instantly and looked around. "How the hell did you call me here? I can't be here. This isn't my building, or anyone's building, and I don't even know how you got to me. You've been officially off my roster for months."

"Shhh," I whispered, afraid she'd alert them before I could get a word in, but she wasn't paying me much attention.

She shuddered as if finding the place utterly unpleasant, and then her eyes finally landed on me for more than a second and she took a step back. "What the fuck happened to you?" She pointed at my shoulder area. "You don't look right."

"I need help." I was gritting my teeth through the words now, trying to move forward.

She nodded, pursing her lips, and said, "I should think so."

"Can *you* help me?"

"I can't help."

Was she really going to just stand there and not help? I was about to break down again. I was *not* having a good week.

Her hands went up. "Not here, not against the leprechauns. I'm out of my jurisdiction. I literally can't help you. It's against the magic that binds me. I do anything while you're here and I'm dead." She patted her chest.

I heard the sounds of footsteps hitting stairs and whispered to Zee, "Get Kane." She was already gone before I got the words out. I was fairly certain she'd heard me. What I wasn't certain about was whether he'd help me.

I looked over at the crawler, who'd moved a couple of feet closer to me, as if it knew how desperate I was getting.

If I didn't take the chance soon, these men might kill me, and that would be the end of it.

I swallowed, my mouth dry, as I heard the footsteps on the stairs getting closer. Did I do it? Did I talk to the crawler and hope for the best? It inched even closer, as if I were calling it to me.

The door creaked open before I'd gathered up the guts to speak to it. Chuck walked in, and headed toward me. Crooked paused by the door, digging out his buzzing phone.

"Yeah?" he said, as Chuck kneeled by me, his gaze moving over my torso and then shifting to my legs. If he dislocated my legs, I'd never be able to escape. Not that there was a great chance now, but it would dwindle to zero.

I looked back at the crawler, knowing my options had run out, and was about to speak to it when Crooked stepped forward.

"Hang on," Crooked said to Chuck. "Don't do anything yet. We're getting company."

"So?" Chuck asked as if someone had stolen the lollipop from his hand.

"So, the big guy said wait." Crooked pocketed his phone and crossed his arms. "We gotta wait."

Chuck glanced at me and then back to Crooked. "He's coming? He told *us* to handle it."

"No. Someone else," Crooked said, and then licked his lips as if this other person was making him nervous.

If he was making him nervous, it was definitely a good thing for me. The crawler was hissing toward me off to the side, as if trying to draw my attention to it. *Nope, not talking to you yet. Hiss away.*

"For what?" Chuck asked.

Crooked opened his hands and swung them outward. "I don't know. Maybe to help?"

Chuck walked the basement, but every time he got close to me, Crooked warned him off. Something was about to go down, and Crooked wasn't looking too happy.

Five minutes later, I heard another pair of feet hitting the stairs. The door swung open and the air was sucked right out of my lungs.

Kane walked in the basement. He hadn't fought his way in. He'd walked downstairs as if invited. He was their company? What the hell did that mean? Was he here to help them or me?

He glanced at me, taking in my condition, and I couldn't see a drop of emotion in his eyes. Had he known they were going to drag me in here? Was he in on this? Did they do it for *him*?

Kane turned toward Crooked. "You said you questioned her."

Had he known or just found out? My attention turned to Crooked, and the way he was trying to causally widen the gap between them.

"We d-did," he said.

Kane's jaw shifted. "Why does she look like that, then?"

Crooked quickly swung a hand in Chuck's direction. "He might've dislocated her arms."

Kane's attention swung to Chuck. "You did the handiwork?"

Chuck tipped his head after a long moment.

And then he didn't have a head anymore. Had Kane just ripped it off? It was there one second and then gone. I might've gasped, but it was lost to the sound of Crooked dry-heaving beside Chuck's head.

Kane waited for him to stop and straighten up.

"You overstepped your bounds," Kane said to Crooked.

Crooked stepped back, lifting his hands in a gesture of surrender as he did. "Complete misunderstanding."

Kane took a step, following him. "Do you understand why I'm letting you live?"

Crooked nodded furiously.

"Good."

Another blur and then Crooked was flat on his back. Blood ran thick down the side of his face from his shattered nose. But at least he still had his head, and his chest was moving. His face...that was another story.

Maybe Kane didn't hate me? The way he'd talked, though, he knew I was here. But for how long? Had Zee gotten to him? How much had he known before her?

Kane took a step in my direction. "Can you walk?" I saw him taking inventory of my injuries.

I managed to get to my feet before he could offer to help. It was bad enough I'd needed saving.

He walked toward the basement door, holding it open for me. I wasn't going to fight with him about how he'd known I was here, or if he'd known why, until I was *out* of here. Why? Because I wasn't stupid. There were more questions rattling around in my brain, but my top priority was to get out. I'd figure out the rest after that.

I made my way slowly up the stairs, managing to grit my

teeth through the pain, the adrenaline from leaving helping me out a bit. The house was empty as we walked through it, except for a few sparse furnishings. A couch in the living room. A couple of chairs and an empty pizza box on the table in the kitchen. This wasn't a home but a place of business—seedy business.

Kane opened and shut all the doors as I managed not to scream.

Fresh air was hitting my skin and filling my lungs, and it never smelled so good before because I knew how close I'd come to dying in that basement.

"Can you make it a couple of miles?" Kane arranged his body to block me from people walking across the street as we made it to the passenger door of his car.

"I can make it as far as I need to."

Without asking, he helped me into the car. It was a good thing he hadn't, because I would've insisted I had it and probably would've fallen on my face.

All my intentions of questioning him once we got out of there went by the wayside as soon as the car started moving over early spring potholes. Each bump in the road felt like a hot poker sticking me, warmed in the fires of hell.

By the time he'd pulled the car into an alleyway several miles shy of the Underground, I was ready to crack my teeth in my effort not to scream out. He walked around and opened the passenger door for me, and I wondered why the hell he was dropping me off here.

If he had come to save me, wouldn't he be bringing me to a safe location, like my home? Or was he going to finish the job, in which case this was the perfect place? It was far enough away from his building that if the fleshy bits got stuck in the concrete, my remains wouldn't stink up the alleyway. It was wonderful how Butch's words chose this moment to pop into my head.

"Why did you stop here?" I'd been nervous around Kane in the past, but never thought he'd kill me. Not even when I first met him had I thought he'd actually kill me. But now, after realizing he'd known those goons had me, I'd be a fool not to consider it.

"Get out." He stood waiting while I debated my next move. It was a quick debate, considering I didn't have one.

Kane helped me get out of the car as I moved a foot out. Didn't seem like he was going to kill me.

He moved so quickly, and the pain was so intense, I thought he was killing me. I would've struck out at him in a feeble attempt, but he'd gripped both of my arms. When he let them go, his hands were at my waist, leaning me against the car. My arms were back in their sockets.

As soon as I could speak, I said, "Thanks. You could have warned me, though."

I forced my head up when he didn't speak, and I saw him staring off down the alley, almost on the other side now, as if he didn't want to be too close. It felt like an act, as if all his senses were still trained on me. I glanced down the other way, knowing that even though it was a short run, I'd never make it. It was a silly thought. He'd saved me; he'd fixed my arms. But the underlying anger I felt coming from him in waves would make anyone fear they might get pulled under.

"Would've made it worse," he finally said. His words echoed in the alley.

I wasn't sure if it was the shade of the alley that was giving me a chill or the coldness of his eyes as he asked, "Have you taken anything that didn't belong to you?

"You too?" What was this? Was there a strange contagion

going around? Was I going to get home and have Asher asking me the same thing?

"Answer the question. Have you taken anything that doesn't belong to you since you left the Underground?" He took a few more steps away and even gave me his back, as if trying to lure me deeper into the facade of safety. Had he fixed my arms for the same reason? Was this all a trap?

No. Not all for show. He'd really killed that man back there.

"Olivia."

"I don't know what you're talking about. I didn't know what they were talking about when they kept asking about their map."

I watched him take another measured step across the alley and then turn back to me. "Tell me you didn't take anything."

He was staring at me in a way that made me thankful I could honestly say, "I didn't take anything."

He nodded once. I'd passed his test.

He walked back to the car, standing beside it and waiting for me. "Get in."

I didn't move. "What would've happened if I'd said yes?"

I wasn't sure if I wanted to get in the car with him. I might be better off on my own. After all, what did I really know about this man? My naivety had led me to believe I was safe with him, but that was quickly changing.

"Get in," he said, his tone suggesting he was growing tired of waiting.

I took a step toward the car but with no intention of getting in. "Would you have killed me?"

His jaw locked, and it looked like he had to fight to get the next words out. "I don't know."

He got in the car as if his answer, his indecision over my

life, was nothing. As if it was not a question of the utmost importance, at least to me.

Three months ago, I wouldn't have worried about being abandoned in an alleyway by Kane. Now I was choosing whether my odds were better being left here or getting in with him. How things had changed.

He'd believed me when I'd said I hadn't taken anything. If he hadn't, I might've already been a mass of meaty bits in the concrete.

I looked around, knowing what walked these streets so close to the Underground. I didn't know why this missing map was so important, or why I was the prime suspect, but I did know I had two banged-up shoulders and not a lick of magic on hand.

I got in the car.

Chapter 7

I SHIFTED ON THE CAR SEAT, TRYING TO FIND A COMFORTABLE
position that didn't exist, and probably wouldn't for at least
a week or so from the feel of things.

It looked like we were heading toward the Underground,
but I wasn't taking anything for granted at this point.
"Where are you bringing me?"

"Underground."

He made a couple more turns and then we were pulling
up to the familiar building.

"I need to get home." I'd already been missing for a day.
Asher would be climbing the walls at this point. Imagining
what he might do was almost as bad as being stuck in that
cellar.

"When I'm done." He shut the car off and got out.

Well, so much for that debate. As much as I worried
about getting home, figuring out why I was abducted in the
first place wasn't a bad thing either. He wasn't the only one
who wanted some answers.

I followed him into the Underground and up to his office
without too many stares. Definitely more than I'd gotten the

other day, though, as people probably wondered if I was working for him again.

Or maybe they were looking because I appeared to have just woken from a nap in a dumpster. *That* might be it.

He sat in his chair behind his desk, his expression not telling me anything.

I moved to the other side of the desk, forgoing the couch. The couch harkened back to the past, a time when this had felt like the safest place I'd ever been. Today, I wanted to make sure I had clear access to the door and a good running start.

Kane gave me a hard look, then shifted his eyes toward the door and back. "You really think standing makes a difference?"

My hand tightened where it rested on the back of the chair in front of me. I didn't have an answer for that—or not a good one that would put him in his place. I'd seen him move so fast that it was as if he'd materialized in a different spot. I might've been clinging to a delusion of escape, but that wasn't something I was willing to share.

"I could give you a demonstration if there's any doubt." He kicked his heels up on the desk and then crossed his ankles, rubbing in the fact that he might have an edge on me—or a mile.

I felt my jaw shifting and locked that sucker down. I walked around to the front of the chair and sat. *There, you win—this time. Now let's move it along.* "What did you want?" I was done with the niceties. I'd tried that and it had gotten me nowhere.

The side of his mouth looked like it wanted to tick up into maybe a smirk, but it didn't. Not that there was any joy here. The easy banter we'd started to have before I left the Underground, the playful pushing and prodding at each other that had become almost ritualistic—there wasn't even a remnant of that relationship now.

As we sat across from each other, there was little doubt what we were—adversaries. It would be nice to know what we were fighting over, but I'd clearly been given my role, and I was fully accepting it now.

"If I was getting what I wanted, we wouldn't be speaking."

I stayed relaxed in spite of the chill in his words, or how they made me want to run out of the room. There wasn't a reason in the world he'd understand why I did what I did. I couldn't expect him to.

And I couldn't tell him why, either, not without risking Asher. As if I didn't feel bad enough physically, the guilt was topping me off.

I shifted, trying to angle myself in a way where everything wouldn't feel so godawful sore, but as soon as I moved, the spot I'd gotten kicked in the ribs acted up. I shifted back, preferring the shoulder pain and easier breathing.

"Lie on the couch if it's so bad." The way he snapped out the order, it seemed like he was more annoyed than I was at the inconvenience.

"I'm fine, thank you." There was about as much warmth in my thanks as his offer.

He nodded toward where I was sitting. "I don't feel like watching you bounce around on the chair."

"Well, you'll just have to deal with it until you spit out whatever it is you need to say." I was hurt, and not just in body. Yes, I'd left, but he didn't once even ask why. It was either rage at him or cry, and I didn't cry. Or I didn't used to. I certainly wasn't doing it again now. My eyes might've burned from the effort, but I absolutely was not sitting here in front of him and breaking down—again. My utter lack of emotional control was becoming a bigger embarrassment than having had eight million dollars months ago and not being able to pay my bills.

"Goddamn it." He was shaking his head and walking toward the supply closet. "Come with me." He turned, expecting me to follow, and I didn't think it was to get more pens.

"Why?" I knew where that closet led, and I was not going into that cellar place. I'd just made it out of one and I wasn't pressing my luck. I was staying above ground for the foreseeable future unless I was dragged below. That might still be on the table, unfortunately.

He stepped back out and stared at me. "You know, you were a lot more fun when you had a death wish."

"Sorry to be such a killjoy. Personal growth and all that. What's down there that you want to show me?"

"Something that'll fix you so I don't have to watch you..." He waved a hand at where I sat.

His annoyance was barely a blip on my radar. "You've got something to heal me?" He had helped me heal before; I'd just been too out of it at the time to realize and remember. Now, that might be worth going into another basement for.

If the shit was about to hit the fan—and looking at the flying turds coming my way, I didn't have a lot of time on my hands to rest up—I needed to be a hundred percent. Even then, without some spells, I was starting at a deficit against these leprechauns and who knew what else might be coming for me.

I stood and took a step but froze. It could be a trick. What if this was all a lure?

No. That didn't make any sense. Kane didn't have to lure me in. He would've killed me in the alley.

While I was still debating, he said, "For fuck's sake, stay here and wait."

I sat back down. I was too sore to keep climbing stairs anyway.

He walked back up a minute later and placed a bottle that looked a little like it could've been olive oil on the desk in front of me. "Rub that into your shoulders."

I lifted the jar and then gave it a shake, expecting something magical to happen. It didn't. "That's it? This is the cure?"

"Yes." His voice was as sharp as a razor.

I didn't care if I was annoying him. I felt like utter shit, and I didn't want to leave with the wrong stuff.

"Will it work on anything else?" It looked like massage oil. Maybe this wasn't so special? I hoped it was better than stuff I could've bought at the bath shop.

"Like what?"

I stopped shaking the bottle and glanced at him. Why was he snapping at me now? "It was just a question."

"Then why are you touching your side?" His eyes shot to my left side, where my free hand had settled.

Damn him. Who noticed every stupid detail? "I don't know. I'm sore?"

"It'll work for broken ribs." He didn't snap this time. "If you need more, let me know."

I nodded, accepting the non-apology.

"So, what am I doing here?" I stood, bottle in hand, and made my way across the office, wondering if I could dab a little bit of this stuff on now.

"There are some things missing, things that cause people to kill other people."

"Like what?" I asked, figuring it was best to know who else might come looking for things.

"A map was stolen from the leprechauns. A vial, containing blood of one of the strongest alpha werewolves to ever live, was stolen last night. A pendant was stolen from the vampires."

I snorted, knowing who'd be upset about that one. Alexandria, the oh-so-pleasant vampire—her boyfriend would surely die way before her without that.

I'd uncorked the bottle as I listened and was trying to dab some on my shoulders while he talked. "What would I do with any of that?"

He stood and walked around the desk and then leaned against it. "Let's just say the rest of us have very well established relationships, built over lengthy periods of time. Now, there's a new girl on the block, a new Shadow Walker who's stronger than any of her predecessors, and things go missing. There's going to be an obvious suspicion in your direction."

"It still doesn't make any sense." I dabbed more oil on my hand and tried to get another spot on my shoulder.

"Do you need help?" He said it in a way that made it clear he didn't really want to help me at all.

"I'm fine."

His lips flattened, as if he was annoyed I hadn't taken him up on an offer he hadn't wanted to make.

"All of these things combined would make it possible for a crawler to survive outside of the Shadowlands."

I nearly dropped the bottle when my hands broke into an immediate tremble.

"It's unsettling," Kane said, as if thinking this was a perfectly normal response.

He thought it was my fear of crawlers. Of course he would. "Yeah, it's terrifying."

Had Asher somehow gotten these things? No. I'd asked

him so many times how he'd gotten out, and every time he said he didn't know. He'd been in the Shadowlands and then in my room. Maybe I was crazy, but I'd believed him when he said he hadn't known.

I dabbed more oil on my fingers and was liberally slathering it on me now. It wasn't like I had to worry about my clothes. They were already filthy. "If you don't think I took them, why am I here?"

"Because you can get a spell to find those things."

Ahhh, and here we were. Maybe I wasn't in such a bad spot after all. Somebody just got dealt pocket aces. "Why would I do that?"

"Because I'm the only one in this world who can keep you alive. You leave here without me backing you and it's going to be one basement after another until eventually someone decides to leave you in a ditch somewhere." Now he smiled, but it wasn't one of his nice, warm, welcoming ones. He was smiling because he had the straight flush.

"What are you proposing?" It was pretty clear, but at this point, I wanted it chiseled in stone.

"We work together, for as long as it takes."

I nodded. This was not the time to go there, and yet, thinking back to how he treated me when I'd come here asking to work together, I couldn't stop myself. "*You* want to work with *me*?"

His eyebrows rose. "I'm throwing you a lifeline. You're not in a position to gloat."

I was the one smiling now. "And yet I strangely feel like doing just that. What a mystery." I wasn't sure if he was amused or annoyed, but I knew I had to lock some more details down before he gave me the boot for being obnoxious. "If we are going to be back working together, it can't only be for what you need."

"You think keeping you alive is one-sided?"

"I need to be able to get some spells, too." Spells that would keep my lights on.

"Then get them. I won't stop you."

I wanted to dance around the office, but I wouldn't. I'd wait until I got out of here and then dance around my building, the one I might be able to keep.

I was back to dabbing oil as an excuse to be distracted while I got my wits about me when I realized the stuff was actually working.

I lifted the bottle, still not impressed by its appearance but nodding in a silent *nice job*. It was as gracious as I was willing to be at the moment, considering Kane might've been willing to kill me in the alley, and might still want to kill me if he found out about Asher. He'd get a thank you when I was sure I was going to live past this week.

He shrugged, as if to say, *Not a big deal*. "You look like shit, by the way."

"Sorry. I didn't have time to pretty up before you stopped by."

"I tried calling ahead of time but you didn't answer."

I shifted and then laughed for no other reason than I was still alive and I had Kane watching my back again. Considering the whopper of a secret I was hiding, I shouldn't have been so happy about that.

"When do we start?"

When he didn't answer right away, I looked his way and caught him staring at where I'd inadvertently lifted my shirt up slightly. I'd been trying to get to my ribs, but let it drop quickly when I saw the bruises he was staring at, the dark purple that ran up my side.

"Soon. Butch will drive you home." He stood and walked toward the door, leaving me in his office alone.

What? Had he expected me to fight them off or some-thing? I couldn't win with Kane. Right as I think we're getting to a place we might be able to work with each other, he gets all weird again.

Butch and Leon walked in a couple of minutes after Kane had left.

Butch walked over and stopped in front of me. "Heard someone needed a ride home?" Leon stopped beside him.

I smiled, happy to see the two of them but not sure about my reception.

Leon gave me a once-over. "Looking a little worse for wear but..."

He smiled, and then all three of us said in unison, "Still alive."

I was back!

Chapter 8

"You're sure you didn't take anything?"

"I told you I didn't." Asher looked up from where he resided on the couch in the apartment. The TV had been one long marathon of *Grey's Anatomy* since I'd gotten back, and there were five empty containers of Ben and Jerry's Rocky Road, the last one lying on its side with a spoon resting in it. A pizza box was beside them, and Asher's stomach had seen flatter days. If I judged the amount of time he'd been sitting here by episodes, he'd been like this since I disappeared.

"You said he wouldn't work with you anymore." He got up and stomped over to the refrigerator and took out another Ben and Jerry's and then walked back to flop down on the couch.

After I left the Underground last night, I'd thought I'd have more time to break the news to Asher slowly. That was before I got the message to be there for a meeting at ten tonight.

"Asher, I have to. I can't keep repeating the whys, not unless you really want to see me lose my mind—for good this time." I'd been explaining since I got back. I'd always thought the crawlers would be the ones to make me lose my mind. Although, technically, Asher might be a crawler. Maybe this had always been the grand plan? Send out their strongest and nag me into submission.

"With him? You have to go back with him?" He dug into his newest Ben and Jerry's.

I leaned over on the counter that divided the kitchen from the living area, wondering what would happen if I knocked my head against it. "Yes. I have to work with him. He's the best shot of getting me in and out of the Shadowlands in one piece." I kept my voice calm as I explained this —again.

A strong person would be able to endure. Apparently, I must not be that strong, because if he kept this up, I might have to pull another disappearing act. Or at least dream of one. Maybe if I could make enough money, I could pay the bills and leave him here? He'd be okay. I'd get his groceries delivered and rig the place with fire alarms. He'd probably survive.

His head dropped and he went silent as I looked at the clock on the wall. If I made it past the next few minutes, I had a shot of some peace tonight. I could always get lucky and he'd lock himself in his room again, but I was afraid to hope for too much.

There was a loud groan before he kicked in again, smothering my dreams. "But you said he wouldn't work with you?"

Nope. This was looking like it would be another marathon. "I told you, that changed."

"And that's where you were all this time? I was worried sick about you."

I didn't doubt he had been. "I'm sorry. I didn't mean to

worry you. I sent you a message on your phone, you know, that little box I gave you? I'd thought you'd gotten it." Now that was an outright lie. I'd had to go get a new phone this morning.

"You know I don't know what to do with that thing." He stood and started pacing the living room. I watched him walk his familiar path. "I should go with you. You shouldn't be alone."

"I won't be alone."

He froze in his tracks, his eyes dropping, as if that was the biggest part of the problem.

"You shouldn't be alone with *him*."

Maybe I could just knock myself unconscious? "You say that, but you don't ever say why."

"You should trust me enough to believe me without explanations. I *saved* you. You're the reason I'm probably here." He turned on his heel and paced in the other direction.

I stayed where I was, my gut twisting. Neither of us knew how he'd ended up in this world, but there was no denying that Asher's theory might hold some water. The timing of when he'd cast the spell to keep the crawlers at bay for me, and him ending up here... It was definitely suspicious.

At some point, the phrase "I saved you" had started to feel like an anchor, the chain attached to it wrapped snugly around my throat. It was true, though. He'd saved me, and I felt like the most ungrateful person ever born, even as I felt like he was drowning me alive.

But I'd protect him for as long as I could, just as he'd protected me. "Asher, you know you have to keep a low profile. Some people might not understand about you."

"*Him*. You mean *he* might not."

"I don't know for sure, but it's safer this way."

I hurried toward the door, in part to get away from Asher and his incessant badgering and also because I needed to call a car if I was going to get to the meeting on time.

"Are you coming back tonight?" he asked with a desperate whine as I opened the door to leave.

"Yes, I think so, but don't wait up or get nervous if I don't." I hoped I wouldn't. If I still had my car, I'd be tempted to sleep in it.

He started moaning again as I left, and I told myself the same thing I'd been telling myself for months. At some point, he'd get the hang of being human-ish, and then he could start a life of his own. If I had to help him until then, I owed him that much and more. But damn was I starting to wonder if he'd ever get the hang of it.

Chapter 9

I ASSUMED THAT THE MEETING I'D BEEN CALLED TO FOR tonight would take place in Kane's office, and would be a small gathering of maybe four or five of us. When Jerry opened the door to the Underground, the place was empty. For the Underground to be emptied at ten at night, there was something bigger going down.

Kane walked out of his office and down the stairs, and from his expression, or lack of it, I knew the temperature hadn't gone up between us at all. I didn't know why I thought things might improve, but tonight's forecast looked like it was ice cold with a chance of frostbite.

Butch and Leon walked down the stairs behind him, looking serious but without the frost warnings. When Leon mouthed, *Still alive*, it took a little of the chill from the room.

As far as Kane? It didn't matter if it got better. I was wasting too much energy worrying about it. I'd dig myself out of this mess and start getting spells I could sell. If Kane hated me, there was nothing to be done about it. We had a working relationship, and that was all I ever wanted anyway, so who cared if he was distant? Actually, it would make things easier. No emotional entanglements, just as it should be. I certainly wasn't going to beg his forgiveness. Nope.

I kept my shoulders squared, my chin up and face blank. I could be just as cold as he was.

Kane didn't acknowledge me and walked over to talk to Jerry as Butch and Leon came and stood beside me.

Butch was looking a little confused now. "Why do you look like you're going to cry?"

"What are you talking about? I do not." I crossed my arms over my chest and glanced over at Kane. It didn't look like he'd heard him.

Butch scowled. "Nah, you definitely look weepy. You and Kane fighting?"

"Shut up. I'm not upset about anything." What the hell? I'd always *thought* I had a poker face. No wonder I lost every time I played.

"You do seem a bit off," Leon said, because of course he had to add his two cents.

"I'm fine. Now shut up."

Kane walked back over to us, and Butch and Leon must've taken pity on me, because they managed to not say anything else.

Kane's expression was as frosty as ever, and then it changed suddenly into irritation as it settled on me. "What? You get into a fight with your boyfriend or something?"

"None of your business," I snapped.

"She's fighting with *one* of her boyfriends," Butch said, seemingly amused at his little joke.

It had the opposite effect on Kane. "How many men are you sleeping with?"

One of the best cures I'd ever found for wanting to cry was wanting to scream, and I was ready to blow my stack now. "Since you're so interested, probably about five, give or take a dozen, depending on the week. That's the problem. I'm upset because I can't decide who to fuck tonight."

He'd ended up only a foot away from me as he said, "While you're working with me, you'll stop whoring yourself out. I don't need to be worried about who you're having pillow talk with."

I closed the distance to six inches. No one was telling me what to do. "I'll fuck everyone in Boston if I want, because it's none of your business and it has nothing to do with our arrangement."

"No, you won't."

"Yes, I will."

Collin chose that moment to walk in the door. I had no idea what he was here for because I didn't even know what the meeting was about yet. "Oh look, another stud I can add to my stable," I said under my breath but loud enough for Kane to hear but hopefully not Collin. I didn't want to give Collin any crazy ideas.

I went to walk toward Collin. It was the only excuse I had to give Kane my back at the moment. When I saw the glimmer in Collin's eye, I realized that he'd probably heard me with his werewolf hearing. Nice going, Ollie.

Kane beat me to him and stopped any awkward conversation from happening, at least between me and Collin.

Kane and Collin stood about five feet apart, but instead of an awkward conversation, there was mostly awkward silence.

Collin's eyes went from me to Kane. "So, I see the two of you are back together."

And now we were back to awkward conversation. The way he said it made it sound like we were *together* together. Boy, was he wrong!

Kane could handle that one. He was the one hovering and making it look bad.

When I didn't hear anything, I looked over where Kane was standing quietly. Nothing?

Butch and Leon joined our little threesome just as two more men walked in. They were both slender and wearing black suits that had a slight vintage look. The one who appeared to be in his fifties had the blackest hair against pale skin.

"That one is Rudy," Leon whispered to me, noticing where I was looking. "You could consider him King Dick of the leprechauns. The loser behind him is his second."

The circle widened, accepting the two newcomers, who nodded at Kane and ignored me.

Alexandria appeared next, with a blonde woman who was already showing fang. Alexandria was all smiles for Kane, fangs tucked away.

We'd all formed a circle of sorts. I had Kane on my right, which I guessed proved that even though he didn't like me, somehow, in this situation, we were still on the same side. Butch and Leon were close on my left. Jerry stayed back by the door, looking much meaner than I'd even imagined he could. Was he waiting for unexpected guests?

Everybody was staring down everybody else, and I wasn't sure if this was going to be a meeting or the beginning of a war.

Collin was shooting daggers at Kane and Alexandria. Alexandria was shooting me the evil eye as I stood next to Kane, presumably because everyone seemed to think I slept with everybody. I must be sleeping with Kane too, because why not? The leprechauns were looking around at everyone like each person was their mortal enemy, except for me, who they ignored.

I might've shot them a couple of hard looks because it was hard to not be bitter when you were held in a basement and tortured for a day.

I did notice Rudy's eyes dropped slightly when he looked toward Kane. Now what was that about? So there was one person here they weren't willing to take on. Vampires? No problem. Werewolves? Got it covered. Kane? Nope, not someone they'd mess with. I tucked that little gem away.

It was starting to make sense of why the meeting was down here, though. With all these guests and plenty of vitriol, the office would've felt like cramped quarters. I wouldn't want this crew in my apartment either.

Alexandria spoke first. "Why is she here?"

Alexandria might've had a couple of reasons to dislike me. First, she was carrying a torch for Kane that would've put Lady Liberty's to shame, and second, I might've turned her current boyfriend into a toddler. Shit happens.

I shrugged in her direction. It was the best apology she was going to get from me. Her eyes narrowed, and I couldn't blame her. It was a pretty lame effort on my part.

"We're all here for the same reasons," Kane said, playing the role of peacemaker. It was sort of like watching a wolf tell a bunny everything was all okay.

Alexandria's fangs dropped. "She's going to find our stuff? Where? In her back pocket?"

I was a second from walking out of here. This wasn't my problem. I would've too, if Kane didn't grab my arm before he said, "She's your best chance at getting your stuff back, so I'd play nice."

Alexandria put both hands on her hips and glared in my direction.

"You *do* want her help, don't you? If you don't, feel free to leave," Kane said, and I guessed he didn't feel quite so satis-fied with just her silence.

She didn't say anything; she didn't move, either. Yeah, that was about as good as it was going to get with her.

Rudy stepped forward. "Is she even capable of getting a spell to find our map?"

Now I was an incompetent? "Well, that's certainly not going to inspire me to get anything for *you*. And considering past events, I'm not sure if I'd be rushing me back into the Shadowlands." I left my meaning hanging in the air. I also made it sound like it wasn't already on my to-do list. There was still at least one leprechaun roaming out there that was going to get a nice surprise once I got some magic back.

"When is she going in?" Collin asked, a little too inter-ested. What? Now he wanted to anchor me? Little late there, buddy.

Kane moved closer until his arm was brushing mine. "When I say so."

"We should all be there when she gets it," Rudy said.

"But you won't be. I'll call another meeting once we have the spell. You can be there for that. In the meantime, no one makes a move on her."

Ahhh, now I understood the real reason for this meet-ing. I'd just officially been placed underneath the Kane protection umbrella.

"You have something to discuss with her, you discuss it with me. No one so much as goes near her. No one touches her—in any way." He walked away and headed up toward his office.

Kane left while I stared at his back. Then I realized we were all staring at his back. It was hard not to after that.

Okay then, he was really serious about me not sleeping around. Good to know. Might've been better off agreeing in private to his terms, and then perhaps my face wouldn't feel like the surface of Mars, but I got the picture. I was pretty sure everyone got the picture.

I stood there, frozen, perhaps even slightly stunned at his upper-handedness, as the meeting's participants cleared out without getting any closer to me than they had been.

"What are you going to do?" Butch asked from beside me, the room empty but for the four of us.

I turned toward him. "What do you mean, what am I going to do? Did you just see what he did? The spectacle he made? Then walks off like it was nothing?" My mouth was hanging open as I waved my hand toward the closed door of the office, my face still feeling hot enough to roast marshmallows.

"Why aren't you following him and fixing this?" Butch asked.

"Fixing what? He barely wants to speak to me."

Butch let out a long sigh before answering. "He's mad about how you left. Now you follow him and fight with him some more until you resolve your issues."

I took a step toward Jerry and the door. "I can't go up there. He doesn't want to talk to me."

"So, you're a quitter? That's what you're saying?" Leon asked, clearly disapproving of my answer.

"I am not a quitter." I took another step toward the door.

"He's up there. Here you are." Butch shrugged. "Looks like quitting to me. I thought you'd given up on quitting?"

"There's nothing I can do." I held my hands up in surrender and took two more steps.

"If you fuck something up, you fix it," Leon said, sounding like my third-grade teacher, minus maybe the cursing.

"I can't fix this."

Leon nudged Butch with his elbow. "She's quitting. She's a quitter."

Butch shook his head disapprovingly. "She's quitting."

"I'm not quitting." I was temporarily retreating.

"Still quitting," they said together.

"No. I'm, 'still alive.' That's the saying, and it's true. I've been surviving against all odds using my own judgment. Still *alive*."

Butch let out a very long and noisy sigh. "Still quitting."

Leon nodded. "Yep, still quitting."

"How about 'still leaving'?"

Butch elbowed Leon. "I think that's the same as quitting. What do you think?"

I already saw Leon's answer coming, but I didn't hear it, since I was out the door.

Chapter 10

I PULLED THE KEYS OUT OF MY POCKET AND WAS JUGGLING A pizza outside my building when Kane pulled up in yet another black luxury car. Or at least it looked expensive. I didn't know cars enough to be sure. He leaned over and pushed the door open.

"Get in. Leave the pizza."

I glimpsed Asher looking down from the window above. Shit. I took a slice out but left the rest before Asher decided to come downstairs.

The car started pulling away before I'd finished shutting the door, and I took a sad look back at my abandoned dinner.

Kane looked over at me, eating my greasy slice without even a napkin. "Don't get grease on my seats."

"Don't worry. I'll wipe it on my clothes first," I said, and then added an eye roll as I kept eating. "Where we going?"

"We'll be there soon."

Okay, then. This was business. Didn't matter if he was unpleasant. It was how I should be viewing our relationship too, and there were no hard feelings in business. I was getting what I needed out of this deal. We both were. Plus, as long as he needed me, it meant I had some security from the rest of the crazies while I rebuilt my finances. That was the only thing that mattered.

He didn't say anything for the rest of the ride, and I didn't either, because I didn't care. Nope, not me. I could do this silent stuff too.

We pulled into a clearing thirty minutes later. Whatever this place was, it looked like nothing but a barren field, except for the vintage Caddy idling nearby containing two familiar faces.

"Why are Butch and Leon here?" I asked, as Kane pulled up beside them.

He wasn't all warmth and sunshine, but at least he answered. "In case we get company. While you're in there, I've literally got one hand tied up keeping you anchored. I don't want to be in a situation where I have to let go."

"Why would we get company? Aren't you sort of in control of the rest of them?"

He turned to me before getting out of the car. This time, he didn't look cold or annoyed. He looked concerned. "There's other things out there that might've heard about this by now. We've got to be ready for an ambush."

He waited for an acknowledgement from me before he got out of the car.

I nodded, as I needed another minute to get my words back.

Okay, so maybe I wasn't as safe as I'd thought. That might've been useful information to have as I was strolling down the street last night, thinking the worst was behind me.

Not that I'd say that to Kane. We had enough beef

between us. I wasn't adding another pound of chopped meat to it, or as Asher would order, beef tenderloin.

I followed him out of the car.

Butch and Leon got out of the Caddy with the smell of fast food accompanying them, and each with a bag of Wendy's.

"I threw out my pizza and now I have to watch them eat Wendy's?"

"What? We can't eat and stand around at the same time?" Butch asked. Leon said nothing, just shoved some more fries in his mouth.

I walked over and put my hand out. "If you don't bring enough for everyone, you don't bring it."

Butch's smile sank as he dug through his bag and grabbed a half-full sleeve of fries. "Thank you," I said, as if he'd really wanted to give them to me.

"What about him? Aren't you going to take some from him?" Butch called after me as I went to look around the clearing.

"Nope. I'm good."

Butch grumbled as Leon laughed. I ignored them as I took a walk around, really absorbing the place.

It felt like I hadn't done this in a decade, but it had only been months. Still, I needed this to go smoothly. There was a lot at stake right now, and I wasn't walking out empty-handed.

As I continued to look the place over, I could feel that something was off with the crawlers. It was subtle—the way they turned their heads away when my eyes landed on them. The twitchiness of their steps.

Kane walked over where I was finishing my fries. "They seem skittish tonight," I said, before I ate the last of the salty goodness.

"I agree," he said, with no attitude and no ego. Even if we weren't going to be friends anymore, it was nice to know in times like this, we could stop biting each other's heads off.

"Any ideas?" I caught sight of a little bunny-looking crawler. Smaller than what I'd need to get in, but that wasn't what caught my eye. It looked like it was fighting with another small crawler. Now that was something I'd never seen before.

"No." He also watched the two fight, and I could have sworn there was a tiny grimace pulling at his lips.

Whatever was going on, it didn't matter—hopefully. It was time to get down to business. I found a nice, big crawler that could open up a doorway into the Shadowlands.

Then Kane's hand on my shoulder stopped me. I turned, expecting to see company. It was still just us. Leon was sitting on a boulder eight feet away, munching on his French fries while Butch gave him dirty looks.

"Stay alert when you go in and get out as quick as possible. If the crawlers are acting strange here, it might be worse in there."

"I doubt it'll be as bad as when I went in and got your spell." If he thought I was going to believe he was worried now, he must've thought I was as green as Ireland grass in the spring. He'd pretty much thrown me out of his office when I asked to work with him again. Then he went to the trouble of making sure no one else would work with me. Not to mention his oh-so-sweet personality lately. Yeah, I could do without the false concern.

I held up my right hand. "If you don't mind, I'd like to get started."

He took my hand without further comment, his expression back to a more palatable reality.

I made quick work of calling the crawler over and entering the Shadowlands.

It was bleak and dreary, and I'd missed the place like a dentist missed cavities. As I breathed, I could feel the potent magic in the air seeping into my pores and filling my lungs. I thought of the retired Shadow Walker I'd tracked down, trying to remember her name. Sherry something or other had been scrawled above the address I'd gotten. The thing I couldn't forget was the craving for magic she'd shown. Was that what it would be like for me after a while? Did it become an addiction? I took another breath, leaned my head back as the magic poured over me, and wondered if I'd care if it did become addictive, as long as I could get this fix.

A squeeze on my hand got me back to business, as if he knew I'd been goofing off a bit. I looked around the place, and just as I'd feared, they were acting strangely in here too. They were keeping their distance and had a twitchy appearance. A larger one, who looked sort of like a gorilla, even curled its lip back at another one of their kind.

What the hell?

Didn't matter. I had two goals. One for Kane and one for me. My goal was more pressing. I needed cash and I needed it yesterday. Maybe I could ask for cash? Who knew? Maybe you really could get a money tree?

I found a slender one that stood about three feet tall and walked on its hind legs. I called it over in a firm voice, not messing around.

"I need a spell to make money." It shifted its head sideways and then skipped off.

So much for the money tree. Probably for the best. I wasn't sure where I could plant it where Asher wouldn't have found it and spent it, anyway.

I targeted my next crawler. A little guy hiding behind a

rock. On the small side, but all the other ones were keeping a healthy distance. I was starting to wonder if whatever Asher had done to keep them away from me in my world had also bled over into his.

Either way, I didn't like the vibes I was getting from them. Time to get what I could and get out.

"I need a spell to find something." The creature gave a little shiver but then offered up the words. The whole time it was saying them, I noticed the other crawlers inching in.

Instead of gathering around where I'd exit, they were circling where I already was. As soon as the spell settled in my mind, I slowly eased away, not wanting to set off any prey instincts in them with a full-out run.

They didn't follow me. They seemed more interested in each other, like there was a division of some sort between the two groups. The handful on my left hissed. The gathering on my right replied with the same, some of them curling back their lips. None of them seemed to care about me.

Either way, I didn't want to be in the middle of this fight. This was going to go bad, and quick. I had way too many problems all on my own. When the smallest crawler shot flames out of its mouth toward a hulking one opposite it, I knew it was time to run.

I sprang toward the place I'd entered, but not before I felt the flames licking at me. I didn't think I was the intended target, but I was definitely getting my share of the heat.

I stumbled out of the Shadowlands and dropped to the ground immediately, yanking out of Kane's grip so I could roll.

Kane followed me down, patting out the flames on my clothes.

"What the hell happened?" he asked once I wasn't combusting any longer. Butch and Leon were beside him.

Kane grabbed my hand, hoisting me to my feet again, and I could feel my shirt hanging open in the back.

"There was something definitely off. I went in and..." Had that been right? "It seems like they're attacking each other."

"Why would they do that?" Butch asked.

I shrugged. I was a Shadow Walker, not the crawler whisperer.

I turned toward Kane. He appeared to be mulling it over, but he didn't seem forthcoming with any answers. He only wanted more information from me. "Tell me exactly what happened."

I laid out every second of my walk: from the apparent division between the two groups to the hissing and flame throwing.

He nodded as I spoke but didn't have any answers.

"But you got a locating spell?"

"Yes." Wait, maybe he did offer up a possible answer. "You think the items missing are related to this?"

"I don't believe in coincidences."

Chapter 11

I'D THOUGHT HE WAS GOING TO DROP ME OFF AT HOME, BUT Kane was definitely heading toward the Underground. I glanced behind us and didn't see Butch and Leon.

He pulled in beside the Underground.

"What's going on?"

"I want to discuss something with you."

Discuss what? I got out of the car, acting as calm as he always did. Or maybe not, considering the way everyone had read me so well the other day.

He was walking into the Underground, and I was following him because I didn't really have a choice. I didn't have a car and I didn't have money for a car. And if I were completely honest, I was following him inside because part of me didn't want to go home and listen to Asher for a couple of hours.

He pushed open the door to his office a few minutes later and Isabella was leaning over his desk, going through papers.

"Are you almost finished?" he asked her in a matter-of-fact way.

Her smile for him was utterly personal. "Just another minute." She shifted a couple of papers, ignoring my presence completely.

That smile she gave him, it had spoken volumes. Something had changed. Something big. Something that made me wish I was in the leprechauns' basement instead of here, because it would've been less painful.

He sat behind his desk, and she shifted a small pile of papers in front of him. "Look these over when you get a chance. I highlighted the areas I thought might be an issue."

I watched as Isabella's hand moved to Kane's shoulder and her body angled toward him. Their relationship had definitely changed. He'd slept with her, and even though she still wasn't looking at me, her smile was for me alone now. There was no faking the tidal wave of gloating this woman was putting out. She'd slept with him and he'd rocked her world—*that* was the face she was wearing.

Okay, get a grip. You don't know if it was good. That was a total assumption.

My eyes dropped to Kane. No, not an assumption. He was good looking in a melt-your-bones kind of way, but that wasn't it. He was raw and vital in a way you felt just by being near him. If he was bad in bed, I might as well give up on the whole gig, because no one else would have a shot.

I still hadn't moved more than a few feet inside the office. I took a step back toward the door, my hand going to the knob, but I couldn't seem to get my eyes to move off the two of them. "Did you want to talk now? I've got other things I could be doing." *Like not watching you and your girlfriend slobber all over each other.* Had he brought me back for this? Why was I even here?

He glanced over at Isabella, who nodded, not nearly annoyed enough to diminish my aggravation.

She smiled as she left the office, as if she knew every dirty, horrible thought running through my mind. To give Isabella her due, she probably did, probably had it down to a ninety-nine percent accuracy.

I stepped out of her way, repelled by her nearness.

He'd slept with her. How long had it taken after I left? A week? A day?

He might've hinted at an interest, but I'd walked out of here after declining him. Not only did I not have a leg to stand on, I didn't even have toes to wobble on.

I walked out on him like a thief in the night. I hadn't even left a note. Then, as far as everyone here knew, I'd shacked up with some guy. Not that he ever brought that up. He clearly didn't care who this live-in was, or wouldn't he have asked me about it? I'd worked out an entire fake background story for Asher, and Kane never said a word about him.

"Well?"

My head jerked up as I was startled out of my imaginary scenarios. "Hmm?"

He was staring at me. "Did you hear what I said?"

I hadn't heard a word. The only thing penetrating my mind was what he'd done. But that wasn't my business. So then why did I say, "Do you really think that's a good idea?"

His eyes narrowed. "Excuse me?"

I pointed toward the closed door Isabella had walked out of minutes prior. "Sleeping with Isabella. Not your brightest move." Also not a bright move? Me, not keeping my mouth shut. I guess we all do stupid things.

"What does Isabella have to do with anything?"

He stared at me, waiting for me to respond, but he hadn't denied it. He'd slept with her. Of *course* he had. Why wouldn't he? He'd slept with that vampire chick, too. That was what he did. He wanted someone, he slept with them. This was why leaving had been the right move. Eventually I would've slept with him too, and nothing good would come from that.

"You like to tell me all about my stupidity," I said. "I thought that was the relationship we have."

"Had."

"Then consider it a gift from me, since you don't seem to understand how women work."

"Okay, let's compare bad moves. Slinking out of here to go shack up with some guy you just met off the street? Bad move."

It suddenly felt like the Arctic in here. I'd been mad he hadn't asked about Asher, but now that he had, it only made me tenser. I had to keep reminding myself that he had no idea who Asher was. This needed to be steered back to Isabella, and it wasn't a hard turn back, considering I was bursting at the seams to get into it with him.

"I'm only saying it because she's going to end up hurt, is all." That was a good line. Looking out for my fellow women made me a good person and definitely not a raging bitch.

"And that's the reason you care? You're concerned for Isabella's mental well-being?"

Obviously he was going to say that with sarcasm, considering he was familiar with our relationship, but I was willing to ride or die on this one. "Yes, as a fellow woman, I am concerned about you damaging her heart." The way I said it, like I was reading a lecture, was probably overkill.

He leaned back and kicked his feet up on his desk, all the while staring at me as if that were the stupidest thing he'd ever heard.

"Who says I'm using her?"

Kane had just introduced a game changer.

"Wh-what else would you do with her?" I asked, annoyed how I stuttered.

"Maybe I'm interested in having a relationship? People have been known to do that sometimes."

His words were like knives stabbing me in the chest, and not even sharp ones. It was like getting stabbed with a butter knife over and over again, feeling every millimeter of pain as it left a jagged wound.

I didn't even try to speak. I didn't have any words. He wasn't the relationship type. That was what I'd told myself. He didn't open up enough to be the relationship type. He'd proven that when I tried.

But here he was, having a relationship with Isabella. That was what he'd just said. He was in a relationship. Or heading into one? I was splitting hairs now. Whatever it was, it was happening.

And it wasn't with me. And I really didn't want it to be. Wasn't that what I'd told myself repeatedly?

I could feel the tremble in my lower lip and bit it. I had to get out of here, and quick, or I was going to make an embarrassing spectacle of myself, worse than the "naked in high school" dream.

I stood quickly and headed toward the door.

"Where are you going?"

"I'll be right back."

I left and shut the door behind me. Except now I was in the Underground, and I didn't particularly want any of these people to see me crying either.

I glanced around, and my eyes were immediately drawn to Flip. She was staring at me as I descended the stairs, her eyes as wide as mine as I tried to hold the tears back.

She was grabbing my arm as I hit the last stair and pulling me with her toward the elevators. I didn't ask where we were going, simply followed her lead.

Flip spoke as soon as the doors closed. "Heard you were back."

I nodded, afraid that if I opened my mouth to speak, I'd start crying.

"It's going pretty well, I see." A small smirk lifted the corner of her mouth as she teased me, contrasting the sharp, concerned look in her eyes.

"Splendid," I joked, knowing I was being ridiculous even as I was on the brink of a meltdown.

"What happened in there? Do I need to go kick his ass?"

"No." That was the only word I got out before the tears were racing down my cheeks.

"I should've kept mocking you. Now look at you. Hold it together for one more minute."

I nodded as the doors opened onto the third floor. The hall was packed with people lounging around in the hallway, and I managed not to explode into a torrent of waterworks while she pulled me into three-Z.

The second the door shut, the tears started again. Then I looked around the place and started laughing and crying at the same time. The walls were bright blue with a rainbow that went from the front door all along the wall, swerving until it landed at a green velvet couch.

"Fun, right?" she asked.

"Yeah." I ran my palms over my face, trying to clean myself up.

"Sit," she said, as she kicked her shoes off onto the purple polka dot rug. I curled up on the green couch beside her.

"Now, what's happened?"

"It's..." I shook my head. It was ridiculous, was what it was.

She did a dramatic head flop to the side before she firmly said, "Spill."

"I didn't want him. I told myself I didn't, and then I walked away because I was doing the right thing, and I was so damn positive of it until I sat there, and Kane's dating Isabella."

"Really?" She appeared very confused.

"I saw them together. It's very clear. I know what I saw."

She didn't look convinced, but nodded.

"I left here without a word. I wasn't with him. I get all that. I don't know why..." I would've kept talking, but I started crying instead. I threw my hands over my face. "And I don't cry!"

"Well, even if I agreed with you that he is with her—"

"He's with her." I knew what I saw.

She nodded slowly. "If he is, he doesn't like her the way he likes...or at least liked...you."

"How do you know that?" Why was I even asking? I shouldn't care. I couldn't care. It was done. That door was officially closed.

"I know these things."

I put my head in my palm. I knew what that meant. She didn't have a thing to prove her theory.

"Seriously, I know for certain, but the way I know...it's a secret."

I looked at her and tried to pretend I believed her. I mean, she was trying to make me feel better. I had to at least put on a show. I ran a hand across my nose, trying to pull it together.

She watched my failed act and shook her head, looking almost as lousy as I did. "Okay, I'll tell you how I know, but you have to promise to never, ever repeat it."

"Okay."

"I've got some Cupid blood in my lineage."

"Cupid? Like bow-and-arrow cupid?"

"Yes. And don't look at me like that. For someone who's seen monsters their whole life, I'd think you'd be a little more generous with the benefit of the doubt."

"You're right. If you say you are related to Cupid, then who am I to doubt you?"

"Exactly."

Cupid was a Fae, right? And she was part Fae. It could happen. I could see a way to get behind this. "This is how you know? Because of this lineage?"

I was so pathetic. I wanted her to convince me. Just like she had Rip Van Winkle blood and that was why she slept all day. I was hitting an all-time low. I was broke, my room-mate was a shadow monster who lived off me, and I was upset a man I'd walked away from had moved on and was dating someone else. A man who had committed murder in front of me not long ago.

But he had killed someone I would've killed myself. Was that really homicidal? I groaned as I wondered what the hell had happened to me.

"Yes. I've known for a while."

"I believe you." Not really, but I wasn't going to make one of my only friends feel bad, even if she might've been a little delusional.

I pulled myself together for what felt like the tenth time in a week. I had to toughen up. I hadn't cried this much when they messed up my arms. It was ridiculous. I swiped an arm over my face as I stood.

"You feel better?" Flip asked, seeming proud of herself.

"Yes. You really helped me. Thanks." When she leaned back and smiled, I was happy I'd lied. "Could you do me a favor? Tell Kane I wasn't feeling well and I had to leave?"

"Sure thing!"

Chapter 12

"No inkling why the crawlers would've been fighting?" I asked Asher for the fifth time today.

"Nope." He was standing back and looking at the dark grey paint and the mess he was making of the wall. Although I wasn't sure he had the same opinion, as he smiled and began painting again. He'd announced this morning that he thought we hadn't found any more Shadow Walkers because the place was too bright, and he knew just how to fix it.

My cell phone began vibrating where it sat on the nearby desk, and I glanced over to see Kane's number.

"I'll be right back."

I stepped out onto the sidewalk before answering, watching through the window as Asher expanded his project to himself and the floor. Not that the carpet had been in great shape, but now it was definitely going to have to get replaced. If it kept him from carrying on about working with Kane, I would've let him paint the place black.

I hit answer on the phone, hoping I didn't have to work tonight. I needed some distance.

"I'm going to be there in fifteen minutes. Be ready."

The phone disconnected before I had a chance to say I needed more time. Not that his tone had brooked any argument.

I stared back inside, where Asher looked like he was just gearing up. It would be a fight to get him upstairs that quickly. And telling him where I was going? No way. He was already getting weird.

Shit. *Shit, shit, shit.*

I called Kane back. "I'll meet you over at the Underground. I was heading that way already."

"No."

No? Just No? Who does that? Gives you one word with no explanation? Only someone with so much arrogance and so much... Yeah, pretty much Kane.

"I'm not in my building." Technically, I was *outside* my building.

"You were as of two minutes ago. You couldn't have gotten far. Go back."

What the hell? Was my phone tapped? How else would he know where I was?

He'd hung up again before I could reply. I looked back toward Asher, who was now staring back at me. Did I call Kane and try again? I could try and empty out the Boston Harbor with a bucket next, too. The only thing that I'd accomplish was making Kane suspicious about why I might not want him here, if I hadn't already tipped him off. That left one option. Get Asher to hide. I hurried inside.

"Asher, it's getting late. Why don't you go upstairs and lie down? I know you've been tired."

"I'm going to keep going for a little longer." He smiled, but his eyes narrowed a hair.

It was like every man in my life knew exactly what I

wanted them to do and then did the exact opposite, just to fuck with me.

"I'm really worried that you've seemed so worn down lately." Actually, he'd been sleeping like a champ and could probably lap me.

He dipped his brush into the paint with renewed vigor. "No, I feel great. I'm going to hang out down here."

Asher had a sick sense like that, knowing when I was trying to get rid of him and clinging tighter than ever. There was nothing else to be done. I'd have to tell him and deal with the fallout.

"Asher, he's coming to get me for work. You need to go upstairs." I didn't need to specify who *he* was. It was getting to the point it was easier if I didn't mention Kane's name, as Asher's body always seemed to stiffen as soon as my mouth formed the K.

His head tilted and he kept painting. "I'm not so sure I do."

"Not so sure?" I'd run from the Underground like a guilty thief to save him from this very fate, and he wasn't sure? "You're not so sure?" I repeated, trying to make the words sink in. I needed to remain calm. He didn't understand he was no match for Kane, especially now.

Wait, he was the one who kept telling me Kane was dangerous. He might not know the man, but he knew enough, according to him. "Asher, you need to go upstairs."

"Why? He might not even know who I am. I've never seen him."

I hadn't heard the car stopping in front of the building, but I heard the car door closing.

Dread, the kind that sucked all the joy from your day, filled me as I turned around.

Kane was heading toward the door, and I could see his eyes narrowing as he looked directly at Asher.

"Asher, I'm leaving. Lock up for me." Because I didn't even want to take the time to dig out the keys. If I stalled that long, Kane would be in the building, in the same room as Asher, and everything in my being told me that was not a good idea. Worse than that. Epic disaster.

"That's him, isn't it?" Asher asked, not answering me about locking up.

"Lock up." I pushed out the door, walked past Kane, and headed to the car. He kept walking toward the building, intent.

"Where you going? Let's go." I opened my car door.

I watched as he paused outside the door. I couldn't see his face, his back to me, but it was obvious his attention was on Asher.

I had run. I'd sacrificed a good situation, and it was on the verge of being for nothing in the next two minutes.

I stood with my hand gripping the open car door, debating whether I should try to call him again or try and tackle him. Then he walked in the building and it was too late for either. I followed in on his heels, forgetting all else and leaving the door to the car open.

There was immediate tension, and I wasn't sure if it was in my head or if it truly existed. Kane didn't know who Asher was. Right? He'd made mention of a boyfriend, but no one had said anything to make me believe they thought this boyfriend wasn't human. Why would there be a problem? But as I watched them standing about a dozen paces apart, it was hard not to feel as if I'd just gone back in time and it was a showdown at noon.

I moved quickly in between them, wishing I was a bit taller and wider and could block Kane's view better.

"Who's this?" Kane asked me, but didn't look away from Asher.

Had I ever told Kane Asher's name? I couldn't remember. If I called Asher "Jon" instead, would Asher go along with it?

"I'm Asher."

Why did nobody in my life listen to me? So many things could be averted if they did. But no, no one had wanted to believe in the monsters, and Asher wouldn't go upstairs when I told him to, either. Now look. I had enough to worry about without this blowing up in my face.

"Well, let's let Asher get back to his painting." My little encouragement wasn't acknowledged as Kane stood stony in his appraisal of Asher, his eyes narrowed, tilting his head back as if trying to smell him or something.

Kane was concentrating way too hard on Asher, and I had no idea what Asher was doing, as I was afraid to turn my gaze from Kane.

Just as I was sure I felt the buzz of impending doom flittering in the air, Kane relaxed. He nodded in Asher's direction and turned toward the door.

That was it? I nearly had a heart attack for nothing? Kane didn't realize he wasn't human.

I didn't turn back to look at Asher until Kane was walking through the door. Asher was watching me, and I waved my free hand, letting him know everything was fine. Not that I thought he'd be able to do anything if they weren't.

Crisis averted, but man, that had been close.

Kane climbed into his car and I got in the passenger side, afraid to speak, afraid I'd blow it and reveal the secret, or he'd smell my nervousness somehow. I swore he could, too. He had some sort of nervous meter. He always knew when I was off, always had. It was a miracle that he hadn't sensed something when he was back there, and it would probably take me a good week to calm down from the close call.

Before the end of today, I was going to have to come up with some excuse to meet Kane at the Underground from now on. That disaster—the almost showdown—could not happen again.

Kane switched gears and the car surged forward.

"What happened to you yesterday?" Kane asked.

Isabella happened. Or Isabella on Kane, to be accurate. "Oh yeah, sorry about that. Something I ate must've been bad."

He didn't say another thing about it.

We pulled up to an old building about ten minutes away, and I got out of the car, trying to sturdy up the jitters still lingering in my knees. I walked a few paces and took in the landscape and the crawlers available, wondering what spell I could get that would reap the most cash, not even worrying about what Kane needed. If I'd had some warning, I would've tried to call Zee and ask her what she thought she could sell now that I was back in action. How hard could it be, though? There were always things people wanted, like eternal youth. That had to be worth some money.

I took a few more steps and then looked around for Kane. He was still by the car, head tilted down as he typed into his phone. I wouldn't have been so impatient, but I needed an escape, even if it was into the Shadowlands.

"We doing this?"

"Hang on a second." Kane was still looking down at his phone.

"Can you do that later?" The earlier tension was leaking out as annoyance. Better that then nervousness.

He didn't budge from his spot, as if he hadn't heard the impatience.

He had. He just didn't care. He was one of those people. He didn't get annoyed unless he felt like getting annoyed. Apparently, he wasn't in the mood tonight, so I could throw an outright hissy fit and I wouldn't move him along any quicker. It was one of the things that drove me crazy about him, and a trait I wished I had.

I turned my back on him, determined to waste as little of my time as possible. He might not be ready, but I'd get everything lined up in the meantime. Over in the corner, there was a really big crawler. Perfect. Kane could text one-handed, couldn't he?

I turned, prepared to drag him over if needed, when I found him only a few steps away.

"I need your phone. My battery died and I needed to finish that message to Butch."

His phone died? That seemed so...*normal*. Maybe even human? This was Kane. How could he have a dead battery?

I glanced quickly at his car. I hadn't seen a charging cord. It was completely plausible that his phone was dead. I mean, even the mighty Kane couldn't keep a phone charged all the time, right? Just because he could do other inhuman things didn't mean he could magically keep his phone charged. There were limits to even superhuman powers; a battery that didn't die might be the one impossible feat. Now that was a spell that could get me some cash.

Kane put his hand out, as if it were a forgone conclusion I would give him my phone.

I pulled it out and glanced down at the battery on mine, stalling for time, not wanting to hand it over for no logical reason. It wasn't like there were messages on it from Asher. He hated electronics.

"Is there a problem?" Kane was looking at me as if I'd donned a clown hat and a red nose.

I couldn't say no. Well, I guess I *could*, but it would blow my *relaxed and everything is super cool* cover. If I hesitated even a second longer, it was going to be obvious I didn't want to share my phone.

I handed it over to him, fighting the urge to yank it back as soon as his hand closed around it.

He held it and looked like he was dialing someone as he walked a few paces away. Then he pocketed the damn thing and turned on me.

"Why did you pocket my phone? I need that." I pointed at the pocket he'd just put it in, praying I'd been wrong and it hadn't been a setup. I knew I shouldn't have given him my phone. I should've said it was dead. Why hadn't I? Dumb, plain old stupid and dumb. Always follow your instincts. I knew that. How many times had those instincts kept me alive? Now look at me? Phoneless, and I had a bad feeling that was the only the beginning of my problems right now.

His hands stayed relaxed at his sides as my phone stayed out of reach. I could try and grab it from him, but who was I kidding? I didn't have a chance. I was screwed.

What was he up to? He was staring down at me in the most unpleasant way, like...ever. His eyes were narrowed again and his attention was intent, as if he was stripping away my layers.

I felt as if someone had slapped me upside the head as it hit me. He'd known Asher wasn't human back at the building. Bile started sloshing around in my stomach like a bad water park ride.

Stay calm. Play this out. Maybe he was just testing me. And even if he suspected, he didn't know. This wasn't as bad as I was imagining. He didn't know who Asher was. It might be paranoia on my part. I took two very confident steps toward him and held out my hand, as he had. "I don't know what game you're playing, but I need my phone back."

He didn't budge, except for maybe a tensing in his shoulders and the veins popping out of his forearms. And the little one in his neck.

This might've been more than paranoia on my part.

"What you need to do is tell me what that thing back at your building is." His words were clear and clipped.

It was a warm day, but not warm enough for my sweat-coated palms and the surge of heat I was generating. If my forehead started beading, I'd really look guilty. I was lucky my shirt wasn't sticking to me like cling wrap. "What are you talking about? He's a friend helping me paint. I want my phone back." And hopefully I'd be able to send Asher a text he would read for once and he'd hide.

Breathe, don't stop breathing. He'll notice if your face turns blue for sure. Stay limber; don't tense. He doesn't know anything or he wouldn't be asking.

"*What* is he and where did he come from? And don't say something stupid like New York or Virginia, because I know he's not human."

"You know nothing of the sort."

He walked toward me, and I didn't realize I'd been walking backward until I hit the car. Okay, so much for holding my ground.

"What is he?"

The game was up. I'd stupidly believed when I got Asher out of the Underground and the weeks had trickled on by that I'd succeeded in protecting him. I should've left the city when I had the chance. Why had I stayed in Boston?

The chance to flee was gone. Brain scrambling up quicker than eggs cooked, I thought back to just a minute or so ago. Kane had definitely messaged someone before his phone had "died." Butch or Leon, probably both, were most likely on their way to my building right now. Would they kill Asher? A hundred percent, if those were their orders. Did Kane tell them to?

What if I ran back? It had been a ten-minute drive to get here. I looked in that direction, and then there was an arm on either side of the car.

"Even if you *could* get past me, which you can't, you'd never make it."

He'd sent people there.

He straightened, giving me my space, and looked east, the direction of my building, and then back at me, before he did a single slash of his head, telling me that trying to take off would be a bad idea.

Message received. I was desperate. Not stupid.

Stand my ground. Then threaten and bluff with anything I could think of if that didn't work. There were no other options.

"If you kill him..." I left the rest of the sentence hanging because I couldn't think of what else to say. I'd shown up at his office begging for scraps not a week ago. What would I do? Say I wouldn't shadow walk now? I guess, if that was all I had. "I'll never shadow walk for you again."

He took his *not dead* phone out of his pocket and held it up, its screen glowing with a healthy charge. "They're going to call me after they have *it* secured. You can explain or you can roll the dice and see what happens if you continue along this path of denial. Work with me, or work against me. Your choice. I won't bore you with the stories of those who've worked against me. I think you're smarter than that."

I didn't realize I was biting my lip until I tasted my own blood. How much to tell him? What could I say that would get both me and Asher out of this? My snug black t-shirt was now stuck to my damp skin. Not even dwarf clothes could conquer this sort of nervousness.

If I told Kane everything, he might kill him. If I told him nothing, he might kill him.

"You're running the clock." He pointed to a nonexistent watch on his wrist.

His phone rang and I could see the look on his face, daring me to move from my spot.

He answered it and held it to his ear as he stood facing me. "Hold on." He dropped the phone and looked at me. "Well? What's it going to be?"

"I'll talk if you promise not to hurt him." I took a few steps toward Kane, getting ready to tackle the phone out of his hand if need be. They do say adrenaline can make you super strong. I might be putting that to the test.

"Waiting."

I looked around at all the crawlers. "I don't think here's the place."

Kane was smart enough to understand immediately.

"Tell me it's not what I think."

I went back to biting my lip as he swore into the air and took a few steps away from me. Finally, he lifted the phone back to his ear. "Keep him secured but unharmed...for now."

I knew what the *for now* meant. Pony up some answers, ones that would make it advantageous for Kane to leave Asher among the living or his time was up. I'd seen Kane kill for less.

Chapter 13

HE DIDN'T QUESTION ME AS WE DROVE BACK TO THE Underground. He was probably saving them all up to torture me with when I couldn't fling myself from the car. I didn't care. Every minute was a gift to come up with a feasible explanation of who Asher was, other than the complete truth. Considering I'd been fearing this for the last three months, one would think I'd have come up with something brilliant. Every story I'd devised had been based on him being human, and that had been blown.

I was still praying for a burst of inspiration as Kane pulled the car in front of the Underground.

He parked the car, got out without looking at me, and headed toward the building. It would've been less insulting if he'd grabbed me by the arm and dragged me in. Walking ahead of me, so confident I was going to follow, was a slap in the face, because we both knew I was so outmatched that it didn't matter.

"I could do it, you know," I said, referring to running, as he opened the door.

"*Sure* you could." He didn't even bother to turn around. He could at least pretend!

Maybe it wasn't so bad to just have it out with Kane over my leaving and what Asher was. Get it all out in the open. It was inevitable, in a way. But I always circled back to the same issue. Then Kane might kill Asher.

All eyes were on us as we walked toward the office. It was either because I appeared to be walking toward my death or because Kane looked like he was about to commit murder. Probably a combination of the two.

I walked into his office first and heard the door shut behind me.

"I'd make yourself comfortable."

His threat was couched in polite terms, but I understood exactly what he meant. I wouldn't be going anywhere for a while.

I walked toward the windows that overlooked the main floor, thinking that if it came to it, I'd probably survive the fall. It might be my only chance of getting out of here. If I landed well, Kane would probably opt for the stairs, because he was dignified like that, and give me a lead.

He sat behind his desk, reclining and propping his feet up. "If you managed to land with your bones intact, you still wouldn't make it out the door."

I leaned against the nearby filing cabinet, pretending I was as relaxed as he was. "I wouldn't be so confident."

He crossed his hands behind his head, still looking pretty confident. "Well? He's not human. Who is he? Or, more accurately, *what* is he?"

"I don't understand why this is any of your—"

"He's in *my* city."

"It's not your city. There's lots of other people who live here."

"Would you like to keep debating this?" He reached over and lifted his phone off the desk. "Because I think whatever that thing is, it's better off dead. I'm giving you a chance to keep it alive, and you're wasting your opportunity."

He would, too. I'd seen him kill before, and he hadn't been nearly as angry as I feared he was now. He didn't even know who Asher was yet, but he was looking for an excuse to finish this.

I opened my mouth, debating how much of the truth I could feed him to make it believable but still save Asher. It was a tough call. Kane's homicidal threshold seemed to be lower these days.

"The entire truth."

I opened my mouth, but fear blocked the words in my throat like I was in a chokehold. I knew it was an accurate description because I'd been fortunate enough to find out exactly how a chokehold felt recently. The clock was ticking on Asher, though, and I had to give Kane something or he'd definitely kill him.

"I'll help you out, since you seem to be struggling so hard with this." He dropped his feet and stood, walking halfway across the room toward me. "I very rarely come across a creature I don't recognize. That means he's something I haven't encountered before." He narrowed his eyes, putting a world's worth of accusation behind them before he added, "But you've somehow become close with this thing in a short time. The possibilities are becoming very limited."

The way he was asking, I had a hunch the size of Antarctica that he already knew. I was holding out for nothing. Still, a couple feelers before I spilled might be in order. "He's what you think." That was, if it was what I thought he was thinking.

His jaw tensed and a strange cord in his neck was

popping out. The last time I'd seen that one come out, a body had lost its head.

"Do me a favor and clarify it anyway. Then, after you do that, tell me why I shouldn't kill him."

His phone rang, buying me precious moments.

He held the phone to his ear and listened, watching me the whole time. "Sit tight. I'll let you know how to proceed shortly."

He tucked his phone in his back pocket and glanced at the clock on the wall. "You've got one minute to start speaking."

"He's the man from the Shadowlands."

He walked away from me.

"You brought him out of the Shadowlands?" The words were gritted out in a mixture of shock and anger.

He stepped back and walked around his desk, and I had this strange feeling that he was looking for a physical buffer between us. I might've been wrong, but I decided to back up closer to the windows in case I was right.

He really thought I'd bring Asher out? "I didn't bring him out. He showed up on his own." I wished my voice was stronger, more confident sounding.

He raked both hands through his hair before he dropped them to his side. "What about the missing items?"

"He had nothing to do with it." I rambled on with more details, hoping to plant enough doubt to keep Asher alive. "He's been out three months. When did their things go missing? It had to be recently."

He took another step, crossing his arms and looking everywhere but me as he asked, "Then how did this happen? How is he out?"

"I don't know how he did it. Neither does he." I walked over to the couch, clenching my hands in front of my mouth. That was it—the truth was out—and Kane was standing there not saying anything.

When I couldn't take the silence anymore, I stood and took a few steps toward him. "You can't kill him. He's the one that saved my sanity. Protected me in the Shadowlands. He got me the space I needed from the crawlers to keep going. I owe him everything." Why wasn't he looking at me? Or saying something? "You can't kill him. I *owe* him."

He turned and said, "Owe him or want to keep fucking him?"

I stepped back, as if he'd struck me. "Go to hell. It has nothing to do with sex." Flashes of Isabella came unwanted into my head as she ran her hands all over him. "*I* don't fuck everything that walks. He saved me and I can't just let him fend for himself. He can't do it. He's not that strong, and it's my fault he's out."

His head jerked back to me. "Your fault? How's it your fault?" He turned, and I felt the full force of his attention on me.

Maybe he didn't believe me? Of all the things that should've caught his attention, it being my fault was what triggered him?

He was silent, almost to the point of it being unnatural, as he watched me. It had the opposite effect on me, and I started to fidget. I felt better when he was seething.

I rubbed a hand on the back of my neck, staring at the floor. "It happened right after he did the spell to keep the crawlers away. He thinks it sucked him out of his world and into ours somehow. This *could* be my fault. I can't let you hurt him." But I didn't know how I could stop him.

He sat on the edge of his desk, quiet, like the fight had completely seeped out of him. Had he made his choice? Was Asher already dead and just didn't know it?

"You left to protect him because you think this is your fault?" He wouldn't stop staring at me in that weird way I hated.

"It probably is my fault."

He didn't argue. He even nodded once, but he didn't look like he believed me.

I wrapped both arms around myself, fighting a chill. "What are you going to do?"

"The situation has to be handled."

"What exactly does that mean?" For someone who was about to commit murder, he seemed very calm. Maybe I was misinterpreting "handled"? Or maybe killing wasn't that big a deal to him?

"Right now? Nothing. Go home. Call Zee. She'll drop you." He turned and walked over to his desk, still seeming very distracted.

What was he up to? "And Asher?"

"He stays here until I decide what to do with him."

I could dig in and fight it out with him, but something told me to leave well enough alone for now. Let this soak in a bit, and tomorrow I could start in on him again, chip away at his resolve.

I left his office, and then it hit me—he knew I could call Zee.

Chapter 14

ZEE WAS OPENING MY BUREAU DRAWERS AND EMPTYING MY underwear into a sack. She paused to hold up an especially cute bra I'd gotten from the dwarves.

I sat up in bed, shoving the hair out of my eyes. "What are you doing?"

She flipped it to look at the back. "I was admiring it." She tossed it in the bag.

"No, I mean dumping all my stuff in a bag in the middle of the night?" I looked over at my clock. It was three in the morning. After getting home and worrying about Asher for hours, I'd finally drifted off—for exactly twenty minutes.

"We're supposed to pack anything that looks important."

I threw the blanket off me. "What the—"

"Kane's orders. Take it up with him." It sounded like that line had some mileage on it.

I grabbed my phone beside the bed, but Zee stopped me. "No need. He's downstairs."

I was out of my room, passing two gargoyles going through my kitchen on the way. Kane was downstairs in my office, flipping my bills like a deck of cards.

"What are you doing?" I moved quickly and grabbed the pile from his hand. "These are none of your business." I would've put them in their basket, but I didn't trust him not to pick them back up.

"You've got a lot of late notices." He casually took a seat on my desk, his eyes skimming down the t-shirt I'd been sleeping in down to my bare legs.

I shifted, suddenly very aware of how short the hem was. "Again, none of your business. Where's Asher?"

"He's at the Underground, where he's going to remain until I figure out what else to do with him."

Kane picked up another sheet from the papers scattered on the desk, and I pulled it out of his grasp. "Is he..."

Now that he no longer had the paper to look at, his eyes were back on me. "In one piece? Yes. Didn't touch a hair on his head."

Kane hadn't killed him, so that was a good sign. I should've been upset he was keeping him. I wanted to be, but the main feeling running through me was relief. Asher was safe and maybe I'd get a little break? Was that really so bad? Did that make me a horrible person? It wasn't like I'd tried to get him caught. I'd done everything to keep him away from Kane. Asher was the one who dangled himself like bait in front of the shark. And I'd probably be upset after the shock wore off. That's all this was. Delayed reaction.

There were loud noises near the stairs, and I looked to see a pair of gargoyles disappearing out the back door. "Where are they taking my stuff?"

"Helping you move. It's not safe here anymore." His voice was a little huskier than it had been a few minutes ago.

"Why wouldn't it be safe? I thought you warned them off?" I'd heard him at the meeting. It was the only reason I hadn't been looking over my shoulder when I walked down the streets.

"When they find out about Asher, they might get unsettled."

"But no one knows about him."

"We don't know that."

"What if I don't want to?" Who was he to tell me what I should do? We weren't friends anymore, or anything else.

He shrugged. "Then stay."

"Fine. Then I will." I didn't want to stay. He wasn't supposed to say stay.

"I'll have the gargoyles return your things."

"Fine." It didn't feel fine, though. It felt horrible. I wanted to go to the Underground. I'd wanted to go back there the very minute I'd left. Why had I said I didn't want to go? I should've grabbed my purse and gone. Now he was going to leave and I'd still be here, alone, while everyone else was over there.

He stayed seated on my desk. "Of course, Asher will remain at the Underground."

I nodded. He'd already said this. Now he was just rubbing it in. Great, everyone was at the Underground but me. Asher didn't even want to be there and he was there. Man, I was stupid.

"All the meetings will be there as well, so until this situation is fixed, you might have to commute."

My mouth dropped. "You can't pick me up? Do you know what it's like to get out there without a car?"

"Maybe sometimes if it's on the way, but I don't like detours. Sorry." He didn't sound sorry at all.

I remembered his detour problem well. Who makes someone meet a bunch of vampires that want to kill them just so they didn't have to drive an extra ten minutes?

It was probably easier to go with him. Truth? I didn't want to be here. I wanted to be at the Underground. What was I going to do? Fight to not get exactly what I wanted? Had I reached that level of stupidity?

"Where are you going?" he asked as I walked from the room.

"Grabbing my purse and getting dressed to leave."

When he laughed, I realized he'd never intended to leave me here anyway. It was more fun for him to torture me slowly.

We walked through the Underground, and I was relieved that the gargoyles had my bags. I didn't have to make a grand entrance with everything I owned at four in the morning, while the party that happened in the wee hours was in full swing.

"Where is Asher? You don't have him in the dungeon, do you?"

"You mean my basement? No. He's in your rooms on sixth."

I nodded. I hated the idea of him locked up, but as far as jails, it wasn't bad. And I'd get him out. I didn't know how yet, but I would.

The sleeping conditions might be a little tight, but my old rooms had a very comfortable couch, so that was manageable.

The elevator opened and I took a step toward my door, which had some guy I didn't recognize standing in front of it. Kane grabbed my arm and steered me toward his apartment. He opened the door and tugged me in behind him.

"What are you doing?"

"You'll be staying here. Not there."

"Why?"

"Because I don't trust him, and it was either there or the basement. That's the only other room available."

I was about to tell him I couldn't stay in this room when I thought of Isabella. It would drive her crazy if I was in here. She'd hated it when I was even on the same floor. It was petty. I knew it. "Fine. I'll take the couch," I said, making it clear what type of roommates we'd be.

"You can take the bed," he said, as if he was being nice to me.

Actually, he was being nice to me. He'd been kind of nice this whole time. What was wrong with him? Was I imagining it? Didn't he remember he'd declared us enemies after I left?

"I still want to see him," I demanded. That should get things back to familiar ground. Enough of this fake nice stuff. I didn't know what the deal was, but I didn't like it. It was hard to figure out where I stood with him when he was acting like this.

"It can wait until tomorrow. Last report had him sound asleep." Kane said everything in a nice, calm manner, as if completely unruffled.

I should poke at him again. I nodded instead, wishing I could put up more of a fight, but I wasn't that eager to see Asher. Kane was being so agreeable that I was afraid he'd relent. Would it really be that bad if I got some sleep first?

He walked toward the door, and even though I was curious where he was heading, I didn't ask. I was afraid he'd be nice and tell me. Then my head would explode.

Chapter 15

I DIDN'T GET UP UNTIL ELEVEN THE NEXT MORNING, AND GUILT drove me immediately next door. The guard moved in front of me, blocking the door. "What are you doing? I want to go in there."

"You'll have to ask Kane." He spread his stance out, as if preparing for a fight.

He might have had some floppy puppy-dog hair, but he was still twice my size. Soft hair or not, he had me beat. Clearly, he didn't know I was all out of magic. There might be some begging or groveling, but there wouldn't be any fighting of note. There might be some blustering, though. "I don't know where Kane is, and it's not up to him."

"I'm sorry, but I can't let you in." He lifted his chin, as if waiting for my worst.

"Who are you? I don't even know you."

"I'm Badger."

"Well, we'll see about this, Badger." He even had a dog name and big, dark almond eyes. Kane was making this one tough.

I dug my phone out, hit Kane's number and typed:

I want to see Asher but your man won't let me in. What's the deal?

A second later, I got back:

I told him not to. You can see Asher when I return.

My fingers flew over my phone as I texted back:

No. I can see him now. Call off your man.

I stared at my phone, waiting for a response. I walked down the hall, still waiting for a response. When I had nowhere left to walk, I called. "What the—"

"No." He hung up.

I called him back.

"Still no." He hung up again.

Damn stubborn man. I called again and somehow in that one minute, while I'd been stewing, he'd changed his ringtone to Meghan Trainor's song *No*. If I wasn't so annoyed, I might've laughed.

I pocketed my phone and glanced at the door, while soldier boy was still girding his loins for magic I didn't have. He'd probably heard about the witches and the monsoon. He was really lucky I was running on empty.

Only one option left, and it didn't leave much room for dignity. I stormed over and got as close as I could, before I hollered through the door. "Asher?"

"Ollie?" I heard some shuffling and then, clearer, "Is it you? Are you okay?"

"Yes. I'm fine. Are you good?"

"I'm okay." His voice, although a tad melancholy, wasn't completely out of the usual range. "What's going on?"

"I'll see you tonight and explain then, okay? Just hang in there and I'll get this worked out."

"Okay."

I stepped back, taking a moment to glare at the guard. I didn't matter if he was only following orders. He wasn't looking directly at me, as if he'd turn to stone if our eyes met. I groaned and walked away. Damn puppy eyes.

This was ridiculous. Asher had the mentality of a little boy, not an evil mastermind. Kane was becoming a control freak. Actually, he'd always been a control freak, but it hadn't been so aggravating until now. I got in the elevator as I thought of all Kane's personality flaws, of which there were many.

I made it downstairs and was relieved to see the booth empty. I didn't need another lecture from Butch or Leon, and I was sure they'd add their complaints to what I'd done wrong or hear them say "still quitting." There was only one bright side to this mess. I'd be able to pay my bills again soon.

Nothing had changed at the Underground, though. I was still getting dirty stares from the witches, slightly less nasty looks from the vampires, and the shifters ignored me. There was a table across the room with food and no patrons, where the dwarves were doing whatever it was they did.

I made my way to the empty booth, alone and happy for it.

Zee, the exact gargoyle I needed, popped up when I called. I took a quick look around to see if there were any heads pointed in our direction before I said, "I need a bagel, and the list of spells?"

"I'm working on it as we speak." She popped back out.

I was taking a bite of my bagel a little while later when a chair scraped across the floor loud enough to cut over the music. Flip was standing a few feet away from a disgruntled witch. She threw the witch a last dirty look for a probably imagined slight and floated her way over to me. Technically her feet were touching the ground, but I could see the Fae blood in the way she seemed weightless.

She slid in opposite me and ordered up some oatmeal, smiling the entire time. She was typically pleased to see me, but she seemed a little too happy today.

No matter how much she smiled at me, I wasn't going to ask. I had enough going on. I'd eat my bagel and mind my business.

"I knew you'd be back." She took a big spoonful of oatmeal with strawberries while she stared at me.

I didn't know I'd be back until yesterday. How could she have known? I nodded anyway.

"I won the bet." Another spoonful of oatmeal went down.

"The bet?"

"Yep, on when you'd be back."

I dropped the bagel and the pretense of not caring along with it. "Okay, so how did you know?"

"I just knew. No way Kane was going to let you go. Not his style. He liked you too much."

"He kept himself busy, though." I didn't have to say with Isabella. Flip could fill in the blanks like Monet filled in a canvas.

"I don't think he was as busy as you think he was."

Sometimes she filled those canvases with pure imagination. "I know what I saw."

"You saw what *she* wanted you to see." She continued to eat her oatmeal, unperturbed.

It would be something Isabella would do. But Kane hadn't denied it. Although we'd hardly been on good terms when I'd asked him. I let the subject drop, filing it away for when I could stand to think of it.

I glanced over at the empty dwarf table. Not knowing dwarf protocol, I asked Flip, "When you get a chance, can you get a message to the dwarfs for me?" I still had a debt outstanding for all the clothes, and considering how ugly the situation with the leprechauns had gotten, it might be good to get proactive in the one relationship that hadn't soured. I had no desire to end up in another basement when they got around to their accounting.

"What do you need?"

"Tell them I'll be able to square up with them soon." *Soon* being sometime before they decided to break both of my legs.

There was a question clear on Flip's face, but she ate another couple bites of oatmeal before it made its way to her lips. "I feel like I should know what you're talking about, but I don't." She leaned back in the booth as she waited for me to explain.

"I know I still owe them for the clothes."

"You don't owe them anymore." Her face scrunched like her last strawberry was too tart. "It was paid months ago."

Settled months ago? Now I was the one stumped. Were they lying to Flip? Maybe they didn't want her to get messed up in their business with me?

"Kane took care of it."

"Kane?" Why would Kane pay my debt? I'd walked out

on him and he turned around and settled my debt? What was he getting out of this?

I leaned forward, thinking of the lack of harassment or contact from anyone. Was that why I didn't have a line of supernaturals banging down my door? "Do you know if he paid anybody else?"

"Not sure, but I wouldn't be surprised." And cue the smirk. "Because he *likes* you."

I held back on asking why she thought that, knowing I'd have to hear about her Cupid connections again. I let out a ragged sigh before I dug in to my defense. "You could see how that's a tough pill to swallow, no?"

And she dug in to her position. "No. I don't see that at all. It's as easy to swallow as strawberry shortcake."

"Flip, you're wrong." I was going to have to give her the nitty-gritty before she'd see sense. "Before I came back here, he almost killed me in an alleyway."

She waved her hand. "Yeah, I heard all about that from Butch."

And she waves it away like it's nothing? "Almost. Killed. Me."

"No one but you actually believes that."

"That he almost killed me? He said as much, or at least didn't deny it."

"He wouldn't have killed you. He would've done it already. Plus, he *likes* you." She was smiling in that cattish way again. "You'll see."

Chapter 16

I'D BEEN WAITING IN KANE'S OFFICE, LOOKING THROUGH THE window onto the Underground for hours. It was near ten o'clock at night and Kane still hadn't come back. What was he doing all day?

Jerry went to open the door. I knew who it was before I could see Kane because everyone in the Underground looked, and pretended not to at the same time.

I was on my feet, double-timing it down the stairs and across the Underground main floor, as Kane walked through the door. There wasn't really a need to rush, as he was still standing beside Jerry when I reached him.

He turned slightly toward me and raised an eyebrow as he continued to discuss some schedule with Jerry.

Please, as if he had no idea why I was there waiting. I had my arms crossed and was tapping a foot, waiting for Jerry to finish with his questions. Kane might've looked ready for a nap, but Jerry grew more restless with the increasing pace of my tapping foot.

"I'll catch you later with this stuff," Jerry said, and backed away.

Kane started walking forward, and I fell into step with him immediately. This was going down now. "You do realize I've been waiting all day for you to get back."

"I was delayed."

I angled in front of him when we neared the stairs to his office and then narrowed my eyes, giving him my best *Don't even think about it.*

He paused, as if he was doing just that.

I grabbed his arm and started tugging him toward the hallway and the elevators. Luckily, he cooperated and came with me, instead of me getting dragged up the stairs.

We'd only made it halfway to the hall when I noticed all the sidelong stares in our direction. "Mind your own business," I yelled over the music. Their heads swiveled back to what they were doing. I knew this crew well enough to know it wasn't that they were embarrassed to stare. They were embarrassed to be caught caring about what a Shadow Walker might be up to.

"You can't blame them for being interested. You do put on a good show from time to time."

Why was he in such a good mood lately? I wasn't, that was for sure, and all because of him. It made me want to stomp all over his Oreos. "This is not funny."

I continued to pull him toward the elevator, not letting go in case he came up with some last-minute detour.

I hit the button and the door slid open. "Get in." I pointed as if he needed the additional instruction.

He walked into the elevator and leaned against the back wall as he waited for me to follow, and said, "You do realize I was going upstairs anyway, right?"

Try to steal my thunder. "Even if you weren't, you would be now." I gave him my back as the elevator rose.

"You seem very upset."

I turned on him, and he remained casually relaxed, his hands resting on the bar behind his hips. The more relaxed he appeared, the better his humor, the harder my blood pounded. It was as if I was being pumped full of gasoline and he was waving a match with his calm demeanor.

"What do you mean *I seem upset*? I've been waiting all day because you gave orders I couldn't talk to Asher alone. That's what. I had to threaten the guard I'd make it rain on him for weeks before I could even find out if he was getting food delivered." Not to mention I'd cornered the dwarves this afternoon and confirmed Kane had paid off my debts. Plus, he was still being nice, even as my personality tanked. What was wrong with him? Of course I was going to be irritable if he was going to keep changing the rules of engagement.

I kept my back to him. I was better off not looking at him in all his relaxed smugness. I couldn't believe I'd missed this man. Showed how mentally unstable I was.

"I don't see why you need to be with me."

"Exactly," he said, as if we were in complete agreement.

"What's that mean?" I turned.

He was still relaxed against the back of the elevator. "That's why I have to be with you. You have no idea the threat he might pose."

"That makes no sense. I know everything about him. The only threat he poses is to someone's checkbook. I should know, having lived with him for months."

The doors opened and he stepped in front of me. "I know," he said, with no lack of bite to the words.

Well, I was glad I wasn't the only one taking this seriously now. What happened? Asher order lobster on Kane's bill?

I stepped out of the elevator and moved toward my old rooms where, hopefully, Asher was okay.

Kane must've nodded or something, because the new guard, who thankfully wasn't so soft looking, stepped aside.

I couldn't help myself from pausing, hand on the door, and saying, "I'd keep an umbrella handy if I were you."

I walked into my old apartment and scanned the living room, all too aware of Kane following behind me.

The apartment door clicked shut.

"Was that bit about the umbrella really necessary?" Kane asked.

"Yes." I heard movement from the bedroom right before Asher poked his head out.

"Ollie!" He met me halfway and was hugging me until my feet left the floor.

"No touching."

Asher looked over my shoulder to where Kane was standing. He put me down slowly, but not slowly enough to merit retaliation.

"Are you okay?" I asked, stepping back and putting some space between us. I moved over to the couch. If he was sitting, maybe he'd be less likely to grab again.

"I'm fine." He shot a nasty look in Kane's direction before settling in next to me. "I missed you."

I could feel the eyes on us from Kane. This was not going to work the way I'd hoped. Kane was supposed to see how simple Asher could be and relax his guard. I hadn't anticipated the passive-aggressiveness coming from Asher, though. He certainly wasn't helping matters. The sooner I could build a bridge between the two of them, the better it would be for him. "Did you eat?"

"They brought me food after they questioned me," Asher said, throwing a dirty look toward Kane.

If Kane was throwing his own glares, I didn't know. I was afraid to look.

"They think I took things. Ollie, I didn't take anything." Asher was speaking to me, but the way he was saying everything was closer to poking at Kane.

"I know you didn't. Don't worry; Kane is getting things worked out, but everything is going to be okay. He's being cautious, is all."

Asher was staring at Kane. I made the mistake of turning around to look at him too. When I did, I was surprised Asher still had a head to speak with.

I seemed to be the only one in the room with a hammer and nails trying to erect the bridge. The way the two of them were glaring at each other, they both had sledgehammers. Except Kane's imaginary sledgehammer was big, thick, and heavy, and Asher didn't realize he had the Barbie Dreamhouse edition.

I smiled reassuringly at Asher and held a finger up to him, gesturing for him to give me a minute as I walked over to Kane.

"Can you leave us? You're scaring him," I whispered.

He glanced over at Asher, as if maybe, just maybe, he was seeing him for what he was: a little boy stuck in a man's body.

He turned back to me. "No."

"That's it? No?" I was about a heartbeat away from piling up my hammer and nails and letting them resolve this on their own.

"Yes."

I put my hands on my hips. "These single-syllable answers have to stop."

He crossed his arms, and I could see he wasn't going to give an inch, even before he said, "Okay, how about this? He might be hiding some of the most valuable items ever created. No one who does that is innocent, and if you think I'm leaving him alone with the most valuable Shadow Walker in a few decades, you're delusional."

Of course he wouldn't. He had his Shadow Walker back and doing exactly as he wanted. Why would he jeopardize something he needed just because I asked? This was exactly why I got annoyed with the fake nice business.

We had a stare-off for a couple of minutes while I racked my brain, trying to think of something that would force him to leave. I didn't come up with a thing.

"I'm asking for five minutes. That's it. He's tense with you staring at him like this. I might be able to get him to open up if you go."

He stood silently for a moment, long enough to make me wonder if I had a shot. Then he leaned closer, like he was going to bend, only to whisper, "No."

I smiled at Kane, as if he hadn't made me want to beat him over the head.

I walked back to Asher. "Don't worry about anything, okay? We're going to get this situation worked out."

"I missed you a lot last night. I can't wait until we can go back home and can be together again."

I was used to the way Asher spoke, but I wasn't so used to it that I didn't know what it would seem like to Kane. I'd told him we didn't have that kind of relationship, and Asher was definitely making me look like a liar.

"Visiting time is over," Kane said from the corner, sounding like I'd guessed correctly.

I could hear the violence in his voice that wanted to leak out into action. Asher certainly wouldn't be his first dead body.

"Don't worry. I'll be back tomorrow and we're going to

get this all worked out." I went to pat him Asher the arm but caught myself before I made contact.

Kane waited for me to precede him to the door. I walked out first. I stopped right outside the door and kept watch, making sure Kane was following me and hadn't changed his mind about leaving Asher in one piece.

We walked out of my old apartment and into Kane's. I made my way into the center of the living room, as did he, as if we'd agreed upon having it out without either of us having said it.

"What is your problem with him? He hasn't done anything."

"You say you didn't sleep with him, but he seems to think differently of your relationship."

"I didn't. He's got a crush on me."

"I'm not sure I'd call it a crush."

"He's barely hanging on right now. There's no reason to be mean to him about it."

He shrugged, which went completely against the tension in his frame or the cord about to burst out of his neck. "Hell, why don't you just sleep with him, then? That should make him feel better. He's your friend, right? Isn't that what you do? Take care of your friends?"

"Yeah, you know, that's a good idea. I'll sleep with him and you can go sleep with Isabella so she stops skulking about."

"You've seen her skulking?" He lifted an eyebrow as if calling me a liar.

Of course I had. All she did was skulk.

Actually, I hadn't seen her skulking the last couple of times I'd been there. I hadn't seen her at all. I was going to have to go track her down tomorrow. I needed to keep closer tabs on that one.

He was still there gloating about something or other, but I had another bone to pick. "Did you settle up all my debts?"

"Why do you ask?"

"Stop answering me with questions. They were *my* debts. How much were they? I'm paying you back." I might've mismanaged my money and had to get saved from the basement, but I was drawing the line somewhere. I wasn't going to be a charity case that needed everything taken care of because he was pretending to be nice to me for some weird reason.

"Really? You are?" He dropped his head as his eyebrows rose.

He wasn't being very nice right now, that was for sure. It was beyond frustrating that he thought he knew my finances—even if he actually did know my finances. He'd probably committed all my bills to memory as he flipped through them. "Stop doing that question thing, and yes, I am." I straightened, acting like he didn't know anything. "How much?"

"You sure you want to know?" he asked, as if daring me to make this an issue.

"I wouldn't have asked," I said, taking up the challenge.

"Fine. You want to handle everything on your own? You don't need anyone? It's four million, six hundred thousand, five dollars, and twenty-eight cents."

"What? There's no way I owe that much. And twenty-eight cents? You're making this up." And what was so wrong about wanting to handle my own problems for once in my life? He acted like I was insulting him. I didn't know where Kane's head had gone, but he was acting crazier than I used to.

"The leprechauns charge interest and keep it down to the penny."

"Did you even try and negotiate?"

"No. I didn't care enough."

Of course he didn't.

"I'm paying you back every cent." Eventually. It was going to be a long time, though, even with spells to sell.

"Good." He walked out, not so gloating anymore. I flopped onto the couch, my hole another mile deeper.

Chapter 17

I STORMED INTO KANE'S OFFICE, GASPING FOR AIR THE NEXT morning. I'd been woken four minutes ago by Butch telling me Kane needed me and it was urgent.

"What happened?" I bent forward, trying to suck more air in than could reasonably fit in my lungs. I'd run the whole way here after Butch had walked in and said there was a dire emergency. I'd been afraid to even wait for the elevator.

Kane was sitting with his head down, reading a paper lying in front of him. No blood, no screaming or crying—not that that would've come from Kane, but no one else was screaming or crying in the vicinity. Which meant there was something bad on that sheet of paper.

He tilted his head to me. "Good. You're here. I'm having the damnedest time."

Damnedest time? "What's the emergency? Butch said it was an emergency."

He stood and pointed to his vacated chair. "Sit."

Oh geez, it was so bad he didn't want me standing when I heard. My stomach felt like I'd had a breakfast of stones.

I did as he asked, afraid of what I'd find on the desk. He handed me the paper he'd been reading, and my fingers were trembling as I took it. What was so bad that Kane couldn't say it? He didn't flinch from anything.

I squinted, reading the small text. Estimated closing cost? Lien search? Yearly taxes? What?

I lifted the sheet toward him and realized he'd already made his way across the office to my couch. He didn't just sit but reclined and kicked his feet up, digging out a ball from the side of the cushion.

I lifted the paper in the air and waved it to get his attention. "You gave me some real estate papers. What's the emergency?"

"That's the emergency." He bounced his tennis ball against the wall, punctuating his sentence.

"This?" I waved my hand with the sheet still in it, making it flap this time. "This is the emergency? Closing papers for some building across town that doesn't even close until next week?"

"It's worse than that." He glanced over, still managing to catch the ball on the return with one hand while he pointed to the pile on his desk. "It's those, too. They're piling up faster than I can go through them. It's bad. Really bad."

Faster than he could go through them? I wanted to call him out on the fact that I hadn't seen him sit down at his desk and look through papers since I'd been here.

I would've called him out on it, but I didn't want him to get any funny ideas of why I'd noticed. He was so arrogant he'd probably assume I was interested in him and what he was doing. I wasn't. Not anymore. He was too high-handed by far. His arrogance could choke out an elephant, and now he kept doing this fake nice act on and off. Who could trust that?

Wait, why was I being called in here for these anyway? This might be *someone's* emergency, but it wasn't *my* emergency. "Why would you call me for this?" I dropped the sheet back onto the pile before it somehow contaminated me.

"Because I need help."

Wait, wasn't there some irritating creature who got paid to do this? She had to be good for something. "Where's Isabella?" I never thought I'd be looking for her. I was example number one of why you never said never.

"Not here." The ball thudded against the wall again.

I looked at the stack again. Great, she was on vacation and he was trying to dump her work on me? Was there no end to the insults I'd endure at the hands of this woman? Well, it could sit and wait until she got back from wherever she was. "When is she getting back?"

"Never." Thud.

Funny. "What? Is she moving to this tropical island? She must've given you a date."

Thud. "She's not coming back." Thud.

"She left?"

When had that happened? I leaned back, trying to think of when I'd seen her. I always noticed her when she was around. She was like having a piece of sand in your eye. Even if I didn't see her, I knew she was there. When had I last seen her? I couldn't remember beyond the office display. She was really gone. I'd been so aggravated and then stressed and just an emotional basket case that I'd missed the fact that she'd stopped stalking me, stopped laying her hands all over Kane like a desperado clinging to the last man on earth.

I hitched a foot up on the edge of the seat and rested an elbow on it for solid purchase as the world tried to right itself. She was in love with Kane. I'd seen the way she'd gaze at him. She wouldn't have quit. She never would've left him. There was a better chance of the sun leaving the sky. Something funny had gone down here.

I was shaking my head as I said, "She didn't just leave."

"She did."

"I find that very hard to believe."

"She's gone either way," he said, seeming more interested in his damn tennis ball than satisfying my curiosity.

This was going to be a big day for firsts, like bigger than when I walked into the Shadowlands for the first time, bigger than when I cast my first spell, even bigger than when I lost my virginity. Well, that hadn't been a particularly good night anyway. Point was, I never thought I'd say what I was about to say.

"Can you get her back?" I couldn't really mean this.

The stack of papers sat looming large on the desk, and I kept going, knowing Kane was going to harass me daily for help if I didn't. I needed him too much to tell him to go screw, and he knew it. "Call her up and tell her you'll pay her double."

"She won't come back for any amount of money. That's your fault, so now you need me to help." He seemed very calm over her leaving. Just thudded his ball. Maybe Flip had been right.

"Wait, how's it my fault?" Yeah, I might've threatened her in the past, but she'd had it coming. Plus, that woman had given as good as she got. I wasn't buying any "poor me" bullshit she gave him that landed me in paperwork purgatory.

"It is."

I walked over to him and grabbed the ball before it returned to him. "Prove it's my fault and I'll help." I dropped the ball back to him, knowing this was my ticket to the shredder. He'd never be able to prove it.

He glanced at me, and I could see something wavering in his expression, and then he threw the ball again. "It is."

He was leaning back on the couch, giving me his best *I'm the boss of this shop* look.

I walked back to the desk, leaned back, and kicked up my heels. It took me less than a second to realize I'd stolen this posture from the man himself, after watching him do it countless times.

I was digging in. There was no way I was getting all that paperwork dumped on me without an explanation.

He finally stopped bouncing the ball. "You know I could make you."

"I'm not so sure about that." That was it. He couldn't prove it was my fault. Ha!

He turned toward me. "You're really sure you want to know?"

"Positive." Big bluffer. I knew this game. I'd played it, stalling for time until you thought something up.

"She acted in my name when she shouldn't have. We had a discussion and she left."

"Like a chitchat discussion?"

"Do you think I kill everyone?" He seemed to find it amusing.

"No. But...well, you don't seem to have a difficult time with it, so it's not like I shouldn't check."

"I wanted to kill her, but I told her if she got out of my office right then, I wouldn't. She did."

I hadn't really thought he'd kill her. He was loyal, I'd give him that. To some people, anyway. "So how is her acting in *your* name *my* problem?" I had him now. I crossed my arms over my chest, smiling wide.

"She told the leprechauns they could pick you up after I'd made it clear you weren't to be touched."

He hadn't turned his back on me? I dropped my gaze as the intensity of that revelation rocked me. When he'd walked down those stairs to the basement, as if invited, I thought the worst. But he'd done nothing. Isabella had, and he'd made her leave because of it.

Why had he not told me this before? It didn't make any sense. "Why didn't you..."

The bouncing finally stopped and I saw the closed expression.

He went back to bouncing, but not before I got the message. I should've known.

He was right. I should've. Yes, he'd used me for his purposes in the past, and I'd used him every bit as much. But he'd protected me too, more times than I could remember now. I'd left without a word, which I knew he'd seen as a betrayal, and he was still protecting me.

Why had he done that? Why was he acting so nice? Or maybe it wasn't an act at all.

When I first met Kane, I'd hated him. Then I'd started to warm up to him, maybe even gotten a little hotter than warm.

Then I left him and he'd hated me, and I'd decided I needed to hate him. Now? I didn't know what I thought anymore.

And where did that leave me and that stack in front of me? I might've been better off thinking he hated me. "I don't even know what to do with all this stuff."

"You've gone over enough of my paperwork before. Just make sure nothing looks outlandish." He was back to thudding his ball as if we hadn't had a moment, exactly as I hoped he would.

I scratched my head, wondering if I needed to read everything or maybe every other page. "I really don't think I'm proficient enough. I'm going to mess you up somehow." Hopefully that would scare him off.

"Didn't you just tell me you were going to pay me back all those debts?"

I placed both hands on the desk and leaned forward. "I'm not paying you back in paperwork, so just get that right out of your head."

"What if that's my preferred payment?" He started humming as he bounced.

We'd see who won this negotiation. "I'll make you a deal. I'll do paperwork, but you're not going to like my rate." Let's see how happy he looked after this.

"Name it."

"Fifty thousand an hour."

He paused and looked at the stack. "Deal."

"What?" I sat back down. How had that gone so wrong?

"That's ninety-two hours of paperwork. You should be able to get through the stack in that time. I'll let you slide on the five dollars and twenty-eight cents."

"But..."

"You named the price."

I started shuffling through the papers, feeling over-whelmed just looking at the foot-high stack.

"You know, ever think of getting involved in a business that has less paperwork?" Had I just teased him? Well, if we were going to be friends, it wasn't wrong. I hadn't flirted; there was a definite difference between teasing and flirting.

"They've all had paperwork. It seems unavoidable."

I took a stack of papers, glancing at my new workload, while sneaking glances at Kane.

I had to say something about Asher, but I didn't want to,

especially not now while Kane seemed like he was in a good mood. But if I didn't, it was going to look really suspicious.

Might as well get it over with. "I need to go see Asher, and since you've got him under lock and guard..." I shrugged as if to say, *You should be able to guess the rest of this.* But that was when it struck me. I wasn't mad. Shouldn't I be mad that I couldn't check on Asher whenever I wanted? Yes, I should. I should be railing at Kane and demanding to see Asher whenever I wanted. But the thing of it was, the shock of the situation most definitely had passed, and I was still relieved I couldn't see him.

Kane tucked the ball back into the cushions and got up.

"When I get back later. I've got somewhere to be."

He hadn't looked like he'd been going anywhere. "Okay."

I knew I should be arguing to see Asher right then and there, but I was too afraid I'd win.

Kane was staring at me, probably wondering where all my fight had gone. I dropped my head, suddenly engrossed in the most interesting numbers.

"You're good with that?" he asked. There was a hint of either curiosity or humor in his voice, but I couldn't tell which. Either way, I'd have to pretend I wasn't good with it, but how to avoid Kane giving in now that he was nice again? I couldn't tell him I didn't want to see Asher. That might make it look like I thought Asher was guilty.

I looked up, making sure my brow was furrowed and my lips were flat. "Of course I'm not, but you call the shots, so what else am I supposed to do?"

"Really? I do?" he asked, leaning a shoulder on the door and crossing his arms as he watched me.

I might've overdone it, plus my cheeks hurt from trying to keep everything tense.

"When did you decide I was in charge?"

Did he have to be funny now? This was hard enough. I mean, everyone else had decided that, but I certainly had never agreed to him being boss, and I wasn't going to now, either.

"I've got a lot of work to do. I can't have this silly talk with you." I kept my eyes on the papers, hoping he'd leave before I had to make up some big lie about how he was the boss of me.

Chapter 18

I WAITED ABOUT TWENTY MINUTES BEFORE I WENT TO THE stairwell off the sixth floor.

"Zee?"

The gargoyle popped in, sporting a side pony and a red Lycra jumpsuit. "Make this quick. I've got a pedicure appointment."

She was not going to be the easiest of partners. "Do you have a list for me?"

"A list?" she asked, half listening as she eyed up a chip on her pinky.

"Yes. Like we talked about? I need to know who wants what spell and who's willing to pay what."

She finally dropped her hand and smiled. "Baby, I don't have a list. I've got a whole damn novel of wants and needs. I just wasn't sure if we were still in business."

"We are not only open but dying for customers. I should be shadow walking soon, and I need to be prepared with requests."

She held out her hand and a legal pad popped out of the air. She licked a red-clawed finger and flipped through.

"I need ones that will pay the most cash," I added. I couldn't be wasting time on frivolities with the amount of bills I had due.

"Not an issue." She flipped another couple of pages and then smiled and nodded. "This is a real goodie. The guy is willing to pay up to a million. Considering you're the only game in town that can supply his spell, that's exactly how much he will be paying."

A million? I'd be caught up on everything and have a cushion. This was it, all I needed. Well, except for the debt I owed Kane, but he wanted that paid in paperwork. "Tell me what it is and I'll get it."

"Raise the dead. How long do you think it'll take to find?" Her overly arched eyebrows went frighteningly high as she waited for the answer with what could only be excitement.

It was a spell after my own heart. I'd wondered many times if I could save my own family. Then I'd remember the book by Stephen King called *Pet Sematary*. What were the odds they'd come back the same? Highly unlikely. And did I have the stomach to kill them again? Even more unlikely. The money was nice, but I couldn't cross that line.

Instead of giving a long explanation that Zee would argue against, I kept it short. "I don't think I can get that one. It would take way too long."

"You sure? I thought you were good at getting things?"

"It can't be done. I'm sure of it." Not by this person, anyway. Not now.

She shrugged and looked back at her pad. "Okay, here's another one. This should be easy. They need a love potion."

I nodded. Love. That was a good thing. As she laid out the details of the who and when, the idea bounced around a bit until it sort of soured. If I did a love potion, someone who wasn't interested in someone else would be compelled to be with that person. They'd probably have *sex* with that person. What if they got married and had a kid with that person, someone they obviously weren't into or the spell wouldn't be needed? The more I walked the idea down the road to its natural conclusion, the more the whole thing started to have an icky, rape-ish feel to it.

"Wait, no, I don't think I can do that one either."

"What?" Zee stared at me like a headful of snakes had popped out of my scalp. "Why? *Why?*"

I threw my hands up and shrugged. "I'll feel like a rapist."

Her mouth looked like she was saying *huh*, but no word came forth.

"If I do this, someone is going to be tricked into thinking they care for someone they don't care for. It doesn't feel ethical." I threw my hands up. There was nothing to be done about it.

"Ethical? We're doing magic, not law. Why are you even thinking about all this? You just get the spells. That's it. You aren't committing the acts." She was tossing her head back and forth, swinging that side pony with it.

"I can't. What else do you have? There's a whole list." I reached out and tried to take the pad from her, but she tugged it back. "There has to be something that won't make me feel sleazy on it."

"I'm in charge of the list. No touching the list."

"Fine." I stepped back in a show of peace.

She watched and then, seeming to come to a truce, looked back at the pad. "Okay, how about this. I've got a female shifter who wants to get rid of excess body hair. Or do you have some problem with destroying hair? Like, you're a hair follicle killer? Or is it okay as long as you don't bring the hair back to life?"

I ignored the heavy layer of sarcasm dripping off each word.

"How much will she pay?"

The way Zee looked down at the paper, I knew the figure was decent. "She's pretty desperate. Hair grows back within an hour of her shaving, and the witches haven't been able to do a thing for her. Werewolf hair is very stubborn. You can imagine the embarrassment during intimate moments. She's willing to pay a hundred grand. Fifty up front and fifty after being hair free for a couple of hours."

Wow, that sucked. "That sounds pretty steep. Maybe we should do it for less?" Good thing she was going through Zee or I would've done it for free.

The pad disappeared and she pursed her red lips, her knee pointing out as she took on a bitch stance. "Excuse me, but I work on commission. You won't raise the dead, you won't let people fall in love, fine. But I draw the line at pricing like we're Walmart."

There were some fights you couldn't win. "Set it up."

"I'll be in touch. I'm late for my pedicure."

"Good talk," I said to the air before I turned around and headed to the doorway that opened up to the hall.

I bounced off nothing before I got there. I tried to repeat the step and nearly fell over this time.

A male said, "Stop shoving!"

I immediately stopped, more from surprise than anything else. I knew that voice. Two dwarves appeared in front of me. The one in the middle I recognized from when I'd gotten my dwarf clothes. He was the DiC, Dwarf in Charge.

"How long have you been here?"

The noncommittal shrug said it had been long enough even before he said, "You won't do dead people or love potions, but you've got no problem with hairy chicks." He looked over his shoulder at his buddy. "Was there more?"

"Other than being a mammy pansy about will she or won't she? Nah, I think that was it." The buddy nodded assertively.

These little guys needed bells on their necks. "Don't say a word about that."

"What's it worth to you?" DiC said, his buddy stepping forward to make sure he heard my answer.

"Nothing. Did you come here for a purpose or just to harass me?"

"We're here to warn you."

I leaned against the railing of the stairs. I should've been more concerned about what the warning was going to be, but as I eyed up the sleekly dressed dwarves in front of me and remembered what they charged for their clothes, I asked, "How much is this going to cost me?"

"This one is on the house."

Free? Nah, that was hard to believe. No one in this place did anything for free. You had to spell it out. "No strings at all? You warn me and we walk away even?"

"Well, you might want to do us a favor in the future," the second dwarf said.

"What kind of favor?"

"There's nothing at the moment, but there might be at some point."

Great, another IOU. I couldn't dig myself out without digging right back in. I shook my head but rolled my hand. "What's the warning?"

"We heard the witches say they needed to even the score with you."

Great. "How?"

"We don't know that."

I found myself raising my eyebrows at them. "That's it? That's all you've got?"

"Yes."

"I don't owe you a favor for that," I said, walking around them to get to the hall door.

"We warned you. You owe us."

I turned, hand on the handle. "You told me the witches want to do me in. Everyone here already knows the witches want to get me. You want to extract favors, you better get me details on *how* they plan to screw me."

DiC turned to his second. "Fine. We'll be back, but you'll owe us then."

"Gladly."

Chapter 19

I walked over to the booth where Butch and Leon were sitting and realized how natural it all felt. I'd been gone for months, but I felt like I'd eaten here every day for the last year.

They both stopped eating and looked at me when I stopped in front of them, waiting to see who was going to scoot over before I had to get pushy.

Butch moved first, dragging his burger and fries with him.

I ordered a turkey club from a gargoyle I didn't recognize. I was taking a bite when Leon brought up a subject that made me wish I'd eaten dinner alone in Kane's office while poring over paperwork.

"Forgot to mention I saw your commercial a few weeks back." Leon took a sip of beer before adding, "It was very nice."

Butch made a suspicious coughing noise that made Leon's lips twitch. It took Leon a moment to get himself under control enough to continue. "It was a good try, anyway."

Flip walked over, and we all shifted to make room. "What's Butch hacking over?"

I looked at Butch as I replied, "He thinks Leon liking my commercial is funny."

She leaned forward, her ear tilted toward me as if she doubted what I'd said. "You mean BBGB?"

Butch stopped laughing, and Leon rolled his eyes and groaned.

Everyone knew what she was talking about but me. "Why is my commercial called BBGB?"

Butch couldn't stop shoving his burger in his mouth, and Leon held a hand up as if something was stuck in his throat.

Flip, socially awkward as ever, didn't seem to pick up on the fact she shouldn't be telling me. "Big Bird Gone Bad. You know, because of the weird-looking puppet thing?"

I leaned toward her. "You gave it an acronym?" Yes, the puppet had been bad, but had it been that bad? Thinking back on it, yeah. It had probably been that bad. Still, what would be the need for a nickname?

Flip looked up at the ceiling briefly, as if contemplating the fate of the universe, before she said, "Technically, it's not an acronym but we had to do something. Big Bird Gone Bad was sort of a mouthful, especially when you're using it all the time."

"Why would you use it all the time?" Was it me? Was I being stupid and missing the obvious here?

The light seemed to finally be dawning on Flip as she answered. "You know, someone asks how something looks, you say, it's not great but it's not BBGB." Her words came out slower and slower until she was finally realizing why maybe telling me this wasn't a good idea.

I was still speechless as she grabbed her plate and started mumbling about having an appointment.

I slumped back, looking at Butch and Leon. "The director had great reviews. He said it would look completely different on screen. I don't know what happened." Or how I'd believed that load of bull.

"Wasn't one of the best commercials, but it wasn't *that* bad," Leon said as Butch remained quiet and very interested in his fries, since his burger was gone.

"Have you guys said that?"

Butch began stuffing fries in his mouth at an alarming rate, while Leon kept opening his mouth but saying nothing.

I leaned an elbow on the table and used that hand to hold up my forehead. "You have."

Butch was choking on fries as Leon answered. "Only because everyone else was using it and it just became a thing. I didn't really feel that strongly about it."

Butch was chugging beer, and if he wasn't sitting in between me and Leon, I was positive he'd be running for it.

"It wasn't that bad." Leon shrugged and then added, "It wasn't as bad as making a deal to shadow walk with Collin."

My other elbow hit the table, as my head needed two hands to hold it up. "Why was that stupid? Kane wouldn't work with me, and Collin was willing."

Leon scoffed loudly. "You're lucky you didn't end up working with him. Collin has killed every Shadow Walker he's ever tried to work with. No one knows why he thinks he can anchor, but he can't if his record is any indication. He couldn't anchor a ship in the ocean with a two-ton weight, let alone a Shadow Walker."

I lifted my head but couldn't quite get my chin out of my palm.

"Why didn't you end up working with him?" Leon asked, and then chomped away on a piece of steak.

Butch stared at me over his beer. "Yeah, what happened?"

Kane hadn't told them? It didn't seem like a secret. "Kane threatened to kill him."

Butch glanced over at Leon, and I saw the silent communication pass between them. I knew what they were thinking. Same thing Flip did. They were wrong. Maybe he was being nice to me again, but that didn't mean he liked me. He had once, but then I'd left. We were work partners now, maybe on the way to being friends again, but that was all.

Kane walked into the Underground. He looked over at our booth, fixed his gaze on me, and then nodded toward the office.

I shoved my uneaten sandwich away. "Excuse me. I'm being summoned."

Butch and Leon shared another *look*.

I made my way into the office, where Kane was already seated behind his desk. "Why can't you ask me to come to your office like a normal person?"

I flopped into the chair and swung my legs over the arm as I waited to hear what I'd been summoned for.

"I did."

His eyes seemed to get stuck on my jumpsuit. It was a really cute black one-piece that did wonders for my shape.

When he kept looking, I said, "I ran out of clean laundry." Well, I was low on laundry. Was it a crime to look cute once in a while? "And no, you didn't call me. You tilted your head."

"If I didn't ask, how did you know to come?"

"It's not the same."

"Same end result."

Instead of staying behind his desk, he took a seat in front of me on his desk, leaning over with his hands resting on the edges. His body folded slightly forward, and it was hard not to notice the way his shoulders were shaped or that he didn't have an ounce of belly fat.

"The meeting to locate the missing items is set for tomorrow." He said it calmly, but the weight of his words was unmistakable.

I'd been expecting this. Had actually wondered what was taking so long, but I hadn't asked him about it. If I did locate the items, then what? The crazy leprechauns might not want to kill me anymore, but would I have to leave the Underground? Would Kane stop anchoring me? Would I be asked to leave?

Kane dipped his head down slightly closer to me. "Are you ready?"

"Yeah, sure." I was definitely ready for the spell. I wasn't ready for what came next.

I unfolded out of the chair before he figured out what was wrong with me.

"Hang on," he said as I had my hand on the doorknob.

I turned, trying to hide any telltale signs about how much the news of the meeting tomorrow had ruined my night.

"You sure you're okay for tomorrow?"

"Yeah." I did a quick nod and left before he could ask again.

Chapter 20

KANE AND I PULLED UP TO AN EIGHT-FLOOR APARTMENT building, barely hanging on to the outskirts of Boston. The place was dark and had sheets of plastic covering various windows. Butch and Leon pulled up beside us in the Caddy as Kane threw the car in park. Besides us, there were three other cars, probably belonging to the most likely suspects: leprechauns, vampires, and werewolves.

I leaned forward, trying to get a better view. It was a good spot. If I messed up the spell somehow, there wasn't that much damage that could be inflicted, since it was only a shell of a building.

I turned to get out of the car, but Kane's hand on my arm stopped me.

"If the spell leads us to Asher—"

"It won't. He doesn't have them." I didn't argue.

Kane didn't move, his hand still on my arm as we silently squared off. He finally let go. I didn't kid myself into thinking he believed me, though.

Butch and Leon caught up to us as we walked into the building.

"Third floor," Kane said, leading the way toward a stair-case over to the side.

The group moved as a swarm as we walked onto the third floor. It looked like everyone had decided to use the buddy system. Rudy, head leprechaun, had his usual escort. Alexandria had brought her backup, and even Collin had decided to bring the guy who had eaten my Doritos. Yes, I was still holding on to that, because who breaks into your apartment and eats your chips? Even a werewolf should know better.

I wasn't used to having an audience, but I didn't particularly care, either. Although this wasn't an audience anyone would want. I was new to this world but I wasn't new to reading body language. Everyone here was wound so tight I was waiting for the sound of snaps.

"Did she get it?" Alexandria asked.

"Yes, or we wouldn't be here," Kane said from my right side. Leon was on my left, and I got a sense of Butch behind me, as if I were being cocooned by testosterone.

Alexandria stepped closer, cutting off Collin's second from view. "We should try for my pendant first."

Collin was having none of it. "The blood is more important."

"No, we all know my map is."

They might've bickered all night if Kane hadn't finally shut it down by stepping forward. "We go for the map first. That's the most potent item."

Rudy looked smug, but Alexandria wasn't going down without a fight. "What if the spell only works once?"

"Exactly why we're going for the map." Kane waited, his posture daring anyone to question his decision. No one did.

He turned his attention to me and I nodded, realizing I was a bit eager to start.

I let the words drift off my lips, a warm, fluttering feeling building within me as they flowed. It filled my chest and spread down into my limbs until my entire body felt alive with the feeling of warmth. The spell swelled in the air. I couldn't see it, but I felt it working, the magic pulsing through me as it built, or perhaps it had started deep inside me. I'd missed this more than I'd even realized. I thought about that retired Shadow Walker, maybe more than was healthy.

I glanced around, and could see that everyone was taken over by the magic, awe on their faces. The air grew thick with it. I kept repeating the words, operating on instinct as sure as birds flying south in the winter.

And I sensed the second the magic started to hiccup, like it was searching for something that didn't exist and was tiring of the pointless job. What did that mean?

It wasn't instinct that told me how bad this meeting might get once the rest of them figured it out. That was plain old logic.

I kept repeating the spell, buying myself a couple of minutes to try and figure out what had happened. I risked a quick glance at Kane, the other person who might sense it. He always knew when my spells had fallen flat on him.

His expression was the same as it had been when I started. But when he glanced over at me, there was the slightest flicker. He knew.

So why wasn't he saying anything? He knew these people better than I did. Why would he want me to tell them? He was the bossy *I'm in charge* person. Not me. Well, it had been my spell. I guess even a bossy person like him might see the merit in me delivering the news.

My words dried up as I stopped pretending there was

any hope left, and the silence grew as everyone waited for something to happen. I was waiting for Kane to talk.

I looked over at him again, not so subtly this time and he gave me a one-shoulder shrug, as if to say, *Just tell them. What are they going to do about it?*

I wanted to reply, *Wait to get me alone and then drag me into another basement and beat the crap out of me?* I didn't. It didn't seem like a good idea to give them any ideas.

Of course, Rudy started, because he had to always be a problem. "Well? Did you get an answer?"

How to word this? Was there some way to say it that would minimize the freak-out? Hmmm. Probably not if the stares were any indication, I might as well spit it out, since they were catching on.

"It didn't work. I don't know where your stuff is." Not exactly a smooth delivery, but the communication was sound. There was no way they'd misunderstand that.

"What do you mean it didn't work?" Rudy said. The rest of them seemed speechless.

Had to love when someone repeated something just because they didn't like what they heard, as if it would get them a different answer.

"It. Flopped. It's saying the map is nowhere. As if it doesn't exist."

"Are you saying I made this up?" Rudy's green eyes were bulging from his gaunt face.

"No. What I'm saying is the spell can't sense your map for whatever reason." *Jump in anytime now, Kane.*

Alexandria interrupted before Rudy could carry on. "Stop wasting time on his map and try looking for my pendant."

I glanced over at Kane, checking to see if there was any reason I might not want to do that.

"If you're up to it," he said in response, not appearing to care either way what I decided to do.

I did a mental stretch, seeing what I had left. For all the magic I'd used the first time, I still felt like I was running on a full tank.

I opened my mouth, hoping the words would start to flow and that this wasn't going to be one of those one-hit wonder spells, where you use it and lose it. That wasn't the case, though, as the magic quickly filled the air and I got another rush.

I could see the awe fill their faces again as they felt the power building. It made me wonder how they were going to react when I told them this one was going to be a bust, too. The spell *wanted* to work. I could feel this magical net of sorts reaching out, searching. And I could also feel the emptiness.

I glanced at Kane and there was a flicker, but this time it was surprise. Well, at least I had that. I knew something first. Should I wait for him to figure it out in the hopes he said something?

Screw it. "Didn't work."

"What? What do you mean?" The same thing Rudy asked was now coming out of Alexandria's mouth.

Really? Were we going to do this again?

"This is a fake, an act!" Alexandria ranted.

Rudy's expression went from annoyed to smug. "Oh, so now it's a problem?" he asked Alexandria.

She ignored him, her full concentration on me. "I bet you know where everything is and you're keeping them for yourself."

"Don't tell me you didn't feel what I was pumping out when I know you did," I said. "Are you magically blind?"

It seemed like the entire group inhaled at the same time.

Alexandria had her hand on her throat, acting like I'd just assaulted her. I heard Butch groan from beside me, but Kane let out a masculine laugh. I knew by now that I couldn't judge the appropriateness of my actions by Kane's standards.

This was why someone else should've been doing the talking.

Alexandria's hand shifted up to her mouth while her companion could've killed me with her eyes while she patted her shoulder.

Collin stepped forward, shifting the conversation. "Or maybe whoever took those things has destroyed them already?"

That didn't make any sense. They obviously needed them for something, or why bother? I wasn't going to be the one to say it, though. I had enough enemies in this group, and I wasn't currently counting Collin among them.

Rudy let out a sigh as his head shook, then topped it off with an eye roll. "That makes no sense, you stupid hairball."

Hairball? Low blow.

"We'll try again in a week," Kane said, drawing all the attention back to him.

I didn't know why he would say that other than to buy us time. I'd felt the spell; we all had. The problem wasn't the magic. It wasn't me. It was the target. Unless he didn't know? I *was* the one saying the spell, the one who was closest to the pulse and ebb of the magic. Maybe he really believed it would work in a week? Nah, highly unlikely.

Rudy wasn't having any of it. He stepped toward me. "I'm supposed to wait a week to see if you mess up again?"

"Yes, that's how long," I said. "Go home and eat some Lucky Charms or shit some rainbows out, or whatever else it is you do."

Rudy's cheeks were flaming. "They should've finished you in that basement."

I felt the heat of Kane's body as he stepped closer. "If I were you, I'd watch your words. You still haven't delivered on our agreement."

My eyes shot from Rudy to Kane. What agreement? It would be nice if my partner filled me in on what was going on.

Rudy's face was growing redder by the moment. I couldn't see Kane's face, but I didn't need to. Those words, soft as they were said, were a warning flair. Rudy wobbled back slightly and then stopped himself. But he kept his mouth shut.

No one said anything after that. There was a nod here or there in our direction, but the party was definitely over. They slowly disbanded, the disgruntled herd of them.

We were the last to exit, Butch and Leon going to the Caddy and me climbing in the car with Kane.

My head flopped back onto the headrest and I reclined my seat all the way back, feeling like I could sleep for a year. All the magic use caught up to me as the questions rattled away in my mind. No one would go through all of that aggravation to destroy the map and pendant. It made zero sense.

If I went on the assumption that they hadn't been destroyed, maybe the spell couldn't sense them? It was the only thing that added up. And how could that be? Unless someone had taken the things over into the Shadowlands.

This could be really bad. I didn't look to my left, but if I was thinking it, Kane probably was, too.

"You okay?" His voice was soft, maybe even concerned.

Where were the accusations? The *I told you so*? Why was he being nice to me again? Was it guilt? I hadn't seen Asher today, and I should've. Maybe the reason the spell didn't know where the items were was because the person who had them was dead?

I bit my lip, wondering if I should even ask, but how could I not? "Did you kill anyone today?" That might've been too vague. "Anyone I should know about?"

He smiled, as if that were amusing. Before I had to be concerned about what was amusing, he said, "No. He's safely resting in your old apartment."

I side-eyed him, wondering if he was lying. It would be a stupid lie, as I'd find out pretty quickly. Kane wasn't a liar or stupid. Arrogant, controlling, and a bunch of other stuff, but I guess we all had our flaws.

He glanced over at me. "Last check, he was watching a marathon of the *Gilmore Girls* and eating his way through five pounds of Lobster Fra Diavolo."

I rolled my head to the side, laughter replacing the anxiety. Yeah, Asher was alive. If someone was going to make something up about a creature that came out of the Shadowlands, it wouldn't be that.

The relief died with the weight that Asher might've had something to do with this. Who else could've? But why would he lie to me about it? There was no reason.

"We've got to come to some sort of arrangement. I can't worry that you'll kill him every day." Because if I was questioning Asher, Kane might be killing him.

"I can't kill him," Kane said, and the weight of his tone made it clear he wasn't happy about it.

"Why not?"

"Crawlers tend to blow things up even when they aren't fully in this world. He might look human, but he's a crawler. He might blow up like an atomic bomb. I'm not going to kill him while he's living in my building. I'm not saying I won't hand him over to someone else, but he's safe...for now, anyway."

The edge in his voice made it clear he wasn't so happy about it, but at least I had something to hold on to now. My eyelids wanted to drift close; all those spells in a row must have drained my energy. The thought of Asher having lied to me kept them open.

Chapter 21

WE WERE BACK AT THE UNDERGROUND, AND ALL I WANTED TO do was run straight to Asher. Then what would I do? If he did have something to do with the missing items, he'd been lying to me, and why would he come clean now? Or he had nothing to do with it. Instead of running to find Asher, and flying a banner overhead with all my concerns, I followed Kane into his office and crashed on the couch.

Kane's gaze was on me, as if he knew what I wanted to do. Maybe he suspected something was amiss, but he didn't know for sure. Now the question was did I look at him and stare down his accusation or pretend I didn't notice?

Damn. Wish I hadn't looked.

Eyebrows raised, he walked over and stood so close it was hard not to look at him.

"Don't pretend you aren't questioning him." He was hovering over my spot.

"I know how it looks, but I still don't think it's him." I shifted positions, making myself more comfortable by not staring right into his face.

"Thank you for not feigning stupidity."

I nodded. I didn't particularly care for thank yous that weren't really thank yous, but I had bigger issues than that to argue over. Plus, it got me some space as he walked over and looked down at the people in the Underground, arms crossed.

The strangest thing about all of this was not accusing me of being in cahoots with Asher. I still couldn't get a handle on why Kane was being so much nicer to me. Well, Kane nice, anyway. It was way too awkward to ask that kind of general question, so I settled for something more specific. "If you're so sure Asher is involved in the missing items, why aren't you accusing me of being in on it anymore?"

"Are you in on it?" His voice didn't hold an ounce of anger or suspicion as he tiled his head, more interested in something he saw downstairs.

"No. But why don't *you* think I am?" I leaned forward, planning on standing but then thinking better of it. My legs were way too tired to bother with appearances or bravado.

"Would you like me to pretend I do? I can if that would make you feel better."

I didn't bother responding to his wiseass remarks and settled into the couch a little deeper, my eyes closing. The bed was calling my name, but that involved standing and walking, so a nap on the couch won.

"Did you get any of the paperwork done?"

The world around us was falling apart, I couldn't keep my eyes open, and he wanted me to worry about the paperwork. "No. I haven't done any more." And I didn't feel a damn lick bad about it, either.

"Until that's done, you still work for me. Don't get any crazy ideas about running off because you located the items."

I pulled the only pillow on the couch over my face, as if I were frustrated. This way he couldn't see my smile.

Kane had just asked me to stay.

I heard his phone buzz against his desk.

"Where?"

I moved the pillow, knowing whatever the call was, it was bad news from that single word. His eyes met mine as he listened. A few seconds later he stood, pocketing his phone. "We need to go."

We stood a block away from the burning building. What looked like every fire engine in Boston lined the street as the firefighters tried to tackle an unrelenting flame that had demolished a ten-story building. It was already licking at the buildings on either side, as if it were a famished beast with an insatiable hunger. Once you saw flames like these, you never forgot the look of them. I'd seen them twice before.

"Did you find the Shadow Walker that let it out?" Not that he or she would've known what they were doing. We never did.

The lines of Kane's face were harsh as he looked on, the flames highlighting his bone structure. "There weren't any survivors matching the description. It was a crawler, but he didn't need a Shadow Walker."

"How do we know the Shadow Walker isn't dead in the building?"

His eyes shifted toward me before one of his *I know it all* comments came forth. "Because in all my years, I've never seen a crawler kill a Shadow Walker that let them out. It's not in their best interest."

I bopped my head back and forth. The logic did make sense. I scanned the crowd for people that fit the description of a Shadow Walker anyway, preferring to cling to a shred of hope. But even if the items were being used to set a crawler free, it didn't mean it was Asher. It proved nothing.

Instead of spotting a Shadow Walker, I saw a group of men off to the side, fifty feet or so from us, set in silhouette. I squinted, catching a glimpse of an angular jaw. "Is that—"

"Rudy," Kane said, answering my unfinished question without bothering to look at the group. "He's the one who called me. This was one of the places on the leprechaun map."

Rudy had been watching us as well, and started toward us.

"Is it gone?" Kane asked once Rudy was within hearing distance.

"Yes," Rudy said through gritted teeth.

I waited for one of them to fill in the rest, but neither of them seemed too chatty over the subject. "What's gone? Anyone feel like cluing me in?"

That Rudy didn't say anything wasn't a surprise. Kane moved closer to me, giving Rudy his back. "That burning building was an ER, short for End of the Rainbow. The crawler leeched the magic from the ground with its fire like a plant would suck nutrients from the dirt."

The sun had set hours ago and it hadn't rained in days. Was this a confirmed ER, or were the leprechauns losing their shit a little? How often were these maps updated?

Rudy shifted a couple of steps back and forth with his hands fisted, staring at the fire like a boxer looking at an opponent.

Kane glanced at Rudy, but the agitation didn't seem to be contagious.

"This needs to end," Rudy said.

Oh yeah, Rudy was definitely losing his shit now.

Rudy had circled around in front of us and looked like he was walking on hot coals. "Are you listening to me? The only reason we won't lose anyone is because you've already taken care of that."

Kane, hands in his pockets, looked down at Ruby and said, "I'll let you know if I hear anything."

It was hard to stay cool when Kane was giving you his *I don't give a fuck* stance. I almost felt bad for Rudy, or I would've if I didn't hate him so damn much.

Rudy handled it better than I. He pulled himself together enough to nod and back away. Bright of him. It took another couple of moments of awkward silence before he walked back to his group.

Kane might've acted like it was no big deal, but I could see the concern slipping back into his features. Kane was worried. Kane, who didn't worry about much.

He rocked back on his heels as he said, "That map lists every ER that exists on this earth. That's a lot of power."

A loose crawler with more power than it normally had, possibly running loose. It was enough to give any Shadow Walker nightmares. At least they weren't carrying bodies out of the charred building.

"Wait, why did Rudy say he wouldn't lose anyone?"

Kane nodded toward the direction we'd parked. "There's a finite amount of ERs. These places are where leprechauns get their magic, their wealth, everything that makes them *them*. But there's a delicate balance between the amount of leprechauns and corresponding ERs. If you could count every leprechaun in existence, you'd know how many ERs there are." He stopped in front of the car. "After a loss like this, they'd have to kill one of their own. If they didn't, one of them would die anyway, and they'd have no control over who."

I went to the passenger side and climbed in. "But you killed one," I said once he got behind the wheel.

"Which would've been replaced. Leprechauns are sterile unless the balance is off. His human girlfriend wants a baby, though, so I don't think he was particularly upset over the one I killed. Leprechauns are replaced. ERs aren't."

I fell quiet as I stared at the still-burning fire in the rearview mirror. "You think it's still nearby?"

"No. I think it's long gone."

It took me about two minutes to realize what I had to do. It took me four times longer to figure out how to broach the subject without Kane taking it as a declaration of Asher's guilt.

All that planning was for nothing when Kane said, "You get five minutes alone to get whatever you can out of him."

What the hell? I'd had this whole conversation worked out, and now I wasn't sure what to do. If I simply agreed, would that mean I was saying I thought Asher was involved? Because I didn't. Or I wasn't sure. Well, if Asher was, he had no idea what he was doing. I couldn't decline. This was what I'd wanted to do!

Maybe I say nothing at all? That might be the best move. I just nodded and hoped he saw me even as he drove.

"I take that to mean you're acknowledging possible guilt."

It was a nod. How had a nod gone so wrong? "I'm not acknowledging anything of the sort." He didn't reply, and as I thought about how I might be able to confirm Asher's guilt, it also occurred to me that there was only one way

Kane would let me go in there alone. "That room better not have had any cameras while I was in it."

I did a quick and painful inventory of all the sorts of things he might've seen. I'd been pretty damn crazy for most of that time. How many days had I walked around with my eyes shut and bounced into walls? And then there was the finale, when I hadn't wanted to leave the shower because it was the only place the crawlers couldn't squeeze in with me. The groan was forming in my chest as I looked out the window, afraid to look at him. I would almost prefer to leap out of the moving car than hear him say yes, he'd seen it all.

"Do you think I would've let you sit in the shower for that long if I'd known what was happening?"

He was making a joke of it, and that was okay. He'd saved my ass, so he was allowed to bust my chops now. And I guessed enough time had passed that it was hard not to laugh a bit at the image I must've presented. "I was pretty far out there for a bit."

"Just a bit," he said, laughing with me.

The laughter faded as I watched him out of the corner of my eye. The palm of his left hand rested on the top of the steering wheel as he drove, his profile catching the light here and there and only making his deep-set eyes seem more intense. His other arm, resting between us, grazed mine.

Why was it that we seemed to be touching a lot lately? When had that happened?

By the time we made it into the elevator at the Underground, I'd counted two more incidents of accidental touching. He'd touched my shoulder when I walked past him into the Underground and he'd put his hand on my lower back when we walked into the elevator.

When had all this touching started?

We stepped off the elevator, and before I took more than two steps toward the door, Kane reminded me, "Five minutes."

Five minutes? He was really going to hold me to that? It was barely enough time to get the hellos out of the way and let the negotiations begin. "You may not have had the room wired when I was in it, but knowing you, you've got it wired now. You can give me twenty."

We stood facing off, a good ten feet from the guard. Enough space for the illusion of privacy.

His eyes seemed even deeper, more intent, in the light of the hallway. "Five. I don't trust him."

"It doesn't matter if you do or don't. You're really fast, and I need twenty." Why was he smiling like that?

"I'll give you ten, but it's going to cost you."

"Cost me what?"

He shrugged. "To be determined later. Take it or leave it."

"Fine. I'm not scared of you." Why was I smiling back? Was he flirting with me? Worse, was I flirting back?

"Agreed." He waved his hand toward my old apartment and his hand grazed the back of my arm, before he headed toward the other door. "I'll be in our apartment listening."

It didn't hit me that he'd called his apartment ours until I was entering my old apartment. That was weird. And he'd touched me again. I wasn't imagining it. I shook my head, ridding myself of all the touching and flirting.

Asher was sitting on the couch, staring at the door when I walked in. He didn't jump up and run to me as he had the last time, and I could see the accusations as clear as if he were screaming them at me.

I sat not far from him on the couch. The clock was ticking, but I waited Asher out.

He stared at the closed door. "Where is *he*?"

"He's coming around. That's why he isn't here. He's trying to trust you." That didn't seem to lighten his mood at all. "Asher, some bad things have been happening, and it's really important that you tell me if you know about them." Even as I asked, I was hoping he'd say no. Did I always like him? No. But I didn't want to see him dead.

"What?" he asked, his attitude going even further south.

"There's some things that have gone missing. We think that—"

"*We* or *him*?" He got up and started to pace in front of me.

"I misspoke. There's many people who are missing items. These are things that could help a crawler get out on its own and cause some problems." He was pacing so fast in front of me that I wasn't sure if he was hearing me anymore.

"He thinks it's my fault. He's probably trying to..." He stopped and looked at me accusingly. "Is he listening right now?"

He tilted his ear toward the ceiling as if he were trying to catch the sound of Kane nearby.

"It doesn't matter."

"So he is and you know it? You're helping him now, trying to blame me for things?"

"Asher, it's not like that. I'm trying to clear your name."

Asher's face morphed from anger to something that stabbed me in the gut.

"I'm trying to help you."

"How could you?" he asked softly, still remaining in one place and killing me with his eyes.

I heard the door opening and saw Kane standing there a

moment later. It had only been five minutes, but it didn't matter. It could've been five hours.

"I'll be back."

Asher didn't acknowledge my words as I walked past him and out the door, knowing this time Kane wouldn't kill him. Not right now, anyway.

I walked next door.

The door shut behind Kane. "He's playing you."

"He's not playing me. He's scared and upset and he doesn't know what's going on."

Our eyes met and I could see he was gearing up for another fight. I fell onto the couch, the guilt weighing me down even more than the exhaustion. "You don't know him like I do. He helped me over and over again. I owe him and he feels betrayed. He's not like the other crawlers." He was my friend up until now.

Kane strode across the room, leaning his shoulder against the wall near the window, looking out at the stars. "He's a crawler that thinks he's human. He's not. He can't be. He doesn't have the same range of emotion. You can't tell me that all that time you spent with him alone you didn't notice there was something off."

I rolled on my side so I had a better view of him. He was utterly still as he looked outside, and he looked as heavy as I felt. We both stayed like that for a while. I didn't know what ghosts were haunting him, but mine was sitting next door at the moment.

He was still staring out the window when he said, "When you left three months ago, I knew where you went within twenty-four hours."

I'd really tried to hide my steps. Was I seriously that bad?

"What does this have to do with Asher?" There was a connection there somewhere. Kane wasn't a rambler.

"I shouldn't have left you on your own." He shook his head slightly, and it felt as if I were hearing his inner monologue.

"You couldn't have stopped me." I thought back to that night when I left with Asher. No one could've stopped me. I'd decided it was what I had to do, and that had been that. I'd dug in.

He looked back at me, his expression making it clear he could've stopped me. He was probably right.

"Fine, let's argue about whether you could've stopped me at a future time." A time that would never, ever come, because it was really annoying when he was right.

"I should've dragged you back here. You weren't ready for this world." The weight of those words settled heavily between us.

I didn't move or say a word. Was too stunned as I caught a glimpse of genuine Kane. He blamed himself for how lousy I felt. He wasn't looking at me right now as he pushed off the wall and headed toward the door, and I had a feeling he felt as worn out as I did, he just hid it better.

As I saw him head toward the door, I fought the urge to call him back, but I couldn't stop myself completely.

"Where are you going?" I asked, realizing how that might've sounded. I hadn't meant it like that, had I?

Hand on the door, he said, "I have a couple of things I need to check on."

I didn't know if I believed him. He probably wanted space, and I'd taken over his apartment, driving him out.

"I could probably crash with Flip if you want your bed back." The idea tasted like ash on my tongue, but it was probably for the best. I could feel myself getting used to this place, to being around Kane all the time. Some distance might be what I needed.

He smiled and then started to laugh. "I didn't lose my bed. You sleep like the dead."

He was still laughing as he walked out the door.

Chapter 22

THE SUN WAS UP, AND HAD BEEN UP FOR A WHILE, WHEN I eventually woke the next morning. I glanced over at the other side of the bed. It didn't look slept on, but I rolled over and grabbed the pillow.

Oh yeah, he'd been here. No matter what he said, I had never slept like the dead, so how was he sleeping in here every night without me knowing?

And worse, why did I like it? Too many questions and not the right time to answer them. I had things I needed to get done today that had to be accomplished alone.

I hit the Underground twenty minutes later and scoped out the place. Office empty. Butch and Leon? Missing. Time to scramble.

I waited until I got into the stairwell, the one nobody seemed to use except for me, and called, "Zee."

Gargoyles were pretty quick. Like, near instantaneous. So when she didn't show up in five minutes, I started calling her name repeatedly, while going up and down a flight of stairs, thinking maybe I needed to find a better spot for reception. "Zee!"

"What?"

I turned to see my favorite gargoyle in a hot-pink skirt, white tank top knotted under her chest, with blonde hair piled high in a messy bun and her face covered in white cream. "I'm in the middle of a facial, so if you're trying to bug me about the job, the hairy were-girl had a hunt. She won't be back for another couple of days. Damn you're needy."

I grabbed on to her arm before she could disappear again. "Wait, it's something else."

Her head bounced around as she spoke to herself. "Well, yeah, of course it's something else. Never calls me to have a glass of wine and shoot the shit. Nope, I need, I want, I gotta have..." Her arms were waving in time with her words.

I was in shock for a moment but managed to keep my mouth shut until my brain formed an appropriate response. "You want to hang out with me?"

She lifted a single shoulder, giving me the side eye. "Why? You too good for me?"

"No, no. I thought you preferred hanging out with other gargoyles." Great, I was insulting one of my only allies, and the one I needed desperately today.

"You *assumed*." She pulled herself up, chin high, as she gave me a condemning look. I waited it out until her posture softened and she was looking at me straight on. "Well? What did you want now?"

My mouth dropped open but I couldn't get the words *I need* out. It was hard after she'd thrown them in my face mere seconds ago.

"You told me you wanted something. Spit it out."

I blurted it out, knowing I had to do this and she was my best shot of doing it with no one knowing. "I need to get somewhere in secret."

Cha-ching was blinking in her eyes. "What do I get in return? I don't work for free."

Why had I been feeling badly? "What's the price?"

The salesperson exterior slipped on. "Do I have to wait for you, or is this a drop-off only?"

"Drop-off only." I'd walk home if needed. Had to keep these bills down.

"I want a higher cut of the spell revenue."

"No."

She relented quickly, knowing she'd aimed too high. "Fine. A spell."

"What one?"

"I want better eyelashes." She leaned her face in really close to me and closed her eyes. "I got these extensions and they're hideous. I have to keep getting them filled, and now some of my real lashes have broken off." She pointed at her eyes and stayed like that, presumably so I'd have plenty of time to look them over.

I didn't even wear makeup these days. When you didn't know if you were going to end up in a basement being interrogated or singed from crawlers in the Shadow-lands, looking pretty dropped fairly low on your priority list.

Still, stupid request or not, I did need a ride. "Oh yeah, I can totally see what you mean. It'll be first on my list. You can't possibly walk around like that." I added all sorts of girly compassion to my voice.

"Right?" she said, straightening up. "I mean, I know it isn't BBGB, but it isn't good."

Was there no corner of the Underground that was safe from mockery? "You too, Zee?"

Her face froze, which probably wasn't saying much, since she was made of cement. "Sorry. Been using that term for months. It slipped." She patted me on the shoulder. "Maybe we should get going?"

I scanned the building around me, paying extra attention to the nearby alleys, before I put my key in the back door. The last thing I needed was Kane to know that I had any doubts about Asher. It was bad enough that I did.

But I wasn't crazy. Just because I didn't think Asher had anything to do with what was happening didn't mean I'd rule it out. I knew exactly what it looked like, and I couldn't afford to take any chances. And if I found something today, I'd deal with it. He'd have an explanation. I just hoped it was a good one.

First nightmare to deal with took me to the office. There was a pile of mail underneath the slot in the door. It wasn't like I had the money to pay the bills. I wasn't handing this stack over to Kane so he could pay them off, too. Perhaps I should pretend I didn't see them until next week? Yeah, brilliant idea, because that'd stop the collectors from taking everything I had.

I walked over, picked up the pile, and shoved them in my purse. I'd look at them after I tried to determine whether Asher was a lying monster. Spreading out my bad news made it easier to swallow.

I made my way up the back stairs. If there was any evidence here of his involvement, it would be in Asher's room. They'd grabbed Asher in a rush, but I would've been surprised if they hadn't searched the place. I didn't think I'd find anything here, but maybe there'd be a hint of something I'd pick up on that they might've missed.

I went for the obvious place first and lifted the mattress.

Nothing there. I pulled the bed away from the wall, then went through the drawers. I took the picture off the wall to examine the back of the frame, and even hopped on each plank of the wooden floor, looking for loosened boards.

I wasn't leaving until I tried everything, so it was time to see what kind of juice was left in that locating spell. The words flowed as I was filled with warmth and asked the spell to lead me to evidence of his guilt.

The words dwindled. I'd felt the potent magic, but nothing was here. Asher was either innocent or careful.

"We didn't find anything either."

I let out a little scream as I turned to find Kane in the doorway.

"Butch and Leon did a sweep of the apartment the same day they picked him up."

I was going to have to get a new cell phone again. I was tired of new phones.

"It's not your phone."

I narrowed my eyes and then realized I'd moved my hand to its outline in my pocket. "If it's not my phone, how do you know where I am all the time?"

"It's your phone line. I have people on the inside." He smiled, quite pleased with himself.

Of course he did. I flung a hand toward the room. "It would've been lax of me not to check. It doesn't mean I think he took anything."

"Of course not." He pushed off the side of the door and walked into the living room.

I followed him out, and that was when I realized he was...off. If I'd been right myself I would've seen the signs immediately, but I was too worried about finding incriminating evidence that could lead to a death sentence for Asher. Although even if I managed to keep Kane from killing him, there was no way I could hold back the rest of the gang.

And now I had Kane all pissed off, as if he had the right. He expected me to lay out every move I made, and I didn't even know if he turned into a bat and hung by his feet at night.

"If you're going to yell about me coming here or something else you think I did wrong, just get it out." I'd thought we were finally at a good place, but here it went again. *This* was why I needed to keep my distance. They either died or got mad and left. You couldn't rely on anyone.

"I don't yell," he said, his voice soft.

Actually, that was so true. I'd never heard him yell. He didn't need to. He could slay you with a couple of soft-spoken words. Worse than his words were when I saw him like this, with anger burning in his eyes right under the surface and waiting to erupt.

"You lied to me when you said you slept with him." It wasn't only an accusation. He said it like he'd already dropped the gavel on me, while I was still trying to figure out where this was coming from.

I waved both hands like a red flag in front of a bull as I stepped closer to him. This might've proved I wasn't quite right in the head, considering the look of Kane right now. "Wait, slept with who? Asher?"

"You're going to stand here and tell me you don't know what I'm talking about?"

"If you are going to accuse me, you can at least give me the details. I didn't lie to you about anything." I wasn't afraid. There was no room left after I accounted for all the burning rage. I spun, taking a few steps away from him, and headed toward the door, thinking I was going to leave. Then the anger drove me back toward him. I pointed an accusing finger at him. "And you can't speak about openness or what I should be telling you. If I slept with all of Boston, it wouldn't be any of your business. I can do as I please. I can sleep with everybody I see, too."

He grabbed my outstretched wrist and leaned in. "So you're admitting you slept with Asher? I can't believe you slept with that thing."

Really? That was what he took from what I'd said? Did he miss the part about it not being his business? Or that I was a free woman?

I gave my arm a yank, but his hand wasn't budging from me. I should've told him to let me go, but between the accusations and his manacle on my wrist, the rage was building. I felt like I was a cartoon character, steam about to blow out of my ears. "Asher isn't a thing." I hauled back a leg and aimed for his shin.

His leg shifted before I made contact. "You're right. He's a monster, and he's playing you."

Missing made me even angrier, and utterly committed to my target. I swung my leg back and aimed. Missed again.

The more I missed, the angrier I got, until I was kicking out at him in a flurry of attempts, knowing I looked more ridiculous with each miss. Instead of wanting to stop, I tried to kick harder and more rapidly. Kane had both hands on my shoulders now, holding me further away than I could kick.

I finally stopped kicking when I was out of breath. "He's not a monster. And not that it's any of your business at all, but I'm not a liar."

"Then why would he say that to me when I just questioned him again?"

"Because I've slept *next* to him. He doesn't realize there's a difference, you dumbass! He's not human, as you keep reminding me. I'd think you'd remember that." By the time I was done, I was nearly screaming. I took a breath to see if any of this had sunk in.

He tilted his head, and I could see amusement budding in his eyes, right before he started a low laugh. He threw his head back and laughed some more.

He was laughing at me while I wanted to rip his head off. I used the opportunity to finally get a good kick in.

"Ow," he said as he let go of my shoulders. "Was it really necessary to resort to violence?"

His face looked so smug that my foot was itching to connect again.

"Very necessary. *Extremely* necessary." I turned and walked from the room, pissed off while he seemed to be in a great mood now that he'd tortured me a bit.

He was still looking way too happy. And he was sucking up all the air in the room, too. Like he needed more space when his mood was good.

"Keep smiling and I'm kicking you again."

He kept smiling. I took a couple of steps away, needing more space than seemed possible to get in Asher's room. I was all the way to the window before my mind moved to how bad this might look.

"Just for the record, I didn't expect to find anything here."

"But you checked." He rested a shoulder on the door, looking dubious and blocking my only exit.

I crossed my arms, keeping my distance. "Of course there's doubt. There's always doubt. You never know anyone fully."

We stood staring at each other, and he took a few more moments before he asked, "Or trust anyone fully?"

I felt like this wasn't some abstract question about some

random someone. This was way deeper, and I was barely keeping my head above water as it was. I shrugged it off. "Same thing."

"I don't agree." He nodded toward the door. "Come on, I'll drive you back."

I grabbed my purse off the counter and followed him out.

I was locking the door when he said, "By the way, I don't sleep with *everybody*. I didn't sleep with Isabella."

My hand paused.

"It doesn't matter."

"Doesn't it?"

Why would it? We worked together. That was it. I wasn't putting myself out there again, not for anyone. It didn't work out. Love of any kind was for suckers, and I was tired of caring. It was better to do your own thing.

I pocketed my keys and turned to find Kane much closer. I banged my back into the door as I watched him leaning toward me.

"What are you doing?" I was barely whispering as he leaned a hand on either side of me.

"Something I've been thinking of doing for too long."

Slowly, his head dipped down closer to mine and I froze. At first, it was the lightest graze of his lips feathering over mine, and even that small touch sent a throb of need through me.

It was because I hadn't had sex in a while. That was all. I kept telling myself that as I stood there, frozen, not wanting to participate but feeling tortured by the idea of not partaking. His mouth dipped again, this time with a little more pressure as his tongue tipped into my mouth, cajoling me into a dance with his.

So what? It was just a kiss, right?

His hand shifted, moving to my jaw and angling my head. Then the kiss bloomed into something else entirely. His body moved in closer to mine, his thigh pressing right at the apex of my thighs, heightening the throb until I heard my moan. His other hand grabbed my ass, lifting me more firmly against him.

I was glad the door was at my back when he moved away, his eyes lingering on my lips and a way-too-smug look on his face.

"So what? You're a good kisser."

"Sure," he said, looking even smugger, if possible. "Come on, let's go home," He walked toward the car as if nothing strange had just occurred between us.

Okay, maybe it *did* matter that he hadn't slept with Isabella.

Chapter 23

I MIGHT'VE SLEPT BESIDE KANE UNKNOWINGLY, BUT I'D managed to avoid him for the rest of the day. Or had he been avoiding me? It was a little strange I hadn't bumped into him at all.

As I'd avoided the world much longer than I'd intended, I realized where I'd gone wrong. You didn't wait for things to happen to you. You made things happen. I'd been on the receiving end for a very long time, and I needed to stop, now.

By the time I walked into Kane's office at eight that night, I wasn't sure who had been avoiding who, and it didn't matter.

He was seated behind his desk, and as his eyes met mine, I wasn't sure if he was going to bring up the kiss or not. I certainly wasn't. I'd had all day to think about it, and it had probably meant nothing to him. It wasn't a big deal to me, either. Mostly.

He leaned back in his chair, his eyes meeting mine.

"I want to go shadow walk," I blurted out before a more uncomfortable subject might arise.

"When do you want to leave?"

"Now."

He hesitated for a moment, and even though his brow didn't furrow, he had that *thinking* look about him. Was this when he brought up the kiss?

"You know what I told them about the week—"

"Was a stall tactic? Yeah, I know. But there might be something else we can use."

He stood and grabbed a set of keys off his desk. That was it? No kissy conversations? Didn't he even care? What? Was he going around kissing everyone? I guessed it was no skin off his lips.

Didn't matter. I needed him and I was going shadow walking today. There was a crawler on the loose, one hairy were-girl waiting for a spa treatment, and a purse full of late notices.

The ride over was quiet, and by the time we got to the cemetery, it was clear neither of us were bringing up the kiss. It didn't take long before he was standing beside me, holding my hand.

I'd been here before, and I found that I still hated the place.

"What are you going to ask for?"

It didn't go unnoticed that he asked me what *I* was going to ask for instead of telling me what to get. "I've got no idea, but it's going to be something fantastic."

"When do you think you'll know what this fantastic spell is?" He gave my hand a small squeeze that felt a little too familiar for people who were just friends.

"I don't know." It seemed like I didn't know much these days. I didn't know if Asher was innocent, I didn't know what to do about the crawler on the loose, and now I didn't know what was going on with Kane. It was one too many not-knowings.

"I'm going to have a chat with them. Worst-case scenario, I get nothing, but if you don't reach for the sky, you'll never know if you can fly."

"You need to stop going to the card store."

He squeezed my hand again. What was up with him? First the kiss, then this?

He needed to stop acting like we were more than friends or clue me in on what he was up to.

"I'm going in," I said, before he said or did something else to thoroughly confound me.

I turned back toward the crawlers, concentrating on a big, ugly one about twenty feet away. Two minutes later, I was in the Shadowlands.

I surveyed the area, my hand still firm in Kane's, his grip feeling stronger than ever. I wasn't sure if it was the trust building back between us or the intimacy, but something was going on there. Whatever the cause, I was grateful.

There were crawlers peeking out from all over the place, plenty to choose from, so that was good. Plenty to block my exit—not so good. Now, to make a pick. My eyes lingered on a large one that walked upright on two feet. Even from this distance, I could feel the magic rolling off him.

Then I felt a tug in another direction. I turned behind me, realizing I should've been keeping an eye out in every direction. There was a furry little guy, not much bigger than a rabbit would be, and it was heading toward me at a full run. It was throwing off magic like I'd never felt, and it was growing stronger as it approached.

I took a step back toward the exit and then stopped. I was a Shadow Walker, the strongest one in decades. The weird bunny Shih Tzu was not going to run me out of the

Shadowlands. How could I possibly explain that one? I'd have to pretend it was the monster still twenty feet away that chased me out.

I've got no idea, but it's going to be something fantastic. Yep, that was what I'd said to Kane before I'd entered. Then furry bunny chased me out. No, that wasn't going to be my story as I fell out of the exit. But damn, I wish this furball would slow down and stop hopping toward me.

It didn't stop, not until it was a foot from me. Then it sat back on its hind legs and chirped. Chirping wasn't bad, especially when I saw its little fangs hanging down and that it wasn't trying to bite me.

Might as well ask it for my spell. What, though? If I asked for a spell to find the loose crawler, it didn't mean I'd be able to do anything with it once I did. I could shoot for a spell to send the crawler back? That had some potential issues too. If it came out once, maybe it would come back. It still had everything it needed.

It started chirping again. It pointed its nose toward me, like an animal that wanted to know my scent.

I squatted down and held out my hand. Who knew, maybe it would give me a better spell if it liked my berry-scented body wash. It sniffed me for a good minute or so and then pulled its head back up and curled its lips back.

I yanked my hand away, but it didn't move. It sat there, teeth on display. Other than two-inch fangs, nothing seemed hostile about the little crawler.

It chirped again and then resumed its teeth baring.

"I'm supposed to let you bite me?"

It went into an excited torrent of chirping, and I had a crazy feeling that it was arguing why that was good for me.

Why I knew that was beyond me, but it felt like more than just a hunch. Every time I hadn't followed my gut feelings in the past, it had worked out for the worst. When I left with Asher in secret, I'd done it because I wholeheartedly felt that I owed him. My gut had told me to stay at the Underground. Now look at the mess.

It was time for a leap of faith. Only issue with that was that I didn't run high on faith. I was more of a worst-case-scenario type. What if it thought it was helping and I ended up stuck in the Shadowlands forever? Just because I believed it, and it believed it, didn't mean this thing actually knew what it was doing.

Time to dig deep and hope this little sucker didn't bite too hard. How bad could it be? Its teeth weren't that big.

I lifted my hand closer to it and it moved slowly, making little chirping sounds as if to ask me if I were sure. I nodded, keeping my eyes averted.

It moved quick, its teeth sinking into the fleshy part of my hand in between my thumb and pointer finger. The thing bit deep. Its razor-sharp teeth felt as if they were hitting bone.

I thought that was the worst of it until the burning started. It felt like engine fuel was being poured into the wound. I pulled my hand back slightly without conscious thought, and then wondered if I should jerk it back completely. Did I really trust this little crawler? Was it poisoning me?

Before I'd decided, the burning began to ebb and a tingling was building in its place, which wasn't altogether bad. It felt like cool water trickling up my arm, and I could trace its path as it slowly made its way to my elbow, then my upper arm. Wait, was this heading toward my brain? My heart? I'd started to panic, wondering if I should rip it off me and risk it taking a chunk of flesh with it, when it pulled its teeth out.

But it didn't stop the tingling inside.

The crawler hopped in the direction I needed to exit, and I instantly knew why as I looked around. The other crawlers were swarming, probably drawn by the magic in the air.

I didn't waste time wondering if they were going to start fighting amongst themselves or come for me. I sprinted toward the exit.

I landed on my knees outside the Shadowlands, Kane still gripping my hand.

He looked me over. "You're not on fire this time, so what happened? You okay?"

"Yeah, I'm pretty sure I'm good," I said, still feeling the strange trickling moving up my neck.

My hand still in his, he pulled me to my feet. "What happened?"

I wavered where I stood and felt his other hand go to my waist. My eyesight grew dark patches. "I'm not sure yet, but maybe I should sit down for a minute."

I saw the car blurred in the distance but didn't make it two steps toward it.

I'd woken from injuries before. It was a slow ache that dragged me back to reality. The pain clung like a pack of leeches and pulled me to the surface.

This was nothing like that. I woke feeling spectacular, as if I'd been injected with the serum of life while I'd slept.

I sat up suddenly, realizing I was on the office couch. Kane was sitting on the edge of the couch beside me. Butch, Leon, Flip, Jerry, and Zee hovered nearby. All of them were staring.

"What happened?" My eyes shifted back to Kane.

"I carried you in. They followed." He scanned me, trying to diagnose a problem he couldn't see.

Everyone was waiting to hear what happened, but it was hard to say when I didn't know exactly. "I was in the Shadowlands, scoping out a good crawler to hit up for some heavy-duty magic, when this little furry guy...maybe girl, can't really tell the sex on those things—"

Kane laid a hand on my hip. "Furry whatever. Keep going."

What was with all the touching? I cleared my throat and continued instead of directing everyone's attention to the intimate act. "It hopped on over to me and paused. I can't say why, but I knew he meant well." Better to prime the pump now before I told everybody I just let the thing bite me on a hunch.

"And?"

"He wanted to bite my hand, and I let him. My hand burned, then tingled, and then I passed out." Okay, so maybe I didn't prime the pump. Kane's hand was resting on my hip in a very proprietary way. I was lucky I could speak right now.

The room went utterly still. Zee backed up a couple of steps while Butch leaned in. "Where's the bite?"

I lifted my left hand and realized the teeth marks were nearly gone, nothing to show for the bite now but two pinprick spots that were barely visible. "It was there. It felt like it broke the skin, but maybe not?"

Butch took a couple of steps back. Leon looked like he wanted to, but seemed resigned. I knew exactly where Kane was because of the heat of his hand on my hip that I couldn't stop focusing on.

"Why is everyone acting as if I've got rabies?"

Zee was the first to speak, but then it was only to make a grand exit. "This is over my pay grade." Zee popped out.

Flip used the opening to get closer and grab my hand, examining it this way and that.

"How do you feel?" Kane asked. I couldn't tell what he was thinking.

I stood and stretched my legs out as they all watched me lap the office. "Incredible?"

Butch and Jerry took a step back when I looped close to them. This time Leon joined them. Flip looked excited and Kane wasn't showing much of anything.

"Could it be?" Flip asked, but it wasn't clear who or what she was asking.

Butch scratched his head. "I never thought it was real."

"What?" Was someone going to tell me what they were talking about?

Kane walked over to where I was nearly bouncing in my spot. "It's called being shadow kissed."

"There was no kissing involved."

"Look down at your hand again." He took my left hand in his and lifted it. "If it's true, those two dots are going to form the top of what will eventually look like cupid's-bow lip line."

I didn't see anything but two tiny pinpricks.

Flip jumped up at my hand, amazed by what I thought wasn't even noticeable.

"Wow," Flip said, the O lasting almost a minute. "This is fucking cool shit. My friend is shadow kissed."

"Call us if you need us," Leon said, before he, Butch, and Jerry exited the office with haste.

I didn't realize Kane had given some sort of silent signal until Flip groaned and said, "I know. I'm going."

Why did he want the room emptied? If this shadow

kissed thing was good, why did we need privacy? I didn't jump all over him until I heard the door shut. "I'm not going to become a crawler or something else weird?"

"You ask after you let the thing bite you?" He sat on his desk.

I spent some more of my endless energy moving about the room. "Is that a yes or a no?"

"No. You won't. I wouldn't let you become a crawler."

I laughed, feeling almost happier than I should've. Kane thought he could stop the world from turning by the force of his sheer will, but even he had limitations, whether acknowledged or not.

"Other than great, do you feel anything else?"

I did a mental inventory, expecting to notice something God-awful upon closer inspection. Limbs, good. Interior, good. Heart beating and lungs inflating. "I feel good. Whatever this is, just tell me." I did two more laps around the room before I planted myself in front of him, tapping my foot and gnawing on my lower lip.

He took in the tapping and fidgeting, his eyes lingering on my lips before he said, "Everything I've heard about being shadow kissed is folklore. I've never known anyone who's been shadow kissed. I don't know anyone who's known someone who has been shadow kissed. But it might mean that the crawler passed some of its magic into you."

"Why would it do that?" I circled the area until I lapped back in front of him, waiting for answers.

He didn't say anything. Kane, my personal know-it-all, didn't seem to know. I thought I'd dislike his know-it-all-ness, but I was missing the hell out of it right now.

"How could this be?" He had to have answers.

"I don't know," he said, but he looked relaxed.

Was he really relaxed? Or was he relaxed because he was

Kane? Maybe he needed more info before he started shooting out answers. "I don't feel any different. And it was a really small crawler. How much magic could that little thing have?" I ignored the fact that I'd felt how much it had. Maybe it had been a trick? What did I know?

"Maybe Asher will know?" If he'd even talk to me at this point.

"No. Don't tell him. Not yet."

My suspicions were so thick at this point, I didn't argue with him. If Asher was hiding something...

"Whatever happens, we'll work through it." He reached out and took my hand, and I could see he meant it.

It might've been the sweetest gesture he'd ever made. I actually felt a little better until he said, "But maybe watch what you say for a few days until we know what's what."

Chapter 24

I walked into the Underground like I had the day before and the day before that. But unlike all those other days, the ones where I'd get a glance here, a quick dismissal there, and a handful of nasty stares, all eyes swung to me. The place was blaring Rob Zombie's *The Devil's Rejects* and yet I thought I could hear a pin drop. The reaction was a bit stunning, since this group hadn't just seen and done it all, they were the aged-wine version of jaded. And somehow, I was the one who'd shocked them?

It didn't take long to figure out that they knew something weird had happened. They'd seen me carried in yesterday and then the rumors must've started swirling. They'd take their look, see I was the same old Ollie, and go back to business as usual, as they always did. The events would unfold like normal, only in slow motion this time.

As I weaved in and out of the tables on the way to the booth, I found the path I normally took was widening. I glanced over and noticed the witches shifting their entire table further away from where I was headed.

Keeping my head up, I focused on where Butch, Leon, and Flip were sitting, while everyone else got their fill.

It took until I sat down and nodded hello to the table that it was clear the rest of the crowd was going to need more staring time. From the looks of it, they might need a few days. If they ever started talking today, it was surely going to be about me. It was the first time I realized how much the conversation added to the din in the room.

I eyed the suspects around the booth. Who'd told? And more importantly, what had they said? Had it been Flip? Nah. Besides this group, no one really spoke to her. Butch and Leon wouldn't say a thing unless they were utterly convinced Kane wanted the information out. It wasn't anyone here.

"Zee?" I said into the air.

She popped into the space faster than normal. She must've been hovering close by and watching the entertainment.

"Was it you?"

Zee put down a plate of eggs, having anticipated my order, as I realized who'd sunk the ship with a pair of bright red lips.

"Girl, you got it, flaunt it." With a shift of her hips, she was gone again.

"Well?" Flip asked, staring intently. She hadn't taken a bite since I'd sat down. Flip might've asked the question, but Butch and Leon didn't seem to be lacking in interest either, although they ate as they stared.

"I'm the same as I was yesterday, minus the shot of energy." I met each of their eyes so they could see for themselves.

Flip's face fell and she shoveled yogurt in her mouth.

"Really? Nothing?" Butch asked, hoping for a different

answer. "Yesterday it seemed a little freaky, but the idea was growing on me."

"There's still time. From what I've heard, it can take some time to kick in," Leon offered, his hand reaching out to pat Flip's.

I scooted some eggs around my plate. "What do you guys think I'm going to become? Aren't I strange enough for you now?"

"Well, you were before you dangled this tasty carrot," Flip said, and Leon and Butch nodded.

I hadn't gotten through a few more bites before I heard a particularly annoying blonde at the witches' table. "She's even a bigger freak now, from what I've heard."

Flip's fingers began drumming on the table.

There was some more muffled talking I couldn't make out, but Flip must've. Her fingers were near pounding now. Butch groaned and Leon shook his head.

"Flip, it's fine," I said.

"No, it's not."

"You guys were just saying how strange I was."

"We're allowed to make fun of you."

"Flip, really, it's all right."

She seemed to be under control for the moment, and I shoveled my eggs in my mouth as quickly as I could. The sooner I got out of here, the better.

I should've kept my head down, staring at my plate. But I didn't. If I hadn't looked over at the witches' table when I did, it still might've been okay.

But I did look.

That was when I saw Dana, a black-haired witch who had taken part in torturing me in the past, mouth, "Shadow scum."

I'd never considered myself a violent person, but I imagined marching over there and punching her in the face. I didn't, though, because I wasn't violent. I looked down at my eggs instead, trying to ignore her.

When I heard a chair crashing to the ground and a feminine howl, I looked up, and someone had already gotten to Dana. I turned to my side, and Flip was still there, the whole table looking at me. No, the whole room was looking at me, as if I'd done it.

"Now *that's* what I'm talking about," Butch said with a smile.

Flip nudged me in the arm. "Now that was some bad-ass shit you did. I thought you said you were the same?"

"What do you mean me? I didn't touch her."

"No, but you chanted some weird stuff right before it happened. She didn't get punched by the air."

I stood, my eggs only half finished. "I gotta get going." I didn't add "before I do something *really* bad and have no idea until afterward."

What the hell was wrong with me now? I had to talk to Asher. He was the only one who might have answers.

Flip's entertainment over, she slid out of the booth with a wave.

I was frozen. Did I ask Kane to get me in with Asher, or did I see what kind of juice I was carrying and go straight there? Kane would try and stop me. Maybe he was right, but he didn't have any answers, either.

I didn't make it away from the booth before a commotion at the door upstaged my freak show.

Chapter 25

Suddenly the only thing anyone in the room cared about was who was at the door.

I turned, curious who could draw the attention away from myself, to see Rudy at the door. Why would the head of the leprechauns be here? Was Kane excluding me from a meeting? No, Jerry wouldn't have stopped him from entering if he'd been expecting him.

The room's attention shifted upward as Kane stepped out of his office. He waved a hand toward the door, and Rudy stepped around Jerry with the disdainful look of one who thought he was above the masses.

As soon as Rudy hit the stairs, I realized I had a meeting to worry about first.

"Where you going?" Butch asked as I took a step toward the stairs.

I'd thought it was pretty obvious, but I turned back to the booth. "*I'm* going to the meeting that's about to happen." Then I made a point of looking at the plates of food in front of them. I didn't *say* the word slackers out loud.

"But...you weren't invited," Butch said softly.

"So?"

I headed off to the stairs but not before I heard Butch say, "If she's going, I'm going."

"Well, I'm not going to be the only one sitting down here like a chump," Leon added, scrambling in behind Butch.

We were all lined up in a row as I hit the stairs.

Rudy looked back at the three of us climbing the stairs behind him. He gave us the same down-the-nose glance he'd given Jerry before he walked in to Kane's office. He made a point of shutting the door. And I'd thought Kane was arrogant.

It didn't slow any of us down. I didn't knock when I reached Kane's office. Didn't want to give him the opportunity to decline entry. I marched in as if I had every right to be there. Butch and Leon, not wanting to seem less than, did the same.

Kane was in a reclined position with his feet up. Rudy was standing in front of his desk, hands on hips, turned to glare at the three of us.

I walked in a few feet more and crossed my arms, not saying anything. Butch and Leon looked around for a moment and then followed suit, stopping beside me as if we'd coordinated beforehand.

Rudy sneered at us and then looked back at Kane. "Is this really necessary?"

Butch, Leon, and I all puffed up together in solidarity. If it wouldn't have ruined the image, I would've turned around and fist-pumped them.

Kane glanced over at us. "I didn't think so, but I guess they do." He turned his full attention back to Rudy. "What are you here for?"

Rudy unlocked his jaw so he could get out the words. "Donald is dead."

Donald who? And why did Rudy think Kane would care? Come to think of it, I hadn't seen Kane last night. I wanted to roll my eyes and groan, but I had an image to keep up.

"And?" Kane drummed a pen on his desk.

Damn, he *had* killed another one. How many leprechauns was he going to kill? I thought we were trying to play nice, or civil, with them?

"*And* you killed him." Rudy turned his attention to me.

What the hell was this about? Why was he looking at me like it was my fault? Did he think I was following him around and digging the ditches or something?

No. There probably hadn't been a ditch. Kane didn't clean up after himself that well.

"Don't look at her. This is between us." It was his *you better listen to me or else* voice. I found it to be optional, but Rudy seemed to think otherwise as he looked back at Kane.

"The only reason you wanted him was because he questioned her."

My chest deflated as some of the air puffing it out escaped through surprised lips. Kane had killed him for me?

"He did more than question her. You said you were going to handle it. You didn't. You should be thanking me for saving you the trouble." He took his time standing. "Unless you weren't going to handle it?"

Rudy wobbled back a little. "I had every intention of handling it. There were things that had to be ironed out first."

"That's good, because I was starting to think you were lying." Kane walked around his desk and stopped a foot shy of Rudy. "And I still haven't gotten the list."

Rudy's nostrils flared as he nodded. He turned and walked around me as if I were a carrier of the plague.

Kane and I were standing eight feet apart, facing each other, and the room was suddenly heavy. Had he really killed that leprechaun because he'd hurt me?

No. That wasn't who Kane was. If he'd killed him, it was to protect an asset, or, at most, a friend. Or send a message like he had in the basement.

As he stood there facing me, it was like he was waiting for me to say something, as if he wanted something acknowledged between us. He stared at me as if I were in on a secret, but I didn't know anything.

The feeling was so intense, I moved across the room toward the window that overlooked the Underground, trying to break the connection. "You could've probably just given the guy a beating." I added a laugh at the end that sounded more brittle than joyful.

He didn't reply, just leaned on the desk and continued to watch me. "I was still in one piece, but I know how you like to protect your turf."

There. I acknowledged he'd done me a solid.

He watched me for another few seconds that stretched out almost unnaturally before he straightened, giving me his back as he seemed more interested in something on his desk.

Was that a dismissal? Was he mad at me for stating the obvious? I'd acknowledged what he did. What was his problem? And *why* did I feel this twisting feeling in my gut as if I'd disappointed him? It was ridiculous. I had bigger problems than imagined slights from Kane that made no sense.

Butch and Leon were making their way over toward the Keurig machine, but my attention was solely on Kane's back.

"I'm not sure if you saw what went down at breakfast—"

"I did."

"Then you know I need to talk to Asher. Tell whoever is

on guard that they have to stand down. It can't wait." I said it in a crisp tone. Screw him. One second we were friendly and now we were barely speaking again? I wanted off the roller-coaster ride.

I didn't care if it was going to be a fight in front of Butch and Leon, either. Kane was the one acting like a jerk. We could fling open the door, kill the music, and let the whole Underground hear if they wanted.

Kane turned back to me and sat on the edge of his desk, not an ounce of tension to be found in his frame. "Why would I do that when you can't?" He stared at me as if he were waiting for a logical rebuttal to his utter high-handed-ness. Everything about his posture said he was relaxed, but his eyes made me want to go on the defensive.

I could feel my temper building as if I were standing in a vat of boiling water. Maybe after what happened down-stairs, I should err on the side of caution. I looked over his left shoulder, thinking that a direct stare in my current mood could go bad. "You don't get to tell me who I talk to."

"Really? Because I think that's exactly what I'm doing." I didn't need to see his expression. His tone was poking at me enough.

"Did you take the last French vanilla again?" Butch asked Leon.

"Shut up. I'm trying to listen," Leon whispered back.

Stay calm. Don't let him goad me into a fight because he was in a sour mood. "I don't know what your problem is, but you're being illogical."

"I don't have to be logical." Kane wasn't paying attention to Butch or Leon either as he stalked across the room.

I turned and pretended to prefer the view of the Under-ground, so as to not look at him and possibly spell him. Having an argument wasn't a great reason to magically punch him in the face. Not yet, anyway. "What the hell are you so mad about? Is it the leprechaun? *I* didn't tell you to kill him."

"You didn't have to. That's what you're missing."

He was right. I was missing something.

"Why aren't you looking at me?" he said before I could respond.

"I'm looking at you," I said, glancing at him and then quickly away.

"No, not for a split second. I mean looking at me."

"I am," I said, lifting my head and trying to un-focus my eyes so I didn't really see him.

Leon chuckled where he stood in the corner. "She's afraid she's going to get you with a spell."

Kane smiled. "Feel free to try."

I unclenched my fists, staring right at him. It didn't help that he looked at the idea of me possibly hurting him with amusement.

"I'm talking to him."

"Be satisfied he's alive. It goes against my better judgment to let him keep breathing."

I ignored the threat, knowing he wouldn't kill Asher right now. I made a concerted effort to hold my ground.

His anger was near boiling up the room.

We stood there, facing off. I wasn't sure what Kane was thinking, but I was considering how a punch or two might be a good idea. Knock his ego down a couple pegs.

I heard Butch whisper to Leon, "Their fights are so annoying. They never even fight about what they're really fighting about, you know? It's no wonder they have to keep going. I mean, really, when I'm mad that you took the last K-cup, I say I'm mad about the K-cup, not that you left the door open or some stupid shit."

I saw Leon nod. "They're not as emotionally evolved as us, is all. You can't help everyone. They're going to have to learn at their own pace, as painfully slow and horrible as that might be for the rest of us."

Kane switched his attention to them for a moment. "What the fuck are you two yapping about? We're not fighting."

Butch and Leon nodded agreement with Kane, until he turned around, and then they shook their heads.

"So that's it? You've dictated and it's done?" How had I punched that witch?

"Yes, until you stop being so naive. He's using your weakness against you, and you keep allowing him to do it." He took a couple of steps away from me and gave me his back again, as if he were too frustrated to have this conversation.

"What weakness?" Had he missed breakfast altogether? Hello, shadow-kissed person here? I was on the upswing.

He turned only partially back to me. "He twists you up with guilt and obligation. You were scared and alone, and now you can't stand to see anyone else like that because it tugs at your own fears. You're going to have to get over it."

I swallowed so loud as I took in the verbal blow that I thought the whole room had heard me. I couldn't think of words to respond with right away. It was as if he'd tripped the breaker in my brain and I was trying to reboot the system. "You're a bastard." That was the best I had.

He walked out of his office while I stood there. I didn't leave the office. I stayed right there.

I thought Leon and Butch were talking to each other, but I wasn't hearing them anymore. I walked over to the couch and dropped down onto it.

Leon walked out, but Butch came and fell into the couch beside me.

We sat a cushion apart for a few minutes, him on one end and me at the other. All the while, I was waiting for him to say whatever it was he needed to say. It was easy enough to know something was coming. Butch wasn't the type to sit in silence beside you unless he was preoccupied with eating.

"Why did you do it? Take off like you did without a word? You could've talked to one of us. Could've talked to Kane. He would've heard you out."

I'd been wondering when this moment would come. Walking out of the Underground hadn't just been about leaving the building, or Kane—I'd walked out on all of them. I wasn't certain that Butch was right about being able to reason with Kane over Asher, but I owed him an explanation.

"Asher helped me so many times in the Shadowlands; he'd kept the crawlers at bay. When he appeared, I owed him the best shot I could of surviving here. I'm not saying it's right or wrong, but there's no denying Kane isn't concerned about Asher living."

Butch nodded, as if he'd known my answer but wanted to hear it from me. If anybody would understand loyalty, it was Butch. Didn't matter what Kane said. I knew why I'd done what I'd done.

When Butch didn't get up and leave, I found myself babbling to him before I knew what I was going to say. It was as if once I'd opened up this part of me, it all wanted to spill out to someone.

"I had to. I didn't think I had a choice. What else could I have done?"

Butch didn't say anything, only nodded as I talked.

"You're standing there and someone who's helped you is in need, you do what you can."

Butch nodded again.

"And it's not like Kane cared so much he came after me. It was nothing to him. I'd..."

What was I doing? There was having a heart-to-heart and then there was spilling your guts until you were lying eviscerated on the ground. What I'd just been about to say was something I didn't even like to admit to myself.

"What?" he asked.

This wasn't something I wanted to admit aloud, but now it was burning in me and I wasn't sure I could hold it back. It was the reason why I hadn't been that sad when I first left, been so-so for the few weeks afterward, and then gotten progressively more morose as the time ticked on. It was ridiculous and embarrassing, and sitting there right now, I felt the emotions and disappointment enveloping me even now that I was back.

Butch leaned forward until he could meet my eyes, waiting for me to continue.

I was teetering on the edge of an emotional abyss, and it swept me right into a tidal wave of words that I couldn't stem the flow of. "I thought he'd come after me. I left because I felt I had to, but I always thought I'd be back. I *wanted* to be back. I thought he'd follow me, but he just let me go as if I weren't worth the fight." I turned from where I was staring at the ground and stared at Butch instead, not knowing what I'd find but hoping that one of the closest men to Kane would be able to give me an answer. "Why does he act like he cares when he doesn't?"

I ran a hand over my eye, not giving the moisture burning there a chance of escape. If Butch noticed my deteriorating condition, he didn't mention it.

Butch scooted over and patted me on the shoulder. "He was letting you live the life he thought you wanted."

Kane hadn't been letting me live my life. He'd been

letting me go. I looked back down at the floor, finally managing to keep my innards where they belonged, inside my body.

I leaned forward, resting my arms on my legs. My hair curtained my face while I pulled myself together. I couldn't go walking through the Underground a blubbering mess.

"You probably don't know this, but he knew exactly where you were twenty-four hours after you left." He cleared his throat before adding, "And what a dump you stayed in that first night."

I glanced at Butch. "I thought it was the less obvious choice in hotels." I wasn't going to tell him how I'd woken up with bed bug bites the next morning and that was why it had only been one night.

"You do realize how many people we trail, right? It didn't matter where you stayed. If Kane wants to find you, he does. And he did want to find you."

Butch thought he was helping, but the more he talked, the worse he made it. Kane had known exactly where I was and hadn't approached me in all that time? Of course, I wasn't going to say that to Butch. I knew it was ridiculous, and I was done spilling my guts out all over the place.

I snorted.

"Look, this is between you and him, but if I could give you one piece of advice, next time you two start getting into it, why don't you actually talk to him about the issue, and not all that other crap you guys throw at each other?"

He gave me a final pat on the shoulder and left me sitting there, while I stewed in his words.

Chapter 26

THE ELEVATOR DOORS SLID OPEN IN FRONT OF ME BEFORE I decided whether to go upstairs to Kane's apartment. He wasn't normally there during the day, so it might be the best place to avoid him. Unless he was there, and then I was screwed.

Zee popped up next to me and tugged me toward a back exit in the hallway that I hadn't known even worked. I'd thought it was welded shut. Could happen. It wasn't like this place got inspected by the fire department.

Her old heap was sitting outside the door.

"You ready to work? I got a hairy were-girl waiting with bated breath and a suitcase full of cash." She headed toward the car as if my answer was a foregone conclusion.

"I don't have the spell."

She froze with the car door half opened. "What?"

I walked over to her side, seeing no reason to get into the car. "I don't have the spell."

"Do you think I was born last century? I know what shadow kissed means. Now get in. Mama needs some gladiator sandals, particularly these black, almost knee-high ones I just saw—"

"Zee, you're not listening. I don't know if I can do this."

She walked around the car door that was between us and pointed at her feet. "Do you see these?"

I looked down. They were wedges with hot-pink straps. Not my taste, but not bad. Plus, I was wearing sneakers and jeans, not a place to judge from.

"Yes."

"I've already worn these out *several* times."

"Um, okay?"

She wagged her finger. "No, not *okay*." She reached into her car and pulled out her purse. "Do you see this?"

Could I say no when it was right in front of me? "Yes?"

"This is so two seasons ago. I bought it used."

"Okay?"

She rolled her eyes. "It looks like I'm going to have to give you the letters."

"Letters?" What letters? Was someone writing and complaining about her clothes?

"*Letters*. In other words, I'm going to spell this out for you." She tossed her past-season purse on the car seat and used both of her hands to wave down the length of her body. "You don't serve up caviar on a hamburger bun. I can't keep going around like this. I have an image, and I'm running through cash like a whore runs through crack. Now this has to happen. If you can't come up with something when we get there then say it might take a couple of tries, but we gotta go!"

I wanted to argue, but as I watched her make stabbing gestures toward her shoes, I realized it was futile. I shoved the hair out of my face and nodded. "Okay. I'll try."

She grabbed her phone from the back pocket of a

miniskirt that was so short I saw every cement inch of her legs, and almost more than I ever wanted to get an eyeful of. "It's on. Meet at the designated place in fifteen." She threw the phone in her purse and got behind the wheel.

I got in the passenger seat, a lamb to the slaughter, or maybe I'd be the slaughterer? Problem was, I had no idea what was brewing inside me, but I was going to find out.

She turned the car on and blasted "Let's Hear It for the Boy," with not nearly enough bass, as we moved down the street. Before we hit the corner, she was screaming the words louder than the speakers.

Zee was singing "Justify My Love" by Madonna and making sultry faces by the time we pulled alongside an abandoned building. I was desperate to get away from the horror show that was Zee's car service. As I watched the rats scurrying through heaps of garbage to safer ground at our approach, I thought about leaping out and asking them to lead me to safety with them.

But, unfortunately, Zee was not the only one in need of cash, so I forced myself to open the car door.

"We're meeting her..." I was trying to get the word "here" out, but it didn't want to be said.

She waited for me by the door of the building. "Yes."

Well, that made one of us comfortable with conducting business in the middle of garbage and rats. What had I been thinking when I thought this was a good idea?

Another car pulled up before I joined Zee, and a single female got out. She was on the slender side and pretty, with dark brown hair and owlish eyes. She smiled as she approached and pulled her hand out of her pocket to shake mine.

"I'm Nance."

"Ollie," I said.

"I know. Everyone knows who you are." Her cheeks went pink. "I mean, you know because you're still alive, and..."

"It's okay." I waved a hand, hoping she'd stop.

That was when I caught sight of the hair on her hand. She must've noticed me looking, and quickly pocketed her hand again.

I gestured her forward and patted her on the back as we made our way to join Zee together. "Don't worry. We're going to fix you up."

She looked like she was about to cry with happiness.

"Zee, lead the way."

Kane was standing in the living room of our—*his* apartment by the time I went upstairs later that night. I hadn't seen him all day. He turned toward me and must've noticed the war face I had on as I walked in.

"You can put away your bullets."

I didn't need much prompting. After being able to help the were-girl, the day had turned a bit brighter. It had taken a few tries, but I'd found something rattling around in my brain that fixed her. I wasn't sure what else was in there, and I couldn't say I wasn't worried. Not only was I tired after working with all that magic, I didn't want to fight, especially not with Kane.

But I would if I had to. I still needed to talk to Asher.

"You've always been arrogant, but this is a whole new level." That had not come out right, if I gathered anything from the look I got. This wasn't the talking Butch had meant. "Let me rephrase. You seem to be overly..." I hesitated. *Controlling* definitely wasn't the right thing to say, even if it were true. "Protective?" I gave that one a moment to see how it would settle. He appeared to still be listening, so I continued. "I don't understand why you are being so protective when I think certain actions are in both of our best interests." Whew, that had been a whole lotta words with no insult. I was getting better at this.

He walked over to the couch and sat on the arm, still appearing calm. "When you left, you moved in with a monster who might've killed you and taken the whole block along when he did. If that hadn't been bad enough, then I found you in a basement where you'd been tortured."

I nodded, mostly because I had to. He had a halfway decent argument. Would it make it all the way to the Supreme Court? Maybe not, but it deserved acknowledgment. Butch might've been onto something with this talking stuff.

"I see your point." There, I threw him a bone before I hit him with *my way's better*. "But I still feel like I've got to keep trying to mine the only source of information available."

He didn't wait long before he calmly said, "Fine."

I didn't move from my spot. He agreed with me without a fight?

"Did you want to talk to him now?" he asked.

Was he screwing with me? "Now's good." I bit my lip as I paused. Did I push it? Yeah, I kind of had to. "I have to talk to him alone. He'll never talk to you."

Kane remained relaxed. "I know."

I nodded and took a step toward the door, then another, waiting for him to yell out "psych" the entire way. He didn't.

It wasn't until Asher's guard stepped aside, as if he'd already been informed, that I completely believed Kane. How long ago had he decided I was right?

Asher sprang off the couch as I walked in. "Ollie, I'm so glad you're here."

There was no trace of the ugliness of our last visit, and his face lit with the biggest smile I'd seen on him yet. The bigger the smile, the worse I felt. Was Kane right? Was Asher playing me, or was he as lost in this world as I'd often felt? He was stuck here, basically in prison, and I'd done nothing to help. As I walked toward him, the feelings of guilt clung.

"I'm sorry. Things have been getting crazy. Asher, I want to get you out of here, but I need your help."

He froze as I got closer, and his eyes searched me. They dropped to my left hand and stayed there. The skin on my hand hadn't changed from a couple of pinprick marks. "You know something happened."

His attention reverted to my face. "Yes."

It appeared I was going to have to drag the information out of him, even when he did know. "What does it mean? How much magic did it give me?"

"It was a gift. What you have depends on the giver. They could've given you a single spell or a treasure trove of power." He shrugged.

He was too blasé by far. Maybe he didn't understand the stakes? It wouldn't be the first time.

"Asher, you need to help me so that I can help you. I need information so I can show Kane he can trust you."

I paused for a moment and thought about my new me plan. "You don't know how you got out; you don't know anything about the missing items..." I threw my hands up. "I need something. You've got to give me something."

"I don't have anything," he whined.

I ran my hands through my hair. There had to be something. "Do you know which crawler might've gotten out?"

This time he didn't answer right away. I took a deep breath before I spoke. It was like the dollar and debt argument all over again. "Asher, I can't get you out of here without a show of good faith."

"There's only one I know of that mentioned leaving the Shadowlands." He took a few steps around the living room.

"This is good." I tried not to pressure him as he got his thoughts together. It took a few minutes before he held his hand up with a finger pointed skyward.

"Do you remember the beast that came to you when you were hurt? The large one with the horns? It was the one I sent to tell you to meet me."

"Yes." The creature had been freakish in its size and also in the power it had thrown off. Really? It had to be that one? He'd looked like a professional wrestler gone bad.

He nodded. "It might be him. His name is Crem."

The idea of going slow went out the window. "Do you know anything else? Like what he wants to do here? Why he wanted out?"

"No. Ollie, I would help you if I could. You know that, don't you?" His eyes were wide and watery, his two hands gripping one of mine. "I don't have anything else. Please believe me."

I nodded. "I'll do what I can."

He dropped my hand and hugged me, while I looked for surveillance cameras. How long would it take Kane to decide Asher was trying to hug me to death? Asher dropped his arms before I had to pull away.

"Stay out of trouble and I'll do what I can." I felt like a fraud saying that. If I was really trying to do what I could, I'd be rifling around in my head, trying to break him out. But I didn't. I couldn't, not until I knew if Kane was right.

A pit formed in my chest during the walk back to Kane's apartment.

Kane was waiting for me as I walked in. I didn't have to

ask. I only needed to look at him to get a confirmation of how much good he thought that had done.

I crossed my arms as I stopped a few feet inside the apartment. "He gave us something. He's trying."

"He gave us nothing but a name." Kane wasn't one to dodge the truth, either hearing it or saying it. The delivery wasn't particularly soft, either.

"Maybe I can use that, combined with a spell, to locate him?"

"Or, more likely, you can't use it for anything, and that's why he gave it to you."

He should've just tacked on *and you're the idiot who keeps falling for it*, for all his subtlety.

I was the one who walked out this time. And that was how the truce of one hour came to an end.

Chapter 27

After spending all morning trying to pinpoint Crem's position with the locating spell, I had to accept the truth. Kane was right. The name was worthless. Had Asher known that? I didn't know. He certainly wasn't helping, though.

I walked back into the Underground, debating whether I would tell Kane I'd confirmed his suspicion or to not say anything at all. Saying nothing at all was lapping the idea of telling him. Mr. Know-it-all didn't need another notch in his belt.

It only took a step or two inside to realize something was wrong. The tension was bubbling over in the Underground, and it wasn't me they were bent over whispering about this time. I was sure of this because as I made my way to Kane's office, no one even paid me any mind. That was a near miracle these days.

Kane was alone with his phone to his ear when I opened the door to his office. I took the chair in front of his desk, as opposed to the couch. I hooked a heel on the edge while I waited for him, quite positive that whatever that call was, it was tied into the reason the Underground was in a tither.

"Keep me posted," he said, and dropped the phone to the desk.

I pointed to the discarded phone. "What's going on?"

He reclined in his chair, but there was tension in his shoulders. "There was another explosion at an ER."

I sucked air in through my teeth. Another End of the Rainbow gone, along with all the magic it held. More magic for the crawler to suck up. "Was anyone hurt?"

"No. But a leprechaun was walking toward the place, only a couple of houses away, when it blew. He caught sight of what he described as a large, dark creature with a pair of horns. Said it wasn't like anything he'd ever seen before." He leaned to the side, resting his chin on his fist as he waited for me to absorb it all.

As far as I knew, other than Shadow Walkers and Kane, no one could see a crawler. Or wasn't able to until now. "He saw it?" This definitely merited confirmation.

"Yes." The word was said with the gravity it was due.

"This mean he's becoming more of this world."

Kane and I stared at each other across the desk, and I knew, even as he sat there looking much more relaxed than I, we were on the same page.

This was too much to sit through. I got to my feet to pace the office. I really disliked that I'd become a pacer. When had it happened? I couldn't remember ever pacing until my life had been upended. Then I'd evolved into one. Or devolved? Either way, I didn't want to be one, so I forced my legs to be still. It lasted two whole minutes before I walked the length of the room again. I'd worry about personal backslides at a more convenient time, if that actually existed.

There had to be some way to stop this before this creature became too strong and started blowing things up just for the fun of it. "We need a list from the leprechauns of all the ERs. We've got to start watching those places."

When I didn't hear an answer, I looked over at Kane. He was clicking and swishing away on the computer, but his arched eyebrow said he'd heard everything.

"If you disagree, say you disagree." Nothing worse than having to guess at someone's opinions as they stared at something on the computer.

There was no hesitation. "It could be a colossal waste of time." Click, click, click, swish.

Well, at least he was decisive.

"It's all we've got." I started working on my mental arguments.

"I know—that's why I've been asking for one. I sent Butch and Leon over there to encourage their cooperation. Now we wait and see how desperate the leprechauns are to save their magic and their lives."

"You sent them over to beat them up?" I slowed my pace. That wasn't a bad idea.

"I sent them to talk it over. You have *very* violent inclinations."

"*I* do?"

He shrugged, seeming amused with himself.

I took another few steps and realized I was pacing to the beat of his click, swish, click. For some reason, it was the thing that made me want to snap.

"What are you doing?" How was I wound so tight while he was playing internet games?

"Playing blackjack." Click, click.

I angled my head and caught a glance at the screen. He had five hands going. "Do you have a gambling problem you haven't mentioned?"

"It's only a problem when you lose." Click, swish, click.

"And I wouldn't comment on other people's monetary management if I were you."

I would've gone back at him, but that was pretty much a slam dunk. Even if he'd contributed to running up the price on my building, I couldn't explain away the rest of it. Another problem for a more convenient day. I was going to need some serious downtime if these evolving and devolving issues kept creeping up.

Click, click, ding. "You're making me dizzy. You might also want to conserve your energy, because if we do get a list, there's going to be some long days."

I didn't stop. "You aren't even looking at me. You're playing your game."

"I'm looking at you and the game."

I looked over my shoulder to see him smiling. "Then *don't* look at me."

"But I *like* looking at you."

My left foot tripped over my right, but I caught myself before I face-planted. I had too many issues to add a flirting Kane to the mix, especially since the kiss was burned into my brain. It was hard enough to keep my equilibrium. Either way, I paced toward the window so he couldn't see the smile that wanted to creep up onto my face. Damn gigolo. He'd probably used that line before, and I'd do well to remember it. *Of course* he'd used that line before. It was a gem.

"Well, look at your cards instead. I don't want to have to call Gamblers Anonymous for you if you start losing."

I leaned a shoulder on the tall filing case by the window that overlooked the Underground. I jutted out a hip and watched the people moving around. This was not a pose for Kane. It was merely the most comfortable position. I tossed my hair over my shoulder because it was in my face, not because it looked fuller that way.

I dug the phone out of the back pocket of my jeans, looking for a distraction.

"Nice phone," Kane said.

It wasn't that nice. It was a year-old model I'd bought refurbished. I hit the screen as if I were checking something, while strategically trying to shield the serial numbers on the back. I'd need a magnifying glass to read them, but considering the surprises Kane had doled out, who knew what he could see. He might have 2000/2000 vision for all I knew.

His laugh was only interrupted by his clicking and swishing.

"What?" I asked, as if I hadn't been obvious.

"I told you, I'm not tracking you through your phone."

"I was looking at the news," I said, playing stupid. He'd said he had a source within the cell company. But maybe he was trying to get me to not swap out my phone and make it easier for him. I'd switched carriers anyway. Let's see how many connections he had.

When the clicking halted, I looked over at him.

"I'm going to come clean just so you don't go to a new phone company again. It's not your phone at all."

"Then how are you tracking me?" Memories of *The Matrix* sprang to mind, and my hand crept over my stomach as I envisioned a creepy worm thing crawling around inside of me. "Whatever you put in me, I want it out."

He let out a low sigh, as if I were proving the reason he should've withheld. "There's nothing in you. It's a spell. Too many people want you right now, so I thought it was safer this way."

"You spelled me?" Okay, this was doable. If he spelled me, I could get something to un-spell me in the Shadowlands. Or maybe I already knew something to un-spell myself? No biggie. I was that cool now.

"You can't undo it. Only I can."

That was what he thought. But to be safe, I should probably try it outside of the building.

"I don't bluff. If I tell you it won't work, it won't."

"Sure." Of course that was what he'd say to stop me from undoing his spell. Very tricky of him.

"If you're going to try to undo it anyway, do it outside the building. And you should work on your poker face. It's going to be a liability one day."

One day? More like every day since I met him.

"Why doesn't the magic I get from the Shadowlands work on you?" And, according to what he was saying, didn't work on his spells. Although I'd test that out myself.

He smiled. I guessed that was the only answer I was going to get.

I crossed my arms as I narrowed my eyes in his direction. "Are you ever going to tell me what the hell you are?"

"As soon as you stop wanting to know." He stopped clicking to smile in my direction.

"What's the point of that?" I had to force myself not to smile in return. It didn't make any sense why it was so hard to do, either.

"That's the point." He nodded to himself as he resumed his game.

"You make no sense."

"I'll make sense once you understand." He was smiling again, but this time to himself.

"Okay, let's stop talking, then, because the riddles are killing me." I turned back to the window, my hair swinging flatteringly through no fault of my own.

"Butch and Leon are back." I straightened. "I don't see anything in their hands."

I heard a slow breath leave Kane's lips, but when I turned, he was still reclining and clicking and swishing away as if all were still good.

The door swung open. "Well? What happened?" I asked, while Kane sat there with more patience than I'd ever have.

Butch reached behind him and raised a hand with a rolled piece of paper. "We've got a list."

Chapter 28

WE WERE SITTING IN A BEAT-UP SEDAN THAT MUST'VE BEEN twenty years old, but blended into the neighborhood perfectly. The age of the car wasn't the problem. It was the interior. It was so small that I could feel Kane's heat or how his arm brushed mine every time he shifted. There wasn't any air left. I couldn't escape the woodsy scent of him or keep my mind from wandering as I stared. It was ridiculous to be this aware of such simple contact. Ridiculous and agonizing how I'd spent the first two hours of my afternoon while we stared at an ER that was on the list.

This was the first time I'd seen one before it was blown up. Now I knew how they flew under the radar. The place was a dump. It was a single-story house, though with the large picture windows on either side of the door, it had sort of a commercial feel. If there weren't blinds on both windows, maybe I could get a better idea. Although the blinds were broken in spots, there wasn't a big enough gap for me to tell from this far back, especially since it was dark inside and the sun was right overhead.

This was a source of power? "Are you sure they gave us

an accurate list of locations? This place doesn't appear to be used, or inhabited, or really much of anything."

"It doesn't have to be used," Kane said. "They're left empty usually. Less attention drawn that way."

He shifted, his arm brushing me again like he knew it agitated me. Although for someone who'd been getting flirty, he didn't seem to have any interest in kissing me again.

I caught him looking over at me when he should've been looking at the house. "What?"

"Is that a dwarf shirt?" His voice was a touch lower than his normal baritone.

"This? Yeah, I think so." One of my nicest. It was a white shirt with a slightly dipping neckline that happened to look fabulous in a way that didn't make me appear to be trying. Which I hadn't, of course. Why would I try to look good to go sit in a car all day? I wore it because it was comfortable. Only reason.

"What do you think our odds are of seeing him before the place blows?"

"Fifty/fifty. More if he keeps going in order."

Crem might've been a resourceful crawler, but he wasn't the brightest. Who stole a list and then targeted the places from the top down?

The worst thing about sitting for hours beside Kane was I couldn't stop the replay of everything that had happened between us. It was like a reel on repeat as I dissected every moment ad nauseam. If I could get some straight answers, perhaps I could get my finger off the replay button. I could figure out what Kane's deal was and move past it.

"Since we've got some downtime, I've got a question for you."

He gave me the side eye. "Since when do you warn me you're going to ask something?"

I needed to remember not to warn him next time. For now, I'd proceed like I hadn't. "Let's say that there was never a chance you would've killed me in that alleyway after you had rescued me away from the leprechauns—"

"Okay, I can go with that theory. I think saving you not minutes prior would be enough to sell it to some skeptics." He shrugged as if he were partaking in my logical conversation and not steeping his words in sarcasm.

"As I was saying, if that were the case, why did we stop in the alleyway after? Why didn't you just bring me back to the Underground?"

He turned toward me, his eyes saying it all even before he spoke. "You really need me to give you an explanation in order to believe that I wouldn't have killed you?"

I used the need to watch the house while he wasn't as an excuse to not keep eye contact. I didn't turn to look at him, even as his stare was leveled on me. I was on the verge of asking him if turning the tables was a hobby, but I didn't want to get side-railed. "You're the one that made it sound like you would've. Not me. *And* it's not a hard question if you have a good reason."

I could feel his eyes narrowing on me, but he answered. "Fine. I didn't want to question you too close to the leprechaun territory because I know they've got ears on the street. I needed to get you away from the building."

"By why not drive right to the Underground? Why stop at the alleyway before we got there?"

"I wasn't stopping to question you. I stopped because you were sucking in air as if it were going to be your last breath. Since we'd stopped anyway, figured I'd question you then."

"Oh." I remembered that night clearly. I'd thought over every detail of it, taking it apart and trying to look at it from every side. After we left the leprechauns, we'd hit a pothole the size of the Grand Canyon right before the turn into that alley. It had shot pain through me like a jet pack. I'd thought I was holding it together pretty good until then.

I'd never connected my gasp of pain with the turn. So he'd pulled over because he knew how bad off I'd been. It checked off another box, but instead of shutting the door on that question, I really couldn't stop thinking about it. That had been...well, almost sweet. This was not supposed to make me feel like a pile of mush. This was a fact-finding mission.

"Anything else you'd like to inquire about?" he asked, and luckily he'd gone back to watching his side of the street.

"No. Definitely not. Absolutely, positively not."

He kept his face forward as he said, "Sometimes you are very strange, even for a Shadow Walker."

I let out a little *hmph*, realizing we'd come full circle again. I'd hated him when I'd first met him, then he'd grown on me, then maybe he'd grown on me a bit more.

And then I'd left. When I came back, it had been even worse than in the beginning. But here we were again, in this strange place, and I didn't know what I was feeling anymore.

I might not have known what I was feeling for Kane, but I knew when a wave of magic hit me.

"He's in there. I can feel him."

"I would've seen him go in."

"I'm telling you, I can feel the energy."

Kane went still beside me, and I knew he'd just gotten a whiff of the magic in the air. I didn't exactly know what Kane was, but I knew he had some power, probably more than I did.

Until I'd been shadow kissed, anyway.

We both got out of the car at the same time.

Kane stopped. "He's about to blow it up."

I might feel magic before him, but I had no idea about the finer points of it. Kane not only felt it, he felt its purpose. I was going to have to get some pointers on how he pulled that off. "Then we've got to stop him."

"There's no time," he yelled, but I'd already taken off running.

I took another step and froze as all of a sudden the air seemed to be sucked out of the atmosphere. I knew this feeling. I'd felt it a couple of times before, but I hadn't known what was coming those times. I did now.

A burst of flames enveloped the building and shot straight toward me. The heat was spreading over me as I turned to run away. Searing heat rushed over my skin like a blanket as I gulped down burning air. I'd thought I was invincible to these fires, but the crawlers had all wanted to keep me alive before. Crem didn't need me. Just as I realized I might die here, an arm reached around my waist and pulled me along.

We crashed onto the ground barely clear of the blast radius. I landed on top of Kane and then was swiftly pulled underneath him until we rolled to a stop. Neither one of us moved other than to look in the direction of where the house had been, my eyes scanning the area as my charred lungs tried to clear out.

"Wait here."

I didn't have the argument or the will to get off the ground. I knew he was going to check the perimeter of the building and try and spot Crem. I also knew that even if I told him I couldn't feel him anymore, he was still going to go check. It was a stubbornness close to my own heart.

I flopped back onto the grass, not caring how I looked or

who saw me. Crem had gotten past both of us while we'd been sitting in wait.

This meant that we might not catch him until he moved on to his next ER. Or maybe it would take a lot more places?

A few minutes later, Kane walked back over and reached down a hand to help me up as he said, "He's gone."

I didn't tell him I'd already known that.

Sirens sounded in the distance as we made our way back to the car.

I didn't say anything until we were driving away. "This might get ugly. He's collecting power. It might get to the point that we can't get rid of him at all, and we don't even know what he wants."

"Exactly."

"Although on the bright side, Rudy is not going to be happy." I only laughed a little.

It was obvious that the entirety of the Underground had heard about yet another explosion. This time, it wasn't because I read the nonverbal hints. It was staring me in the face. As we walked in, there was a screen that would do an IMAX theatre proud, hanging on the wall over the bar area. The house we'd just left was burning on the screen, adding a glow to the faces turned toward it. All we needed was the heat cranked up and it would've felt like we'd stepped into the waiting room of hell.

Butch, Leon, and Jerry were huddled together in the corner with Flip floating herself around them. They fell in behind Kane and I as we walked up toward the office.

"Any change?" Kane asked as soon as we were all in the room with the door shut.

Jerry stepped forward, looking nothing like an amiable beach boy now. "No. He's been in his room all afternoon."

Butch moved toward the Keurig, clearly needing an

extra French vanilla today. "I still say he's connected somehow."

Butch started grumbling, but Leon reached below him and opened a cabinet, placing a new case of French vanilla K-cups beside the coffee maker.

Asher might've been sitting in his room all day, but I could read *this* room. No one believed he had nothing to do with today's explosion. My doubts about his innocence were growing almost daily.

I walked into the center of the room as I tapped a finger to my lips. "There might be an easier way to get Crem. Let me take Asher out of here, give him a taste of freedom again, and see if I can warm him up a little."

I could see everyone thinking it over until Kane shot it down. "No."

And we were back to the days of one-word answers, because God knew how I loved those. "Yes."

"This is my call."

"I'm the Shadow Walker. I'm the one who has walked beside these creatures. I say yes."

"This isn't shadow walking anymore. This is hunting. You aren't a hunter."

"I might be a better hunter than you."

"Now you're just talking crazy."

"Does it never end with them?" Jerry asked.

"No. It really doesn't," Butch. "Probably won't until they either kill each other or do other things."

I looked over at Butch, as he was elbowing Jerry with a smirk on his face. Jerry was about to laugh, but stopped as he saw me staring them both down.

I turned back to Kane. "We need to exhaust all avenues. You know I'm right."

His jaw twitched a few times as we squared off. "If you

want to exhaust all avenues, then let's talk about how we could kill him."

"No. You're not killing him."

"And you're not wasting any more time on his lies."

We broke apart like two boxers at the end of a round that neither of them won, each going to our corners to regroup. Everyone else went back to their coffee break, Leon mumbling something about not using up all the creamer.

I was over by the window when I saw Zee flash into existence at the bottom of the stairs and point toward the back hallway.

I glanced about the room. Everyone was quiet, deep in their own thoughts or fighting over the last of the sugar. I edged toward the door. "I'm going to go grab a sandwich," I said softly, not looking to attract too much attention.

I got a nod and a few grunts.

I ducked into the back hallway, nearly invisible to the crowd now that there was bigger drama going on.

Zee was waiting by the door. "What?"

"I've got a surprise." She grabbed my arm and tugged me out the door with her.

I climbed in her car, hoping it might be another hairy were-girl looking for some relief.

"Where are we going? I hope it's not that dingy building again. I swear I've got flea bites." The place had been much worse on the inside than it had appeared, the carpet insect-ridden.

The plus side of places like that was no one would come snooping around while we were working. Not that we were doing anything wrong, but this wasn't something I wanted to broadcast.

I scratched my legs, feeling suddenly itchy. Capris might've been a bad call for today.

"Nope. Somewhere much better." She reached out and patted the air in between us. "It's not prime time, but I felt that we needed to up our game."

I felt like I'd swallowed a rubber ball that, after lodging in my throat for a moment, bounced around the walls of my stomach. "Up it how? We've only done one spell."

We turned the corner, into Bay Village. It was a middle-of-the-road neighborhood that made up for any shortcomings with a lot of character.

She slowed her car as we approached a building and then stopped right in front. It was a brick-faced two-story building with a pink and white striped awning over the door and window. A green neon sign above read, *The Magic Box*.

She got out of the car and waited for me to join her in front. She bent forward, watching me as I didn't budge. She must've seen something that made her decide to change her course and head over toward my door. If I had to guess, it was my puke-green face that tipped her off.

She swung my door open as I tried to hold it closed. "What are you doing? Get out."

I didn't move. "What is this?"

She grabbed my hand and started tugging me out of the car. I would've resisted, but she was freakishly strong. Must've been all that cement.

"It's our new place. I wanted you to see it before the adverts go out next week."

"Adverts?" I tugged back as she pulled me toward the building. I wasn't sure if she realized I was still fighting her as she kept moving forward without pause.

"Yes. To grow the business."

"No. No advertising."

She stopped at the door and put in a key with a flower

decal on it. "I can see how you'd be worried about advertising."

Okay, we had a storefront. Maybe that wasn't the end of the world. It was better than fleas. But she had to be crazy to think of advertising.

"After your commercial, it makes sense you'd have cold feet." She patted my shoulder before she opened the door and said, "But I'll handle it and it'll be much better, and we won't show you in it. I thought we should keep your identity a mystery."

I followed her into the building. "No, absolutely no advertising." Although if I wasn't in it, it might not be too bad.

"We'll discuss it later."

I stood still inside. Damn, this place was adorable. There were white couches in the front that looked delicate and scrolled, with pink cushions and silver tables. The place made me want to have a tea party. "This *is* cute. How much is this costing?"

"I negotiated the first month's rent for free in exchange for the renovations."

"And what did the reno cost?" I didn't have the money to lose.

"Not bad. Me and my girls did most of it. You might need to dig around in that head for some eyelash and weight-loss spells when you get a chance, though."

So not exactly free, but I could live with that.

She walked over to an interior door. "This will be your domain. You can greet people or stay in there and not be seen at all."

I walked over and looked inside. This wasn't too bad. Actually, it was the nicest little setup I'd ever seen.

Zee walked over and pointed to the grey velvet lounge.

"This is where the client can relax while you work your magic. This is for you, in case you need to rest before or after." She pointed to a leather armchair in the corner.

There was a console table against another wall, with a water dispenser sitting on top that had floating lemons, limes, and oranges inside it. The words *We make dreams come true* were painted in silver on the wall above.

"This is..." *Not too bad* really didn't measure up. "It's absolutely beautiful."

Zee smiled so brightly it was like a blast of sunshine in the place. "Are you ready?"

I sat down on the lounge and stretched out. "I think I am."

Chapter 29

I was yawning as I got in the car with Kane the next morning. Knowing how close death was hovering near Asher had proved to be a real sleep deterrent. Kane was driving to our next stakeout, but I didn't bother asking where it was. The location didn't particularly matter.

I was yawning again as the Rolling Stones came on the radio and Kane's mouth formed all the words to "Sympathy for the Devil." Unholy shit, was that what he was? Everything else seemed to exist, stuff no one even believed in. Lots of people believed in heaven and hell. I held back the question for one moment, thinking he might get insulted by it if he wasn't. If he was, maybe he'd drag me into the underworld with him for figuring it out.

I asked anyway, because if that was even the slimmest possibility, how could you *not* ask? "Are you the devil? Okay, maybe not the devil, but some relation to the underworld, like an imp or something?"

"Because I like the Rolling Stones?" Each word almost sounded like its own question. "And if you thought I was the devil, what does that say about your standards for working with me?"

It was very irksome to think that even if he were the devil, this somehow implied a deficiency in my character. "I wouldn't say it means anything about my standards. Maybe you had a reason to become the devil? Even if you were the devil, you'd still be you."

He pulled the car over and parked it. "Is that how you feel?"

My hand edged toward the door handle. Why did that question make me want to run from the car? "What do you mean, is that how I feel?" And why was he staring at me like that? I'd just asked him if he was the devil. Insulted, yeah, I'd get that. Not this warm gleam in his eyes.

"It means would it really not bother you if I were the devil?" He was staring at me, near demanding an answer.

"You pretty much said you weren't, so I'm not sure why this is important."

"But it wouldn't matter."

I was getting a weird feeling from this conversation, and an even stranger one from the way he was looking at me. It was the same feeling I'd had after I found out he'd killed the other leprechaun. It was definitely time to go stretch my legs.

His hand on my arm stopped me from making a hasty exit.

"What?" I asked, looking down at his hand and then his face. "Are you going to tell me what you are now?" I asked, trying to cut through some of the tension.

"No. But maybe I'll knock the waiting period down." He shot me a half-smile, and I settled back into my seat, knowing I was out of the danger zone.

"Thanks." Great. I'd become one of those annoying fake thankers just to move on.

I took a look around. We were sitting across the street from a building that resembled my own. Well, almost. I had cute copper awnings over my picture windows. They had striped fabric ones. But they both had an old-world charm that lured you in. It had lured me in. It was one of the reasons I'd overpaid.

One of the reasons. I turned away from the building, my attention on the other reason I'd overpaid.

"Why did you do that?"

Kane groaned.

"Why are you groaning?" I knew my tone was snappish, but my blood was boiling simply from the memory. That had been really uncool of him.

"Although I have no idea what you are talking about, I know this is going to be another one of *those* talks." He shifted, like he needed to get more comfortable for what was to come.

"Why did you run the price up on my building?" I shifted my body so I wouldn't get a cramp in my neck as I stared at him.

"Because I didn't want you to get it." He was stating the obvious and he knew it.

Oh, so I could get questioned but not him? "It was mean. Why were you trying to be mean to me?"

"It wasn't mean. I thought you leaving was a mistake, and I was right."

He was staring forward, and I had a feeling that I was actually getting under his skin. It didn't make me stop asking him questions, though. "Why didn't you keep going up?"

"Because I felt that if you wanted to leave so bad that you

were willing to spend that much on a building, I should let you go." Kane, Mr. Know-it-all, Mr. Relax, I've Got Everything Under Control, was riled.

And all because I'd left? Somehow, seeing him like this, tense and not looking at me, vulnerable, it started to knit together all the little tears I'd felt in our relationship. He really did care about me. It wasn't an act and it wasn't to keep control of an asset. He liked me.

Both of us settled into a peaceful quiet for a while, just long enough to take the raw edge off the recent emotions.

It was a good twenty minutes before he spoke. "Are we going to keep having these conversations? Because I'm going to make you take your own car for the stakeouts if you say yes."

"It's called communicating." I yawned again, hoping he wasn't being serious. Even though I could drive now without crawlers rubbing shoulders with me, I preferred to look out at the scenery and relax. And I didn't want to take my own car. "Would you like to discuss some of my transgressions?" I hoped he didn't want to. That would suck. It wasn't like I wanted to dig up everything he'd ever done to me. I couldn't seem to help myself, and now I was glad I had.

He sat silently for a moment, his eyes meeting mine, and it was as if I could see them softening, warming. "No."

Didn't he care about what I did? I agonized over everything that had gone wrong between us, each one ripping a little piece of me. But he didn't care? It didn't matter to him? Maybe I didn't matter to him? Maybe I'd read his agitation wrong?

He tucked a lock of hair behind my ear before his eyes shifted to my mouth and my insides started to warm.

His thumb grazed my lower lip, and my breath quickened. He wasn't acting like he didn't care.

"Wh-why not?" I asked.

"Because I understand why you've done the things you've done, and I accept you."

His other hand wrapped around the back of my head, his eyes shifting to my lips.

And then I felt it. Crem was here.

"What?" Kane pulled back a bit, studying my face.

I held up a finger, silently asking for a minute so I could pour all my concentration into what I was feeling. Crem was definitely here, but could I pinpoint where the feeling was originating from?

The feeling was growing so strong, but I couldn't read the direction. I glanced over at Kane, and I knew he was feeling it too now. We got out of the car at the same time, both of us scanning the area.

How was I not seeing him approach? Crem was right here. Had to be, from how strong the feeling of magic in the air was.

Then it was gone. It was as if the magic had vanished.

Did Kane still feel it? When I turned to ask, he was looking at me with the same question.

I was still shaking my head as I scoured the area, not believing what my senses were telling me. "I think it's screwing with us. I don't know why, but I've got this niggle in my brain telling me we're being played."

He nodded. "I've got that same feeling."

"Why leave this ER intact?" I asked, hoping Kane would have some brilliant idea that was escaping me.

"I don't know, and I can't figure out how it keeps getting by us." We both stood staring at the building for another minute before he said, "I'm going to lap the place and make sure we aren't missing anything."

Kane headed off, and I took a couple of steps back,

trying to take in the whole picture, find an angle to this that we'd missed. Was it dipping in and out of the Shadowlands? Was that how the magic turned on and off?

If I shadow walked now, would I find Crem hovering nearby? If I did find it in there, what would I be able to do about it? I didn't even know what I was capable of doing yet. Still had to try.

Kane was walking around the building, peering in windows, as I headed back over to him.

That was when a shadow on top of the building drew my eye. There it was, horns and red eyes. It must've been muting its power somehow. Then a wave of magic hit me so hard I almost fell to my knees. Its mouth opened, and I knew what was about to come. I looked down and realized it was hovering right above where Kane was standing. I knew in that second that Crem wanted to kill Kane.

I opened my mouth to scream as flashbacks rolled over me. It was just like the night I'd lost my family. I couldn't let it happen again.

With no time to spare, magic flew over my lips as I ran toward him. I didn't know what I was saying, but my legs were moving at a speed faster than I'd imagined possible, and I could feel the soles of my shoes growing warm.

I caught an astonished look on Kane's face right before I plowed into him and kept moving. The heat came, but I was outrunning the blast. We landed in a thump a block away, my landing a little rougher than when he'd done me a similar favor.

Debris flew around us, and I heard the fire raging before I lifted myself off Kane and saw it.

I fell back on my ass, barely holding myself up with my arms outstretched behind me. However I'd managed to outrun the blast, it had used up everything in my tank.

Kane sat up, watching the flames as I watched him. My eyes started to burn as I realized how close he might've been to death. As the series of events ran through my mind, I knew that had been the point.

"I think Crem wants you dead. He was luring you in."

"It would seem that way."

Chapter 30

KANE WAS LEANING BACK IN HIS CHAIR AS I LAY ON THE COUCH, bouncing his tennis ball off the wall. I could see how this could become addictive, especially if you were wound up, which I was after Kane had nearly been blown to bits in front of me.

We'd already been hashing it over for an hour, with no ideas why. The lack of motive made it worse somehow.

The usual suspects had come in and out, chiming in, but no one had a solid idea. They'd grab a cup of coffee from the Keurig and mumble about whose turn it was to stock the French vanilla—I wasn't sure why, but the gargoyles wouldn't touch K-cups.

Butch had left a few minutes ago, leaving Kane and I alone again. He'd been staring at me strangely the entire way back. I'd been rehashing the newest events, looking for crumbs in the forest, so to speak, when I caught him staring at me again.

I hated when he stared at me like that. That look was like my on switch, lighting every cell in my body. It was irritating when I was trying to relax and wanted the lights set to dim.

I made a circular motion toward his face. "You have to stop doing that. I don't know what idea you've come up with, but it's unsettling."

He didn't stop, just kept staring at me. "You saved me. You could've yelled a warning and I would've had plenty of time to get out of the way, but you saved me." He held up a finger. "I didn't technically need saving, but you did it anyway."

"Excuse me, but you wouldn't have had time. I definitely had to save you. But to your point, you've saved me enough. I didn't get all weird about it."

"It's different," he said.

"Why? Because I'm a girl or because I'm a Shadow Walker?"

"Neither. I usually do the saving, is all."

"And the killing, don't forget that part." I bounced the ball a couple of more times, amused with myself.

He let out a laugh as if me calling him a murderer was somehow funny to him. It wasn't long, though, before he was looking at me in that weird way again.

"If I'd known you were going to get all weird about it, I would've let you die." I dropped the ball by my side and grabbed the stack of magazines that had started showing up again. I flipped through one, not seeing what was on the pages but having the luxury of being able to block his stares with it.

"I'll make sure to remember that for next time."

"You do that, because I am not bluffing. Next time Crem tries to blast you into oblivion, you, sir, are on your own." Even if only the idea of it ripped me into itty-bitty pieces.

"Accepted," he said.

I knew he didn't believe me. I didn't believe me, so why would he? I peeked over the magazine to see he was still looking at me strangely, like he'd seen my soul or something. It was altogether uncomfortable, worse than the world watching you run down the street screaming like a lunatic. I'd done that, so I could speak with conviction.

I'd just ignore him until he became normal. That was the thing to do.

He made a *hmm* noise, and when I peeked at him this time, the weird look was gone. His eyes were sharp and focused, like he was in the midst of a discovery.

I dropped the magazine onto the table and went back to the ball. "What? You come up with some idea why Crem would want to kill you?"

"No. But I've got something else."

Whatever it was, it was a biggie from the way he was focusing. I stopped bouncing the ball and sat up. "Are you going to tell me?"

His head tilted to the side, his eyes never leaving mine. I went back to bouncing the ball while I waited. It was easier than maintaining eye contact while he was sucking up all the oxygen in the room.

"You didn't leave here because you wanted to save Asher."

Great. Now he was back to some theory where I had something to do with the missing items? "What are you talking about?" I jerked my head back to him, irritated by the notion and expecting to see a matching anger. "Are you saying I was involved in the missing items?"

"No." He had a slight smile, and my tension eased with it. At least we hadn't gone back to that again.

"Please share your insight, then, because I'd love to hear why I do what I do. It's so enlightening for my feeble brain to be able to listen to the All-knowing Kane." I bounced the ball again as I thought of how amusing I was.

"You used Asher as an excuse to leave." It wasn't a question. He was utterly confident in what he was saying.

After a near miss catching the ball, I forced myself to keep bouncing it. He had no idea what he was talking about. "I know you're bossy and all, but I never thought you'd try and tell me what I was thinking, too."

I kept my eyes on the ball as I tracked him getting out of his chair and walking around his desk to perch on the corner. He crossed his arms, looking like a cat with a bowl of cream in front of him. "You didn't run for him. You ran from me. I made it clear I was interested in more. You didn't know what to do with your feelings, so you ran. But you just couldn't bring yourself to run too far."

I bounced a little faster, refusing to look at him. That wouldn't help my nerves any. "That's hogwash you're making up so you don't feel bad that I'm going to let your ass burn next time."

"No."

He was digging in, which meant it was time for my exit. I tossed the ball on the seat and got up as casually as I could fake it, when I wanted to run for the door.

He leaned back, watching me. "Look at you, even now, with me bringing the subject up, you're ready to make a run for it."

I stopped in my tracks. "I wasn't running. I've been on that couch for a while and I was stretching my legs."

His eyebrows rose as he nodded slowly. Placating bastard.

I crossed my arms and shook my head, as if that could undo all his nodding. "You're so wrong that I'm nearly embarrassed for you."

"Okay, let us examine the facts for a moment. See who's right?" He lifted his foot and kicked the chair toward me, practically daring me to sit.

If I didn't sit, he'd say I was running. I had nothing to lose. He had no facts. You couldn't lay out evidence of feelings.

"Sure, I'll play your little game for a while if it makes you feel better." There, how'd you like that placation, buddy?

He smiled, not seeming to mind.

I walked around the side of the chair and slumped into it, hooking a heel on the edge so I could use my knee as an armrest.

He hooked a foot around one of the legs and dragged it closer while I pretended I didn't mind.

"If you had such a dire fear for Asher's life, why did you stay in Boston? Common sense would've told you to get farther away." He sat, arms folded, waiting for his reply, as if I were on the stand under cross-examination.

"Excuse me, but Boston is my town, too. Maybe it wasn't the smartest move, but it had nothing to do with you. I'd lost enough and thought it could work. Miscalculation on my part, but nothing to do with you."

He didn't seem to miss a beat as he continued. "Fine. Let's move on to you trying to work with Collin, someone you knew I didn't trust and had warned you off."

"Oh, sure. Now even my talking to Collin is about you." I scoffed loudly in case he hadn't picked up on my disbelief.

He stood, paused as he passed my chair, and then walked over to the window that overlooked the Underground. "You know one of the reasons I keep this place going is the information I get by allowing everyone here. There's countless shifters downstairs that owe me favors.

You knew that, and you were forcing my hand after I refused to work with you."

I stood and turned to face him. "I didn't have a choice."

He nodded again in a way that made me want to slap him. "Did you go the retired Shadow Walker to see if she could point you in the direction of other anchors?"

I shrugged. I stood then stopped myself. I was not going to pace the room. "I understand that you know everything, so you should be aware she was too unstable to rely upon for anything." And it hadn't really occurred to me. Why hadn't it? Why had I run right to Collin after Kane shot me down? I'd known it was going to get back to him. Was he right? And how embarrassing was that?

"So? Is that all your proof? That I stayed in Boston and didn't ask a nutcase for help? Your case is looking pretty thin." At least on the surface.

"No. Actually, it's not."

He looked way too pleased with himself, and it sent shivers through me. Why was he so sure of himself?

Had I held my ground long enough to make a run for it now without being utterly obvious? I leaned back on his desk, trying to keep calm as he walked back to me. I scooted farther back on the desk to keep my space as he leaned forward, a hand on either side of my legs.

"Do you know I have surveillance for five blocks in every direction from here?"

My eyes shot to the door and then I forced them away. I should've run when I had the chance, because I knew why he was so sure of himself now.

"Getting that running feeling again?"

"Absolutely not." My lungs wanted to kick into overdrive, and trying not to breathe was making it harder. I was doing all I could to not show my hand, but the way he was looking made me think my cards were marked and he knew exactly what I had. "So what? You've got some cameras?"

"I'd gotten some reports that you'd popped up in the area a few times, hovering a block away. They told me you'd drive up, pause, and then drive away after five or so minutes."

"I got lost a few times. I'm not used to driving." I edged to the side and forward, seeing if he'd move out of my way.

I leaned back when he didn't.

"I asked my guys to go back over the footage. Do you know how many times you got 'lost'?"

I knew exactly how many times. I'd driven this way about twice a week since I'd left. I'd leave my building to go buy paint and find myself driving here. I'd pick up takeout only to drive here. I'd force myself to stop a block shy, even though all I really wanted to do was keep driving, walk into the Underground, and speak to him. Just see him for a minute. I wanted to sit right here, in front of him like I was now, and be close.

I'd told myself it was only because I felt over my head with Asher, and Kane had always known exactly what to do. Except even on the good days, when everything was perfect, I'd wanted to come here. I'd always wanted to come here, and it had always been about him.

Only now, as he faced me down, forcing my truth out, it felt like harsh sunlight when I wanted to retreat into the dark. And he was right. I wanted to run, fast and hard. I didn't want to think at all.

"What are you so afraid of?"

I turned, looking anywhere but him, which was hard when he was right in front of me, his legs brushing mine.

He lifted his hands and cupped my head, bringing my gaze back to his. "I've seen you walk into the Shadowlands as if you were going for a walk in the park. You stare down creatures a hundred times stronger than you. You ran in front of me to save me from a burning blast of fire, but now you're afraid?"

I dropped my eyes, avoiding his stare. "Saving you doesn't mean I want to be with you."

"No, but the way your breath hitches every time I touch you does. The way you lean into me without even thinking about it."

His hand moved to my hip and then my lower back, making it clear I'd done it. And he'd noticed.

His fingers splayed on my back, as if trying to touch as much as possible. "What you did today, it changes things."

I shook my head as my lips parted. His mouth moved past mine, and I felt an ache until it settled further down to whisper along my neck.

One hand stayed on my back as the other grabbed my ass and shifted me forward until I was perched on the edge of the desk and he stepped in between my legs.

His hands held me there as his hard cock pressed into me, and a deep moan escaped me. The roughness of his jaw grazed my cheek as his lips came to my ear.

"I can wait until you're ready, but I won't pretend anymore." His voice was gravelly with the same need that I felt building within me.

He stepped back, putting air between us when I wanted none. He walked out of his office, and I knew he was giving me a choice.

Accept what we were honestly or live in a delusion and lose him.

Chapter 31

I STEPPED OUT OF THE ELEVATOR ON THE SIXTH FLOOR AN
hour later, still off kilter from the conversation with Kane. It
was hard to be honest about your feelings for someone
when you had buried all those feelings in a twenty-foot
hole. The last thing I was prepared for was the howling
noise coming from my old apartment.

It was Asher, repeatedly shrieking "Ollie" and sounding
like a wounded animal. Badger was the guard on duty, and
he was standing stone still, as if he didn't hear the noise
filling the hall—or really didn't want to.

I got as close to the door as I could. "Asher? Are
you okay?"

"Ollie, I need you." It was a wailing noise, but
softer now.

I tried to get closer to the door, but Badger wasn't budging. "What's wrong?"

"I can't say it like this."

Shit. I pulled my phone out. I'd wanted a little space
before I spoke to Kane again today, but there wasn't much

choice. His phone went right to voicemail, and I didn't bother with a message.

Straightening my shoulders, I put on my firmest expression and faced Badger. "You need to move."

"I can't—"

"Yeah, yeah, I know. I need you to move anyway, because I don't want to do this the bad way."

Badger tilted his fluffy head as he squinted. "What's the bad way?" The slight tremble in his voice said he knew exactly what the bad way was. Through him.

Why did he have to look like a big puppy? Of all the people to have to threaten. "Please, just move out of the way?"

He grinned in a sad sort of way. "I really want to, but I can't. What are you going to do to me?" He grimaced, turning his head to the side and closing his eyes.

"Hopefully only put you to sleep for a little bit?"

He nodded and then sat down against the wall.

"What are you doing?"

"I don't want to hit my head when I pass out," he said, eyes still firmly shut.

Smart move. I dug around in my head, keeping two ideas prominent: no harm, just sleep. At least this wasn't a rush job, so as the words formed, I felt out their potency before I completed the whole spell.

The guard slumped.

"Badger?" I whispered. He didn't budge. I reached down and felt a strong pulse. Satisfied, I stepped over his legs and walked into the apartment.

I shut the door quickly so Asher couldn't see the condition of the guard outside, if he hadn't already felt the spell I cast. I wasn't convinced Asher was guilty, but that didn't mean I was confident enough to let him go waltzing out of here.

He was standing a few feet from the door. I felt like I'd gotten punched in the gut when I saw the sickly grey tone to his skin, almost as if he were still in the Shadowlands.

"I've been waiting for you. Where've you been?" His voice was soft, and he looked absolutely dismal.

"Are you okay?" I reached out toward his face but halted, afraid it might cause him pain.

He took my outstretched hand, pulling me deeper into the apartment. "No. I can feel myself getting weaker here. You need to help me get out of here. We need to go back to the Shadowlands."

This world was killing him, and I'd been a part of leaving him locked in this apartment. I hadn't known he wasn't feeling well. I hadn't wanted to know. "I'll get you back."

Badger was knocked out cold. Did I take Asher out of here now? Find a crawler and see if I could walk him back in? It might be my only chance. Kane would be furious, but he'd get over it. I hoped. He'd have to. I couldn't let Asher die. We didn't know if he'd done anything wrong.

"No, *us.*" He gripped both my arms and was pulling me farther into the apartment. Determination mixed with desperation coated his words. "You need to come with me."

I froze, or tried. He kept pulling me with him. Bad. This was bad. Trying to calm him, I softened my voice and tried to remain calm myself. "Asher, I don't belong in that place."

"Is it him?"

Him being Kane. Asher still didn't want to say his name. I must not have answered fast enough, because he gave me a shake that rattled my teeth.

"No. It's not about Kane. This world is my home. I can

visit the Shadowlands, but this is where I belong." I could already see where this was going, and dropped the softness in favor of a firmer voice. Asher's stubborn face was coming out. Hopefully he wouldn't take so long to see the point that we'd miss our opportunity to get him out of here.

"It'll be better. I'll take care of you there, like I couldn't here." His grip tightened on my arms. "I know what you need now."

"Asher, you're hurting me." I refused to let the fear I was feeling show in my voice.

I'd spent months alone with Asher and I'd never been frightened until now. He'd always been like a harmless little brother I had to take care of. Maybe he hadn't been altogether there, but not once had he felt like a threat.

He didn't loosen his grip as he steered me toward the couch. "You don't believe me, but I'm going to show you. I can be everything for you."

He shoved me down on the seat cushion so quickly I was disoriented from suddenly shifting from standing to lying on my back. That moment of hesitation was all he needed to climb on top and begin tearing at the waist of my yoga pants with his hands while I tried to push him off.

"Get off me!" I kept telling myself that this was Asher as I screamed at him. He wouldn't do this to me. But it was as if he didn't even hear me speaking. He planted one hand on my chest and started to undo his pants with the other, and no amount of tossing and turning dislodged him. He was freakishly strong, and I wondered if he'd hid this from me on purpose.

"Asher, you need to get off me or I'm going to have to do something really bad to you." I had this crazy idea that if I could just get him to listen to me he would return to the slightly childish man he'd always been.

He didn't even look at me as I spoke, so intent on his purpose. Nothing was getting through to him.

I started chanting the sleep spell I'd just given to Badger, but I felt it fall flat immediately. Shock that the magic didn't work added an extra edge of panic as I flailed underneath him.

He managed to shove his pants down while I struggled, to reveal a flaccid penis. Not knowing how long it would stay that way, I searched for another spell. This one had some serious teeth behind it, but it fell flat again.

Desperate enough to try anything, I whispered, "Zee." When she didn't appear, it became clear Kane must've done something to ward this room from the rest of the building.

My call for help and spells weren't the only things not working. Asher was staring at his limp dick as if he knew something wasn't right but not sure what he was supposed to do about it. While he was puzzling out his next move, I looked over my head and realized the lamp was within grasping distance.

I might not have been able to do a spell on him, but I might be able to do one on myself. I uttered the same words I'd used the other day when rushing to Kane's aid. The magic surging through my body made me want to sob in relief.

Using the burst of accelerated speed, I grabbed the lamp and hammered him over the head before he realized what the waves of magic rolling off me meant.

Asher's eyes rolled back in his head and his body toppled over to land in a loose sprawl on the floor.

I slammed my way out of the apartment, afraid to look back. Once outside, I grabbed Badger by the shoulders and shook him hard enough to bang his head against the hall wall. I didn't get so much as a groan out of him. Great, that spell had worked too well.

"Zee?" I hoped whatever ward had prevented her from hearing me in the apartment didn't spill out into the hall. She popped out of the air in a second.

She moved her head sideways, taking in my torn clothes and the panic in my eyes. "What the hell happened to you?"

"Can you secure that door somehow?"

The light bulb went off for her. "Ahhhh, gotcha." She hooked a thumb toward Kane's door. "Go get together a bit."

I nodded, more than willing to leave her to secure the door on her own.

A shower was the first order of business. A shower that entailed a lot of scrubbing and a wish for something stronger than coconut-aloe body wash.

Out of the shower, I made sure to put on a long-sleeve shirt so the bruises wouldn't be visible. Kane could get rid of them, but he was the one I was hiding them from. Pair of jeans and a light sweatshirt, and voila, I was as good as new. On the outside. No one would be the wiser to how bad it had gotten in there, except maybe Zee.

I left the bathroom and headed next door, prepared to face the wrath of Kane. There was no way Zee hadn't called him in by now.

I walked into the hall and saw Badger still slumped against the wall, the door to Asher's apartment wide open. I realized the cavalry had already arrived when I heard Kane's voice. "I want every camera in the area checked, screen by screen."

Butch, Leon, and Kane were all standing in the living room as I entered. But where was Asher?

I thought Kane would rough him up, but did he kill him while I was trying to scrub the top layer of my skin off?

"Did you..."

"He disappeared."

"What?" Gone. Asher had just performed his second escape act since I'd known him.

The rage that was flowing off Kane filled the room.

No one said anything else, but the place emptied, except for Kane and me. He walked over to me, looking me over.

"You came in here alone, after you knocked out the only available help?" His jaw shifted.

What did I say? Yes, I heard Asher in distress and I went running to his aid? Oh yeah, then he tried to rape me. I didn't want to believe it, let alone talk about it yet.

"Perhaps you were right about him being a little bit dangerous. But no real harm was done." *Mostly.* Kane didn't need to know what it had taken for me to make it out of the room.

"Are you okay?" The question was considerate, but the voice was still furious.

Big-mouth Zee. She couldn't have played it down? My arms were sore and I wanted to scrape all the skin from my body, but I was in one piece. "I'm fine." I looked at the floor where I'd left Asher, still stunned by everything that had gone down. How could he be gone? Had everything been an act? The helplessness, the friendship... "Do you think he could have left at any point?"

"Probably. Stay in the building. He might be able to get out, but he won't be able to get back in. I don't want you alone until we find him." He was walking toward the door before I agreed, not that I had any desire to argue.

"You're leaving?"

"Yes."

"Hang on, I'm coming with you."

He stopped by the door. "You can't. It's a long shot, but

there are people I know who might be able to give us answers. They won't talk in front of strangers."

I nodded. We needed any kind of shot we could get right now.

He walked out of the apartment.

Chapter 32

I WAS SITTING IN KANE'S OFFICE, IN HIS CHAIR, FOR NO REAL reason other than he was gone, when I didn't want him to be. Asher was still missing, and that didn't help matters.

Plus, I was drop-dead tired. Although I never saw him in bed next to me, I somehow slept better when he was there.

Butch barged in the door and looked at me, and his face changed. "Saw the light. Thought you were Kane."

"Nope. He's not back yet."

Butch nodded and walked over to the couch. I didn't need him to say he hated that Kane was still gone. It was right there in the way the corners of his mouth were down and in the weight of his fall as he dropped onto the couch.

I rocked back on the chair, having a hard time keeping still. "Does he do this a lot?"

"Every now and then."

What was every now and then? Once a month, couple times a year? Once every ten years?

"Do you know where he went?" Kane had been gone for three days, and this was the third time I'd asked.

"I told you I don't know." Butch had his head relaxed back as he stared at the ceiling.

Leon barged through the door, looked around the office, and immediately seemed to lose his burst of energy. "Just came to see if—"

"We know," Butch said.

Leon's head dropped as he walked over to the Keurig, not bothering to complain when there was only hazelnut left.

When Jerry walked in the door, all three of us said, "He's not here."

"Yeah, doorman here? I know." He pointed at his chest. "Alexandria wants a meeting."

"With who?" Butch asked.

Jerry pointed at me.

I shrugged. "Send her up."

Leon spun so quickly he spilled his coffee. "Don't send her up."

"We have instructions to keep everything under control," Butch said, standing.

I kicked my feet up on the desk. "Send her up. I want to see what she wants."

For some crazy reason, they listened to me.

Alexandria strolled in, looking splendid in a slinky pastel-blue dress with a slit nearly up to her hip. Why did I think it was a good idea to alternate yoga pants with jeans? And a brush, that might've been a good move. I'd been operating on a messy bun since Kane left.

She folded her body into the chair in front of the desk with the grace of a cat. I'd seen plenty of vampires at this point, but she was so graceful that she must've been a dancer in her human life.

She crossed her legs in a way that had Butch doing a double take. Until I kicked him, anyway.

Why didn't people ever look at me that way? Oh yeah, that's right: yoga pants, sweatshirt, and lack of a brush. Actually, Kane looked at me that way—even better than that, to be honest.

She flipped her hair in a come-hither way that made me worry she was going to take out Leon next.

It didn't work.

She gave up and finally got to the point. "I've heard no one has seen Kane. That he's missing?"

Deny or ask why it was any of her business? Defensive probably wasn't a good move. "He's allowed to leave the Underground." Had that been defensive? It had only been three days. He wasn't gone. He had told us he was leaving.

"He hasn't been gone this long in twenty years."

How did she know that and I didn't? When Kane did get back, we were going to have a little heart-to-heart over what his relationship with this vamp was. As soon as she left, I was talking to Butch and Leon.

"Who's in charge?" She looked at Butch, then Leon, before her gaze rested on me. "Surely it's not you?"

I sat up a little straighter and then forced myself to slouch back into the chair because I didn't care what she thought. "Really? You think I'm not up to it, do you?"

She looked me over slowly until her gaze stopped at my face. "No, I'm certain you aren't."

"You think I'm weak?"

"I'd like to see what happens when you lose your babysitters."

She was baiting me. It was so glaringly obvious that it was laughable. She was also doing it at the worst time possible, as my nerves were on edge. Everything about me was on edge, and the last thing I had tolerance for was this jerk sitting here and calling me weak. Yeah, it could possibly have a little to do with how helpless I was feeling at the moment, not knowing where Kane was, if he was even alive. Didn't matter. She was pressing my buttons, and I was fine letting off a little steam in her direction.

"Butch, Leon, give us a moment alone."

Neither of them moved. Way to blow my image, guys.

Butch stepped a little closer. "I don't really see the need—"

"I'll be fine."

Leon coughed. "I think that for the—"

"I said, it's quite all right." Neither of them budged. Wonderful. This was exactly what I needed to enforce the image of me being capable. Two babysitters.

Alexandria laughed softly. "Aw, they're afraid to leave their little ward. How sweet."

"Butch, Leon, please step outside so that I don't have to go into the alleyway with Alexandria, unless you want me to do it while you're napping." I knew I was getting the evil eye on both sides. Maybe that had been a little low of me, but couldn't a girl protect herself once in a while?

They were both grumbling as they left, Leon saying something to Butch about how I was bluffing. Butch was physically urging him toward the door anyway, saying he didn't want to take the chance. Thank God for Butch, because I was pretty sure I had been bluffing.

I waited until the door closed and I saw them take a few steps away before turning on Alexandria. "What did you come here for?"

She stood and circled the chair until she was resting both hands on the back of it. "I was concerned for Kane, is all."

"Nope. Try again."

"Why is that surprising to you? We have a very long history. And now look at him. Slumming it with the poor little Shadow Walker who's so fragile she can't be left alone."

"As fun as this verbal swap is proving to be, I've got other matters I need to handle today. Get to your point?"

She leaned forward. "You need to leave, and I'm going to give you the opportunity to do it on your own."

I should tell her to fuck off and get out of here, but instead I asked, "Why is that?" Stupid. You don't engage with crazy. As someone who used to be crazy, I knew this all too well.

"Because Kane is getting attached to your pathetic little life, and I'd hate to see him hurt when you die." She stood and leaned over the desk, all done in super speed.

I knew it. She still wanted Kane. "Don't you have a hairy little man already?"

"You must know you don't measure up. It will never last. I mean, look at you."

Fucking yoga pants. "And if I don't take this gracious opportunity you are affording me?"

She looked toward the door, where Leon and Butch had left. "Then that was a really stupid move."

Common sense was screaming to tell her I'd think about her offer and get back to her. Or better yet, tell her that I agreed and then do nothing. I was too tense to choose those options. Had too much pent-up anger toward myself over the fact that Kane wasn't here and I didn't know what to do about it. So, instead of using common sense and stalling the problem until the future, after I had some time to ponder it, I said, "Get the fuck out of my face."

"Bad choice."

She was a blur until she materialized in front of me and I felt teeth sink into my skin.

It was painful as hell, and I realized this bitch wasn't messing around. She was going to kill me. Here and now if I didn't do something. "Get off me," I said, feeling like I needed to offer her a warning as spells I didn't know I possessed were filling my head.

She pulled harder on my vein, and I felt a weakness spreading through me fast. I wasn't going to last long enough for another warning.

The words spilled out of my mouth, and I knew as I tasted the spell on my tongue that this wasn't weak magic. I'd pulled from the top shelf.

Her fangs loosened their grip as she staggered back, grabbing her stomach. Her eyes were wide in horror. Her mouth opened as if she were trying to speak but couldn't.

She was doubling over as I wondered what I'd done. How had I done it?

She fell to her knees, one hand wrapped around her throat now and the other planted on the floor as she looked up to me, agony showing on her face. And shock. Complete and utter shock. I recognized the expression, because I was feeling a good dose of it myself.

Was she dying? Oh shit. *This*...was not good. I scrambled inside my head for something to save her, but now I was drawing blanks.

I ran to the door, making sure I kept my still-bleeding neck out of sight. I forced a fake smile as I caught the eye of Butch, who was standing five or so feet away with Leon, still on the upper-level walkway. I nodded toward the inside of the office, and they did their best to not mad-dash it inside.

I shut the door as soon as they came in, and then all

three of us were staring at the vampire in the middle of the room as the last twitch left her body.

Butch leaned down and flopped her over while trying not to touch her at the same time. "Holy shit! What did you do?"

I thought about the words I chanted as she'd sucked away on my jugular like she was having an afternoon smoothie. Thinking back, I might've said something along the lines of "final death," and something or other about "hell and no return." Yeah, definitely not worth repeating. "I don't think I should repeat the spell."

Leon nodded. "Very good idea."

Butch looked at me. "Why'd you kill her?"

"I didn't mean to. She started sucking on my neck. The words just came out," I said, pointing to where I could still feel blood dripping. I was glad I'd worn a ratty sweatshirt now. If I'd been prancing around in a good dress, I'd be mighty upset.

Alexandria was completely still now, my blood still red on her lips. If she hadn't been trying to kill me, I might've felt worse about it.

Leon started shaking his head. "Fuck. This is all we needed."

"We shouldn't have left her alone. I was afraid of this," Butch added.

My head jerked from where Alexandria lay to them. "You mean you weren't worried for me?"

"No. Her," Butch said, pointing at the body. He stared for another few minutes before he groaned. "We've got a room full of vampires downstairs that all saw her come in here. Now what are we going to do?"

"What about the dungeon?" I pointed toward the closet that led to the door.

Leon squatted beside her. "Her body isn't the issue. She's going to be a pile of sludge soon anyway. The problem is, she goes missing and the last time she was seen was up here." He was shaking his head. "The vampires already don't like you."

"If you're going to dredge up the past, let me remind you that the first vampire I killed was in defense of a young girl who was being fed on, and—"

I had to hold my hands up before they started that same old argument that she wasn't going to be killed.

"We don't know whether or not she was going to survive. I did what I had to. And this was not my fault. If Alexandria had kept her teeth to herself, none of this would've happened."

"If you'd let us stay in the room, none of this would've happened. You were itching for a fight, and you got one," Leon said.

"Excuse me, but who were the two people who warned me about leaving little fleshy bits in the alley?" I waved my hands dramatically. "Oh, no, not *you* two? You never get your hands dirty."

Butch glanced at Leon, who shrugged.

Leon straightened, wiping his hands on his pants. "Okay, so maybe we've done a few things. Now what?"

I walked over to the window, trying to get a head count. At nine in the evening, the place was already starting to fill up. "We create some sort of emergency that sends everyone running."

This would still be her last known location, and I'd learned this wasn't like human law, where you needed proof beyond a reasonable doubt before they threw you in jail. It was more along the lines of *she was last seen at the Underground with the three of us and now she's missing so let's go fucking kill them this afternoon before we have our tea and cookies.*

But it would buy us some time.

"Like what?" Butch asked.

"I don't know about this," Leon said.

Butch turned to him before I could. "It can't get any worse. We're already fucked. Load up on French vanilla and man up."

"It can always get worse," Leon said, right before he headed over to the Keurig. "There's only hazelnut."

Chapter 33

Leon walked around the main floor of the Underground, kicking debris out of his way and shoving at an overturned table with only two legs left. "What did I tell you both?"

I glanced at Butch, who did a swift shake of his head. Yeah, he didn't think we were actually supposed to answer either. I brushed some cement dust off my leg and kept quiet.

"I told you, it can always get worse. I know this from life-long experience. What did you two say? No, we've got this under control. It's just going to be a flash of light, all smoke and mirrors to scare them off. Well, now look at us." Leon stopped walking long enough to throw out his arms in dramatic effect that sent out a dust cloud. "What are we going to say when Kane gets back? Sorry, we destroyed your building? We had to cover up a murder that never should've happened?"

"The whole building isn't destroyed. It appears to only be this main floor." I patted the air in front of me. "We'll get it fixed."

My reply didn't seem to have the effect I'd hoped for, as Leon ignored me and turned to Butch. "What did he tell us? Don't let her do any magic in the building."

Butch didn't respond as he picked up a stray piece of metal and looked over at the window, as if trying to determine if it was from there.

Leon kicked another piece of cement. "And what did we do? Say yeah, good idea. Do your magic."

I didn't know who he was speaking to anymore, and I definitely didn't remember the conversation sounding like that. Although he had a valid point.

Leon paced another circle around us, kicking up more dust as he moved. I leaned back on my hands, trying to evade an especially bad swirl, and immediately sat back up to pull a splinter out of my palm. "Let's look on the bright side. The place looks like it was hit with a nuke—"

"That's the bright side?" Butch asked, appearing to think I'd lost my marbles. "You were making more sense when you were hiding in the shower stall afraid of the crawlers."

"First off, that's just plain ole mean. I understand this didn't work out so well, but what I was going to say was, we're lucky the beam of light went off first and they all ran like hell. We could be sitting in dust and guts instead." I was going to need tweezers for this.

Leon huffed. "Yeah, who knows what your body count would be up to by now."

"She was sucking me down like I was her favorite afternoon smoothie. What was I supposed to do?" Oh, maybe I could suck the splinter out?

Leon circled around. "We are so fucked."

"No, we aren't. I'm going to get this fixed." I gave up on the splinter and dug into my back pocket to find my cell phone had a smashed screen. I'd forgotten I'd landed on my ass during the blast. "Anyone have a working phone?"

"For what?" Butch asked.

"A contractor."

I heard some cement shuffling around and a cough before DiC, Dwarf in Charge, walked in through a newly made hole in the wall.

"Seems like you've got a problem here," he said, surveying the room. He pulled out a small spiral notepad from the inside of his impeccably tailored suit and started writing on it.

"You're not getting the job," Butch said.

DiC ignored Butch and continued around the room, making more notes.

"You can fix this?" I tossed Leon his phone back.

DiC stopped writing to look down his nose at me where I was sitting on the floor. "Of course I can."

"I don't want any part of this," Butch said, and headed toward the office stairs that had survived the blast.

"How much?" Knowing the dwarves, it was going to cost me through the nose in spells. I had spells, though, and I didn't want Kane to come back to his home looking like this.

"I'll let you know after it's done." DiC scribbled some more.

Leon dipped his head in my direction and mouthed, "No."

I ignored him. "How quick?"

"Couple of days."

"Done."

Leon was rolling his eyes when Butch poked his head out of the window in the office that overlooked the Underground. "The office is still mostly intact, other than missing windows."

Leon leaned back to look at him. "The Keurig working?"

Butch ducked back in and then yelled, "Think so. Its light is on."

The three of us were sitting up in Kane's office a couple of hours later when I realized we'd fallen into this unhealthy pattern over the last few days. We'd all sit around in silence, as if we were mourning Kane, which was ridiculous.

I was standing by the window, distracting myself by watching the dwarves starting work below. I glanced over my shoulder. "Are we nervous about Kane missing yet?"

"Not yet." Butch said it with less confidence than he had yesterday. Every day it got a little shakier.

"He said he was leaving. He didn't just disappear," Leon added.

I nodded. He was right. Too soon to panic. I looked back at the construction when two witches made their way in. It was the one I'd accidentally punched with magic and the one who'd run my memories like it was a cinema. I'd had a special hatred for Cinema Queen after she'd shared all the top hits of horrible moments from my life.

They stepped through the blasted door and made their way across the floor, swerving to avoid dwarves carrying supplies. They headed right for the stairs to the office. If they were here to screw with me, they'd picked the worst time.

Butch caught a glimpse of them climbing the stairs.

"Oh no, we can't do this now," Butch said, his words slightly mumbled as he ran in front of the door.

Leon obviously thought this was a bad idea too, since he ran and stood beside Butch, physically blocking the door.

I saw Leon's hand shifting to the knob and locking it. "What are you doing? Let them in."

"Oh no," Leon said. "Not until you promise no more magic."

The two witches were fast approaching, in clear view, since there was no window or shade on the door. "Let them in and I'll try."

Leon glanced over his shoulder. The witches were almost here. "Promise."

"What if they try to kill me?"

"Everyone tries to kill you. That's not good enough," Butch whispered as the witches closed the distance.

They politely knocked on the office door, which struck me as a bit ridiculous. After all, we were all staring at each other, nothing separating us but dusty air.

"If you don't let them in, I'm going to go out there." I waited for that to scare them a little before I added, "And I won't hose down the alley afterward."

They gasped.

I nodded. That's right. Stinky, fleshy bits in the alley.

They stepped out of the way.

If the witches had a clue what *not hosing down the alley* meant, it wasn't obvious, as they said my name in a soft, polite tone. "Ollie?"

I opened the door and motioned them in.

"Do you mind if we call you Ollie?" Cinema Queen asked.

I shrugged. "What do you want?"

Broken Nose visibly swallowed, showing herself as the weak link. "We think we got off on the wrong foot."

I nodded slowly. "Really? You do? That's very interesting."

Butch and Leon had worked their way around, so they were at the witches' backs, and I quickly realized why. Leon shook his head, mouthing, "Don't do it."

Butch's hands were in the prayer shape, and I'd love to know what god he prayed to. These two were way too dramatic. I wasn't going to kill more people today.

Most likely.

Cinema Queen took a half step toward me. "When you first came here, we didn't really know what your intentions were, so we might've been harsh on you. Then, after the rain, we were understandably upset. We both took some shots at each other, but we'd like to bury the hatchet if you are willing."

Leon and Butch vigorously nodded.

I made a *hmmm* noise. Butch and Leon might've been desperate for peace, but I saw some wiggle room here. "I don't know. I might have to think about it."

"Maybe we could…" One witch looked at the other witch as they scrambled to come up with a bribe.

Seriously? They didn't have anything planned? They thought I'd roll over that easy?

"We could…" Broken Nose trailed off, as if she couldn't come up with anything. She stepped a little closer to Cinema Queen, and I thought they might start hugging each other and crying soon.

Really? I was going to have to walk them through this? "How about you write me a check? I'll consider it payment for past damages." And my bank account could certainly use it.

"Definitely. How much would you like? Ten thousand?" Broken Nose asked.

My upper lip lifted, as if there was an odd smell in the room.

Cinema Queen jumped in. "A hundred thousand. She meant ten a week until we paid you a hundred."

I didn't look like I was smelling something funny anymore, but I wasn't quite smelling roses either.

"And fifty. One hundred and fifty!"

Cinema Queen waited for my reaction to her latest offer. I probably could've upped it a bit more, but I had made it rain on them.

I smiled. "I think that would be very generous of you."

They ran from the room and Leon shut the door, locking it again, for whatever good that did.

Chapter 34

I GREETED BUTCH AND LEON AS I SAT AT ONE OF THE TABLES the next morning. The dwarves hadn't gotten around to fixing the booths yet.

Didn't matter where we sat, though. The view was still the same. I couldn't look anywhere but up at the dark office. It had been four days since Kane left. No word and he wasn't answering his phone. Didn't call back after countless messages.

I ordered food.

I looked up at the office.

I toyed with my food and glanced over at the door, hoping to see him walk in.

Kane had said he'd be back soon. Four days was not soon.

It took about thirty minutes for me to concentrate long enough on Butch and Leon to realize I wasn't the only one staring upward.

"This is normal, right?" I asked, hoping I'd get the answer I wanted. I got a halfhearted grunt and a shrug. "So, this is *not* normal?"

Another shrug and two grunts.

"Answer me. I need actual words right now, because I'm walking the edge here." I was on the brink of jumping across the table and strangling the first one I got my hands on if they didn't give me a verbal reply.

Leon looked at Butch but then saved himself from physical harm by talking. "We're worried too."

That wasn't what I wanted to hear. This was definitely not the normal, but in my gut, I'd known that already. I dropped my fork, not bothering with the pretense of eating anymore.

There hadn't been any explosions, so that was good. If Crem had blown Kane up, we would've heard about the explosion. But Kane disappearing right after Asher did? When I knew Asher hated him? It didn't sit well.

I looked around and realized that we'd started to attract attention. Or I had. I adjusted my voice before saying, "Office."

They nodded. They'd probably noticed all the tilted ears in our direction.

I made my way up to the office, with Butch and Leon on my tail and everyone in the place watching our every move. We weren't the only ones suspicious about Kane's disappearance. The apartment upstairs might have been a better idea, but it was as if now I'd decided to act, I didn't want to waste one more second, even to be less obvious about it.

I pressed my lips firmly together until we were all in the office and the door was shut. "What's the policy when someone goes missing?"

Neither of them spoke right away, but I didn't get nervous until I saw them shoot each other questioning looks. Then I was ready to climb the walls. "There is a plan in place for when someone goes missing, right?"

"Kane was always the planner. He's never gone missing before," Butch said.

Leon walked to the Keurig. "This is too much. I need a French vanilla, not a hazelnut, and I can't handle this today." Both of his hands were running over his scalp and his psyche seemed to be frazzled.

I spun around to Leon, heart in throat and my pulse going from sixty to one fifty in two seconds flat. "Drink a hazelnut and deal with it." I took a step closer to him and took a hold of his forearm to make sure I had his full attention. "You can't fall apart on me. Not now." I watched as my words sank in and then waited for some sort of acknowledgment that he was going to keep it together.

His head bobbed rapidly a few times before he said, "I'm good. I'll drink the hazelnut."

I gave him a pat on the back. "Good man."

"What about the locator spell you have?" Butch asked.

"I tried it last night, along with everything else I could think of. He's not showing up." That was the worst part. It meant maybe he was already dead. Or in the Shadowlands? Lured in by Asher somehow? The weight of the over-whelming possibilities made my legs feel like they wanted to give out.

Butch's eyes dropped to the ground.

"What are we going to do?" Leon asked, holding on to his coffee with both hands.

I looked at Butch, thinking he'd answer, to realize they were both looking at me. *Me.* They thought I could do something to save Kane? I was calling the shots?

Screw it, I was good with that. I could do this. Kane had saved my ass over and over again. He wasn't going down even if I had to dig up his grave and drag him back from the dead.

But I had to be smart about it, and not go all Death Angel or Bomber Girl on everyone and everything. I had to think this through. What would Kane do? He wouldn't panic. He'd assess the threat first. Intelligence gathering. That was what we needed.

"Reach out to all the people you can think of and find out if they've heard anything. Don't make it obvious that Kane is missing and we're searching for him. We don't need any other issues popping up because we seem vulnerable."

Leon was making another coffee, having chugged the first. "How are we not going to make it obvious?"

I thought about that for all of half a second. "Then be obvious. Just get it done." God help anyone who got in my way right now. So much for pulling back on my inclination for destruction and mayhem. "Call everyone you can think of and hunt down anyone you can't get on the phone. Report back here by tonight."

"What happens tonight?" Butch grabbed the keys for the Caddy off the desk.

"If we have no other leads? Something drastic."

"Still crazy," Leon said, plucking the keys out of Butch's hands.

I turned to Leon. "Wait a second. First it was 'still alive.' I liked that. It was good. Then you two thought you could switch it to 'still quitting,' which was just obnoxious. Did I give you a hard time? No. I could see your point, so I let it go. But you can't change my tagline every week on a whim."

Leon looked at Butch. "She's right. Maybe we should make it 'still crazy' and leave it at that."

Leon took a sip of his coffee, thinking it over. "I can live with 'still crazy.'"

"No," I said. "That will not be my tagline. Now go."

The door to the office shut and I watched as they left the building. The minute they were gone, I called for Zee.

As soon as she popped up, I got right to the point. "Have you seen Kane or heard anything in the last few days?"

"No. No one's seen Kane."

"What do you think?" It was strange to realize how much I'd come to trust this often rude and utterly absurd gargoyle.

Her normal stone face softened like I'd never seen. "I don't like it."

I turned around and pretended that I needed something on Kane's desk, buying myself a couple of seconds to get the billboard of emotions off my face. I needed people to listen to me right now, not think I was a basket case about to fall apart. There'd be time to fall apart tomorrow, or next month, or at some other time that wasn't this very moment.

"Well? What are you going to do?" she asked.

Had there been some sort of secret meeting I didn't know about that had placed me in charge?

"Well?" Zee said. "What are you going to do?"

I turned around and leaned slightly on the desk, enough to appear like I was somewhat relaxed and to not broadcast the fact that I was scared to death.

How did I accurately describe what I had in mind? "What I'm going to do is something probably pretty stupid and definitely desperate."

"I like it already."

Chapter 35

THE DAY HAD DRAGGED BY, AND I FOUND MYSELF WITH nothing to do but run through the events leading to this place I now found myself. Kane had been right. I'd underestimated Asher.

Butch walked into the Underground, and the set of his shoulders, his slow pace as he crossed toward the office, said it all. He walked in the room, shook his head, and dropped his eyes.

He glanced over at Kane's empty chair before he took a seat on the couch. I leaned my shoulder back against the wall as I stared down at the floor of the Underground, waiting for inspiration to arrive, among other things.

"Any word from Leon?" I asked, keeping my eyes trained on the main door.

"No, but he should be back soon." He let out a deep sigh.

I glanced back in time to see him lean his head back and close his eyes, looking ten years older than he had a few days ago. I returned to watching, but not for Leon.

Butch didn't seem like he had any energy left to move, but he asked, "What are we going to do now?" When I didn't answer right away, I heard him sit up. "Are you waiting for something?"

I bit my bottom lip, knowing the reception I was going to get. No one was going to think this was a good idea. It was my idea, and *I* didn't think it was the brightest. But it was the only option we had right now. I'd rather be doing something, which might not work, rather than nothing, which definitely wouldn't. "I'm waiting for someone."

"Who?" Butch sounded skeptical and he didn't even have a name yet.

He was going to find out soon enough anyway. "Collin," I said as I saw Leon walk through the main door, looking as downtrodden as Butch had.

The couch creaked, relieved of Butch's weight. "Collin? The werewolf Collin?"

"Yes." There was no hesitation in my voice. I'd been waiting to have this fight all day.

Butch made his way to my side, squinting at me. "Why is Collin coming here?"

I lifted my eyebrows and tilted my head toward him. "You know why."

Leon walked in the office. I looked past Butch's squinty eyes and asked Leon, "Anything?"

Leon shook his head. "You guys?"

I shook my head and looked back down at the main door again, still ignoring the squint I was getting from Butch.

Butch's eyes widened and he started shaking his head. "You're really going to do that?"

"Yes, I am." I crossed my arms and prepared to take them both on.

"What is she doing?" Leon asked, walking halfway across the room towards us.

"Shadow walking with Collin as the anchor." My words were firm.

Leon looked like he was pushing it around in his brain a bit before he surprised me by saying, "Okay."

"Kane will kill us," Butch told him.

"It's her choice, and he'd do it for us. How can you tell her not to take the risk?" Leon asked.

I piled on. I'd go it alone if that was what it came to, but I'd rather have Butch watching my back. "If I don't, Kane might not come back. He might be lying somewhere bleeding to death while he's partially stuck in the Shadow-lands. What if Asher lured or trapped him somehow? I have to try and find him." Butch didn't answer. "When you asked me what we were doing, you put me in charge. As the one in charge, I made a decision. And I need you to back me up, because we have to save him." I braced my hands on my hips and tilted my chin up as I waited for him to say something. Butch was scratching his chin and looking at his feet.

When he finally looked up, he said, "Okay. I'm in."

"Thank you." I punched him gently in the arm, because we weren't the hugging type, and went back to my spot to watch.

Collin strolled into the Underground like he owned the place twenty minutes later. He crossed the room toward the stairs with a look that clearly said, *Don't screw me, or else.*

Butch rolled his eyes. "There was no one else?"

"If there was, I would've called them." I shrugged and threw up a hand.

Collin walked through the door, his chest puffed out like he was sizing up his new turf. Yep, he definitely knew Kane was missing.

"Thanks for coming," I said, hoping to make this as painless as possible.

He nodded then looked around the office. "I thought Kane needed something? Why isn't he here?"

Butch groaned. I wanted to but held back. Could the guy be more obvious? Everybody knew Kane was missing. If I didn't need him so much, I would've hit him with a magical punch in the gut.

"I need you to anchor me." Need, not want.

"Why would I do that?" His eyes shifted to Butch and Leon as they went and blocked the way out. Collin was officially trapped, and there was only one way out of here.

"Because I'll owe you." Ugh. Another one I'd owe.

He shook his head as he eyed the door. "Dead men don't collect debts. My life is easier with him gone."

I walked over until I was a foot from him. "I'd rethink that. If you don't help, Kane might never come back. Do you know what that means?"

It was a rhetorical question, or should've been for anyone with two brain cells to zap together. As Collin stood there, nothing flickered across his expression. He'd known Kane was missing and had already thought this out. But I had a feeling he'd come to the wrong conclusion.

There'd be a power struggle as everyone tried to fill the gap left by Kane's enormous footprint. But he was very wrong on one point. "You won't be next in line. I will. And you will be persona non grata."

He blinked rapidly, showing his hand even before he spoke. "No one will ever follow a Shadow Walker. I'll let you be my second, though." He smiled as if he were being gracious.

"You seem very sure of yourself." I took a step back and quickly went through my head for some magical tricks.

He knew what I was doing and seemed way too smug about the whole thing, as if I couldn't possibly show him anything impressive. It made me switch from my initial plan of a small show to something with a bit more oomph.

I let the words flow out of me in a torrent of emotions. The papers started fluttering. It was only a mild breeze at first, and he laughed, as if that was all I had.

With a push, the wind hit him so hard he fell on his ass and slid across the room. Unfortunately, there was some collateral damage, and Kane's desk slid as well. Butch and Leon were hanging on to the doorframe for dear life, and the windows cracked—the new windows.

"Let me know when you've had enough," I yelled.

"Stop it!"

"What? I can't hear you so well over the wind."

"Stop!"

Suddenly everything dropped to the ground, all of us looking a lot worse for wear. And Kane's office, whoa. Well, once I saved his life, he'd get over it. As long as I did save his life.

I looked out the now broken window, and the entire lower floor of the Underground was staring upward. I used my elbow to knock out a loose piece.

"Everything is fine. Go back to your meal." Busybodies.

Collin was getting up from the floor. "I get everyone's word here that if I do this, there'll be no retaliation against me if it goes wrong?"

"Deal," I said, no hesitation. It wasn't like I wanted to hurt the guy, or not usually.

Butch and Leon weren't so quick.

"Deal." Butch was the first to cave.

Leon held out longer, but finally gave a nod. "We're all going down together, now, fur boy."

Satisfied everyone was finally on board, I walked over to the desk and ended up having to dig through the papers on the floor before I found the map I'd marked. I handed it to Collin. "Be there in an hour or we'll come and get you."

Collin took the map, and I was pretty certain he was scared enough to show up of his own accord. He exited the room like he thought he was about to be the star in *The Wizard of Oz* remake.

Butch was smoothing down tufts of his red hair. "Now that was a show."

"Thanks." It hadn't been perfect, but I was feeling somewhat smug. I'd used my magic, no one had died, and the building was *mostly* still standing.

Leon nudged Butch. "If she makes it through this, she gets to go back to 'still alive.'"

"Agreed."

Chapter 36

BUTCH AND LEON STOOD BESIDE ME AT THE CEMETERY, ONE OF the first places I'd ever shadow walked.

Butch ran his fingers through his hair. "I don't like this."

"Shut up. She's nervous enough," Leon said.

I'd deny the nerves, but I was too jittery to talk. I might be willingly walking toward my death, and Kane might already be dead. That thought gutted me. There was no such thing as calm right now.

"Maybe you shouldn't do this?" It was the fifth time Butch had said that.

Leon tensed. "What are you, stuck on repeat? She feels like she's got to, so let's support her."

"Does she, though?" Butch asked, stepping around me and closer to Leon.

Leon matched his move until they were standing in front of me, face to face. "If a person I loved was in danger and I could do something, I'd take the chance."

I coughed. "I'm not in love with him. I'm concerned for him."

Butch threw his hands up. "See? She's fucking delusional. That's why she shouldn't be doing this."

Leon stood his ground. "She's just not in touch with her emotions. It doesn't mean that she's making bad choices."

I was relieved when a white SUV pulled up. Their debate was cut short as Collin and two of his people got out of the car. I squinted in the dim light. I knew these two. They'd tried to recruit me before Butch and Leon. Somebody owed me a bag of Doritos.

I met Collin halfway as his sidekicks continued toward Butch and Leon. Each side did an appraisal, feeling their counterparts out.

"Big wheels you got going on," Leon said, motioning toward the SUV. "Overcompensating much?"

"Maybe we can afford a new car, is all," one of Collin's guys said.

Butch squared his shoulders. "Don't disrespect the Caddy."

There was a tense moment, and then it was over for no reason I could figure, and they appeared to be shooting the shit. It might've been guy code, or some sort of thug code. Either way, it was a mystery to me.

Collin nodded to the side. I followed and held up a hand to Butch and Leon when they would've followed.

Collin crossed his arms and couldn't seem to find a comfortable position to stand. "We really doing this tonight?"

I looked about the place. I'd thought the message and location had made that pretty clear, so what was going on here? I centered my attention on him and realized there was a slight sheen of sweat on his forehead. Ah shit. He was scared. That didn't bode well.

"Yes. You good?"

"Yeah, I was just thinking maybe we're jumping the gun a little. Maybe we should wait a couple more days." He swiped a palm over his temple.

What was up with him? It was hard enough to keep myself calm. "What's the problem? Are you still worried about Kane? I told you, we'll be square. Even if I don't make it out, Butch and Leon won't go back on their word."

He shrugged in a way that didn't inspire any confidence. His eyes shifted to the guys, and then he turned to give them his back. "I don't have a good track record. I'm afraid I'm going to kill you."

Now he wanted to tell me he was inept? Now? "You won't kill me."

He was still sweating. "You don't understand. I might've been more talk than action."

"Then why do you go after all the Shadow Walkers?" I took a deep breath and dug in. He could be scared. I could be terrified. Didn't change anything.

"It's more for show these days. I've killed all of the others." He spoke so softly that I almost didn't make out the words.

Shit, so that was true. I'd really hoped it wasn't, but there you go.

My choices sucked. I could walk away, wait it out for a couple of days, hoping Kane might show up, and basically do nothing. Or I could go in anyway and hope for the best. "Listen to me. I've been informed that I'm the strongest Shadow Walker in decades. That means you aren't going to kill me." I waited for my words to work some sort of magic on his confidence, unlike what they were doing for me.

He was nearly dripping in sweat, and I saw him visibly swallow. "You're positive we can do this?"

"Yes." I sounded confident, although it was forced bluster on my part.

I turned and looked to Butch and Leon, giving them a small nod. I was going in.

I grabbed hold of Collin's hand. "Don't let go."

"I won't." He nodded rapidly.

Stupid or not, I believed he would try.

I scanned the area, found the largest crawler I could, and called it over to me. I knew right away that even they sensed a big difference between Kane and Collin, but I wasn't going to be deterred.

"Let me in."

There was no hesitation as it opened up a doorway for me and I stepped inside.

The second I went in, I felt the difference. Whenever I'd gone in with Kane, I felt his hand firm around mine. I hadn't taken more than one step, and it felt like Collin's hand was a mere feather brushing against mine.

A smart person would've turned around and left right then. I'd always been more stubborn than smart. As long as I sensed some form of bond, I'd get back. Time was of the essence, though. I found the first crawler inside. It was about three feet tall and stood on its hind legs, and there was no animal equivalent to it.

"I'm looking for a human in here."

Its head tilted sideways as if it was not sure what to do with my request. It walked away, as if it didn't care to hear anything else.

After only a couple more steps, I tried gripping my fist around where Collin's hand had been, but there was nothing there. It was like trying to hold water. I kept clinging anyway. I knew where the exit was. It was a simple matter of keeping track of where I went, and I'd be able to get back. The logic made me feel better, even if it might've been my own made-up bull.

I needed to find Kane. If that meant lying to myself, then I'd lie with the best of them.

I called over every crawler I saw as I walked further from the exit. I tried a larger one next. It reminded me of a grizzly, from what I'd seen in pictures.

I got the same non-response before it headed off.

I'd been walking for a little while, and had tried crawlers in every shape, when I turned a corner and saw Asher standing there. "You came."

I took a step back. I'd known I might see him in here. Figured I would, but it was a chance I'd had to take.

I tamped down all the anger that wanted to erupt from me. Kane was the priority right now, and I'd do whatever was needed. "Is Kane in here? Did you lead him here?" I asked, trying to keep my voice calm, as if I were asking what the score of a game had been.

"I knew you'd come back."

"Of course I would. Is Kane alive?" I'd tell Asher whatever he wanted to hear.

His eyes went to my hand. He wanted me. I wanted Kane.

"Come with me and I'll take you to him."

Whoa, this was too easy. He wouldn't just hand over Kane. He hated him. Why would he offer to lead me to him with nothing in return?

Then he held out his right hand to me, and I understood the cost, what he was asking. I looked down at my own hand, where I was still gripping air, hoping that when I turned around and got close to the exit again, I'd feel Collin's hand.

I reached out my left to Asher, hoping I'd misunderstood.

He shook his head.

If I let go, I might be giving up any chance of getting out again. If I didn't let go, Kane would be stuck here forever.

I let go.

Asher smiled slowly as he took my free hand. "You made the right choice, Ollie."

I nodded, while wishing he'd shut up. I didn't want to hear him talking. I wanted him dead for forcing me to make a choice. For doing this after I'd tried to save him. I didn't want to hold his hand. I wanted to rip his head from his shoulders.

He rattled on about how I'd made the right choice, but I tuned him out. If I didn't, I would've tried to kill him then and there.

I didn't know how long we walked. It felt like a couple of hours, but I was losing my sense of time in this place of perpetual gloom.

He stopped in front of a small house that looked like it could only hold one room. It was rustic, and the door and single window showed nothing but blackness.

"Is Kane in there?" If he was, he was being eerily quiet.

"No. This is for you. I built it after I first met you." He watched me as if waiting for some sign of approval. As if he actually believed I was going to be pleased he'd done this for me.

"You're not leading me to Kane, are you?"

"Kane isn't here." There was no doubt in his voice. He was absolutely certain of it.

I'd made the biggest mistake of my life. Kane wasn't in the Shadowlands. But if he wasn't here, then why hadn't I felt him when I cast the locating spell in my world?

I'd come here for nothing. Kane might be lying hurt and trapped somewhere, but not here. I pulled on Asher's grip on my hand. I had to get back.

"Ollie, I'm doing this so we can be together. I can give you everything here. It's better for you. I know what's right. Kane doesn't. You need to stay here where I can protect you and take care of you. You'll get used to being here. You'll learn to love it." He was dragging me toward the door.

I feared if he got me in that house, I'd never leave it again. There was a pulse of magic coming from the place that felt enormous. He was leading me into a jail.

"Wait...wait! Give me a minute here. Just tell me why you're doing this." I was stalling for time to think, to come up with an escape. And if this was going to be my end, why he was doing this to me.

He didn't release my hand, but he stopped pulling me toward the house. "Because from the moment you walked into my world, I knew we were meant to be together. Look around you, Ollie. There's nothing but grey and shadows wherever you look. Then one day you walk in to my world and it's like you brought the sunshine with you. You were light and warmth and I'd never seen anything like you before. I helped you to survive my world. Helped you find the magic you wanted, but you always left. So I went to your world.

"But I didn't belong there. I was a burden. I knew this. My body didn't work right in your world. I went looking for more magic, but even that wasn't helping. I couldn't be what you needed me to be, so I had to bring you back to my world. Here, we can be the way we should be. You see that, right? This is how it has to be."

He turned away from me and began to again pull me toward what would be my prison.

"Asher, you need to let go of me." I dug in with my heels, but he was overwhelming me. "I don't belong here. If you make me stay, I'll fade away like you were beginning to in my world. There won't be any light or warmth from me, because I'll die."

"We're meant to be together."

He kept pulling me, no matter what I said. His mind was made up and he would keep me here if it destroyed the very thing about me he was seeking.

I knew it was useless, but I didn't care. I'd try anything. I grabbed for the most potent spell I could find in my mind, and started forming the words.

The magic buzzed around me, through me, tingling in every part of my body. Something was happening. I focused on where he was gripping me, and he suddenly yelped.

Asher dropped my hand. The magic was working on him. It had to be because I was here, in the Shadowlands. That was the only thing that had changed since I'd last used my magic against him. He was vulnerable here.

His mouth opened, and I knew he wanted to speak, could see the thoughts in his eyes, but nothing came out. His face scrunched as if in agony, his eyes growing watery. Violent tremors racked his body, and I could feel the magic seeping deep into him, twisting at his insides. The magic felt like an extension of me as it wreaked havoc on what he was made of. I wanted to pull back, remove myself from the dark and slimy feel of him, but I couldn't. He was an abomination, even in this dark place.

I finally stopped chanting when I knew the damage was too much to repair. He crumpled to the ground, and then he was changing into a crawler, a large one, with two horns. A shell of a body lay beside it.

He was Crem. His eyes squeezed shut, a shudder went through his body, and a rattling sound came from his chest.

He was dead.

I knelt beside what was once Asher. I realized I didn't know how I felt anymore as sadness warred with relief. He'd saved me more than once, but then he'd used my gratitude to bind me to him.

When it had all started falling apart, he'd tried to trap me. What hurt the most was Asher might have succeeded with at least part of his plan. I might be trapped in the Shadowlands.

A movement off to the side pulled me out of my thoughts. The small bunny crawler that had given me the shadow kiss hopped over. It must've been following us.

"He wasn't allowed to leave, was he?"

It chirped back. I didn't know what it said, but it didn't matter. I knew I was right.

"That's why you gave me this?" I held up my hand, noticing that the skin had started to change colors where it had bitten me. "You knew he was going to lure me back."

It didn't pay me any attention now as it sniffed the clothing that had shredded when Asher shifted to Crem. Fabric flopped to the side, and I saw the corner of a piece of parchment.

I pulled it out and opened it up, hoping it would tell me how to get out of here. It didn't. It was the leprechaun map. I lifted the shredded shirt, and the vampire pendant fell to the ground. The blood was probably long gone, but I didn't think that mattered anymore. The creature that had drunk it was dead.

"Wait, can you help me go home?" I yelled as the bunny left.

It didn't stop or acknowledge me. It had gotten what it

wanted. I pocketed the map and threw the pendant around my neck. If I ever got back, these things might come in handy.

I'd get back to the exit and I'd find Collin.

Then I'd find Kane.

It took me a few hours to find the place I'd entered. It was right beside a boulder I'd mentally marked. I flexed the fingers on my right hand, but felt nothing.

There weren't any crawlers trying to block the exit on me, either. Maybe that had been more of a Kane thing? As if they knew he was there holding the exit open for me?

I walked the few steps to where I'd entered and then kept walking, right through where I should be able to get out. It was gone, or shut, I didn't know, but I was stuck. I was never getting out of here.

No. Screw that. I'd given up on life before, but I wouldn't again. My tagline was not going to end up being "still quitting." I'd keep going until I couldn't. I'd find another way out.

I didn't know how much time had passed. The sun didn't rise or set here. It was like perpetual dusk.

I didn't need to eat or drink. It was as if all bodily functions had ceased to exist as I wandered. The crawlers paid me no heed anymore, and that was the scariest part of it all. It was as if they'd accepted my being here, as if I were part of this place now.

I slumped, not knowing where to go or turn. I'd already found myself walking in circles. Maybe if I found the little bunny crawler again, I could force it to help me this time? But that had been hours ago.

I looked at the notches I'd made in the ground, looking for a direction I hadn't gone yet. There was only one. I'd only walked a few hundred feet when I felt a breeze flow over my hand, and nowhere else. I froze, gripping my hand. Nothing.

I took a few more steps, and invisible fingers feathered across my skin. It was Kane. He was on the other side somewhere, reaching out to me. It had to be him. I stood, not sure which way to go. I grasped the hand that was barely there, and it was like a fist around water.

I didn't know which way to go, but I could do this. I'd get out of here. I dug into the ground with my foot, marking my spot with a 1 before I took a few steps. Concentrating on the slightest change of feeling in my hand, I rushed back to my starting point when I realized it was fading. If that way lost him, it had to be the other way.

I took a few steps in the opposite direction. The change was so slight that it was hard to tell if it was stronger, but I knew it was there. I dragged my heel into the ground until I'd carved a 2.

I took a few more steps, retreated to my starting point, and did it again in each direction until I was sure which way to go and marked a 3 into the ground.

What felt like a day later, I dragged my foot, marking the ground with four hundred and fifty-two. I took another few steps and fell through an exit that I hadn't known was there.

Chapter 37

KANE WAS THERE, SCOOPING ME INTO HIS ARMS AS SOON AS I crossed over. He shifted me until I was against his chest, my head in the crook of his neck. His arms wrapped around me. I was cocooned by his heat, the smell of him. When he held me like this, I almost believed nothing could ever hurt me again. He must've held me like that for five minutes, and I didn't complain.

"Where were you?" I asked, my arm wrapped around his neck.

"I'm so sorry." His arms tensed around me.

He placed me down on a nearby rock, leaving his arm around my waist to steady me as his other ran over my limbs. Butch and Leon huddled nearby. Butch handed me a water bottle, and I guzzled it down, all my thirst coming back with a vengeance.

"How long have I been gone?" I asked between gulps, noticing the way they were staring at me. It had to have been a while.

"Two days," Kane said, and then motioned for Leon to hand me some protein bars.

Kane, having done a full perusal of my body, asked, "What happened in there? How did you end up so far from the exit? I could barely feel you."

I gave them a rundown as I chewed my way through three protein bars and chugged another bottle of water. The three of them nodded as the story unfolded.

"So Asher was Crem?" Leon asked. "How was that possible?"

"It was just a shell he used. He was probably leaving it behind in the apartment when he slipped out."

Kane had an *I told you he was bad news* expression on.

"You're going to gloat now?"

"Why not? You're okay," he teased.

I forgave him when his arm tightened around my waist, and I saw him watching my chest to see how well I was breathing.

I knew that was what he was doing because I was doing the same to him. I thought I'd never see him again, and now I was having a hard time dragging my eyes from him.

"What happened to you?" He looked okay, but that didn't mean anything.

He was still smiling, but a hardness was in his voice when he spoke. "I think there may be some people that wanted me away from you. I was lured into a trap."

I lifted a hand to his arm, barely holding back the urge to check him for wounds. "Is that why I couldn't find you? I tried every spell I could." I had some good spells up my sleeve, but that locator was a real dud.

"I was lured into a building by a creature I thought was Crem. It took me a long time to get out, but I wasn't harmed."

"Who?" My mind ran through the possible suspects, but I couldn't fathom who would go after Kane.

"There was no one there. It was a magical barricade. Doesn't matter. I'll find them." He didn't need to add what would happen then.

I looked about the clearing and didn't see anyone else. "Where's Collin?"

"I didn't kill him," Kane said, smiling because he was crazy enough to think me accusing him of murder was funny. "I honored your agreement."

Kane didn't have to tell me how hard that had to have been. "Thank you."

"Come on, let's go home."

I got up on shaky legs, feeling almost as bad as when I'd left the leprechauns.

Kane's arm still around my waist as I walked toward the car, I watched as Butch and Leon hesitated a moment before going over to the Caddy. They both smiled.

I didn't have to ask why. I smiled back.

"You really earned it this time," Butch said.

Butch, Leon, and I all looked at each other and said in unison, "Still alive."

I woke up, the sole inhabitant of the bed, and I hated it. Why wasn't he in bed with me? He said he slept here. It was the middle of the night, and I was flopping around alone. Now I couldn't sleep. Definitely his fault. If I hadn't unknowingly gotten used to him being here, then I wouldn't be having trouble now. He'd started this whole mess and left me holding the bag.

After another ten minutes of lying there and tossing, I got up. I went into the living room, hoping that watching TV would dim the recent memories so I could fall back to sleep. Who doesn't have a TV in their bedroom?

Someone who doesn't watch it.

Kane was there, leaning by the window, sweatpants hanging low on his hips. He looked like a living sculpture, and I wasn't sure anyone real had ever been created so perfectly. Or maybe he wasn't perfect to anyone but me.

He glanced over. "What's wrong?"

I got used to sleeping next to you and now you won't come to bed, damn it. I wasn't sure if I was ready to be that blunt. Way too fast. "Nothing. Just wanted to watch a little TV."

I walked around to settle on the couch, grabbing the remote.

"Nice renovations you did while I was gone."

"You're welcome." The dwarves had done a nice job fixing up the Underground.

"Do I want to know what the place looked like before?"

I shook my head. "Probably not."

He nodded. "I heard there's a vampire that went missing."

I shrugged. She'd had it coming. "Bad things happen when you treat people like they're Slurpees from 7-Eleven."

He sat on the corner of the couch beside me. "Put that other show on. The one with the guy in a kilt and some chick who went back in time."

My head swung to him. "*Outlander*? You want to watch *Outlander*?"

"Yeah, what's so funny about that?" He was smiling, as if he knew exactly why I thought it was funny.

I clicked on demand and hit play while he was stretching out. I put the remote down, and before I could lean back, he looped an arm around my waist and tugged me down beside him. He shifted and then was behind me, spooning me.

I felt ready to drift back to sleep, and another piece fell into place. "Do you snuggle with me when I'm sleeping?"

"It might have happened on occasion."

No wonder I couldn't sleep without him anymore. He'd been secretly cuddling with me for weeks. I hadn't woken up once. I didn't need to ponder why. I knew. Even in my sleep, I'd known it had felt right.

Keep an eye out for *Kissed by the Dark*, Ollie Wit, Book Three.

Sign up for Donna's mailing list.

Find Donna on the web at Donnaaugustine.com

ALSO BY DONNA AUGUSTINE

A Step into the Dark

The Keepers

Keepers and Killers

Shattered

Redemption

Karma

Jinxed

Fated

Dead Ink

The Wilds

The Hunt

The Dead

The Magic